Praise for Taylor McCafferty's
Second Haskell Blevins Mystery
RUFFLED FEATHERS

"*RUFFLED FEATHERS* IS TAYLOR McCAF-
FERTY'S LONG-AWAITED SEQUEL TO HER
BRILLIANT *Pet Peeves,* which introduced us to
Haskell Blevins, the premier (and only) hard-boiled
private detective in Pigeon Fork, KY. And it's hard to
be a hard-boiled P.I. in Pigeon Fork."
—*Washington Times*

"Blevins struts his stuff solving the murder of a
poultry millionaire. . . ."
—*The Poisoned Pen*

"Small town mysteries have an undeniable charm.
The microcosm lends a tidy, nostalgic intimacy to the
story. . . . *RUFFLED FEATHERS* takes a whimsical
look at a tiny Kentucky town."
—*Lexington (KY) Herald-Leader*

"A light-hearted piece of entertainment . . . recom-
mended."
—*Mystery News*

"McCafferty writes skillfully. Blevins's narrative
voice is convincing, and McCafferty manages to avoid
the trap of building humorous character solely
through lumping together a bunch of idiosyncrasies.
The dialogue develops both plot and character; the
scene where the social-climbing daughter-in-law de-
mands proof that Jacob is dead is a virtuoso turn. . . .
AN ORIGINAL COMIC MYSTERY."
—*Publishers Weekly*

Available from Pocket Books

Books by Taylor McCafferty

Pet Peeves
Ruffled Feathers
Bed Bugs

Published by POCKET BOOKS

A HASKELL BLEVINS MYSTERY

BED BUGS

Taylor McCafferty

POCKET BOOKS

New York   London   Toronto   Sydney   Tokyo   Singapore

This book is a work of fiction. Names, characters, places, and
incidents are either products of the author's imagination or are
used fictitiously. Any resemblance to actual events or locales or
persons, living or dead, is entirely coincidental.

An *Original* Publication of POCKET BOOKS

POCKET BOOKS, a division of Simon & Schuster Inc.
1230 Avenue of the Americas, New York, NY 10020.

ISBN: 0-671-75468-8

First Pocket Books printing May 1993

10 9 8 7 6 5 4 3 2 1

POCKET and colophon are registered trademarks of
Simon & Schuster Inc.

Cover art by John Zielinski

Printed in the U.S.A.

To Gene Taylor,
my favorite brother,
whom I bugged mercilessly when we were little.

Acknowledgments

As always, I want to thank my twin sister, Beverly Herald, for her editorial help. I also want to thank John Horlander, a medical student at the University of Louisville, for taking time out from his studies to answer my questions.

BED
BUGS

1

Word travels fast in a small town. I'm not exactly sure why. Folks who live in big cities will tell you that it's on account of there not being much else to do in a small town except gossip about your neighbor. This isn't really true. I'd say the fifteen hundred or so inhabitants of Pigeon Fork, Kentucky, are just about as busy as anybody anywhere else. Busier than some, in fact, being as how a lot of folks around these parts are growing their own food and sewing their own clothes and building their own houses.

All the same, folks around Pigeon Fork always seem to have the time to spread a rumor or two. It's not just the womenfolk, either. The men gossip every bit as much. Fact is, I've heard it said more than once that one of the reasons we always seem to have a nice breeze blowing through town is on account of all the tongues wagging.

I'm pretty sure that's an exaggeration. It was knowing, however, just how fast rumors get spread in this town that made me in such a hurry to explain things to Ruta Lippton the minute she finished climbing up the stairs to my office.

My office is over my brother Elmo's drugstore, so Ruta had quite a few stairs to climb. Ordinarily I would've seen her coming, but on this particular Wednesday morning in May, I was a little preoccupied. That's why when Ruta finally got to my door, I was still standing in the middle of a big puddle of water, holding a large potted philodendron. If I'd heard her coming, I would've moved faster.

As soon as I saw Ruta, I knew I had some heavy explaining to do.

For one thing, Ruta made no move to knock on my door. She just stood out there on my landing, peering at me wide-eyed through the glass of my office door.

I'd seen Ruta around town, so I knew who she was. In her early thirties, Ruta was the head beautician and sole proprietor of the Curl Crazee beauty shop. She was a walking billboard for her shop, too, looking more than a little curl-crazy herself. Her shiny brown hair was done in large corkscrews all over her head, and every one of these corkscrews stuck out at least three inches all the way around.

I couldn't help thinking what I always did whenever I saw Ruta. This woman must've attended the Stick-Your-Hand-in-a-Light-Socket School of Hair Design.

One of her classes at the Socket School must've also been Makeup 101—How to Apply with a Trowel. Ruta's face was at least two shades darker than her throat, the apples of her cheeks were the same shade as real apples, and her eyes—outlined heavily in black—reminded me of that dog, Spuds, that's in the beer commercials. Only, unlike Spuds, Ruta had gone for two black eyes, instead of just one.

Surrounding Ruta's face were also what I believe used to be called "spit curls" back in the sixties. Ruta must've used quite a lot of spit on her curls, because they appeared to be stuck to her face. She also must've just walked over from her shop, because she was wearing a bright pink uniform and pink Reeboks.

After Ruta stopped staring at me and my philodendron through the glass door, she stared at the puddle on my floor. Her black eyes widened even more.

As soon as I saw Ruta's eyes do that, I remembered that the Curl Crazee beauty shop could probably be called the headquarters of Gossip Central in Pigeon Fork. Melba Hawley, the secretary I share with Elmo downstairs, does most of what she calls her "networking" during her weekly trips to the Curl Crazee.

Networking here in Pigeon Fork, as best as I can tell, is not exactly what networking is elsewhere in the United States. Here in Pigeon Fork, judging from what Melba has told me, it's like being on a television network, broadcasting to anybody who'll tune in, telling everything you know—and some things you can only guess—about everybody else in Crayton County.

Standing there, holding that philodendron, with a quarter inch of water lapping at my shoes, I knew full well that if I didn't talk fast, Ruta was going to spin on her heels and leave. And if she did, there wasn't a doubt in my mind that by nightfall, she would've told all of Pigeon Fork that she knew for a fact that the only private detective in town was not toilet trained.

Now, *that* ought to be real good for business.

"My air conditioner's been leaking," I called to Ruta through the closed door.

Ruta continued to stare.

I wondered how fast it would take to explain recent events.

Even though it was only eleven-thirty, and it was only mid-May, for God's sake, it was already eighty-eight degrees outside. Kentucky weather is like this—it always seems to be going for the surprise. In the middle of summer, all of a sudden it'll feel like fall, and in the middle of spring, it'll sometimes try to convince you it's summer.

Yesterday afternoon I'd finally gotten convinced. May or not, it was summer. Hot, sweltering, brain-bubbling summer. So this morning, bright and early, I'd brought in my air conditioner. I'd lugged it up all those steps outside, stuck it in the window, balanced it like you're supposed to, plugged it in, turned it on, and then—while I was going through a stack of mail consisting mainly of bills—the air conditioner quietly and efficiently wet all over my floor.

I didn't notice the puddle until it had crept under my feet. Then, of course, I scrambled for a bucket to catch the overflow. The only one I could find was pretty small, and it happened to have the philodendron growing in it, but it was the best I could do on short notice. Besides, I figured this would, no doubt, be a real good way to make sure the philodendron always got watered. It was just as I was grabbing up the philodendron that Ruta appeared at my door.

I decided that it would probably be in my best interest to give Ruta the Reader's Digest condensed version of all this. "My air conditioner must be broken or something, because it's sure made a mess," I said. "I was just going to put this under it to catch the water." Ruta's black-eyed stare must've rattled me a little, because as I spoke, I actually held up the bucket full of philodendron. For proof, like maybe I expected the philodendron to back me up on this.

Ruta looked like the testimony of a philodendron wasn't going to make much of an impact. Her eyes traveled uncertainly back to the puddle.

My eyes followed hers. "Yep, it's sure a mess, isn't it?" I said. I knew I was repeating myself, but I couldn't think of anything else to say. "This thing's been leaking up a storm, all right." I said all this a little louder than I ordinarily would have, being as how Ruta had not yet seen fit to open the door to my office.

Out there on the landing, Ruta looked like maybe she thought I was trying to shout down any doubts she might have about the air conditioner story. She continued to stare, not yet saying a word.

I started wondering if the woman knew how to work a door. Maybe the complexity of the thing was completely beyond her.

At that moment—thank heavens—a couple of fat drops of water appeared at the corner of my air conditioner and slid down the wall to the floor. Ruta looked over at those drops, blinked, and then apparently decided that we'd covered the air conditioner subject all we needed to. She cleared her throat and said, "You Haskell Blevins?"

I may have been imagining it, but to my ears, Ruta sounded as if she were hoping I'd say no.

She already had to have a pretty good idea who I was. Even if Ruta hadn't noticed me around town like I'd noticed her, I've got me some real fancy lettering now, painted right on the glass of my office door. The exact same door Ruta was now looking through. The letters on my door are printed real big in a typeface that the sign painter called Times Italic. The letters say, HASKELL BLEVINS, PRIVATE INVESTIGATIONS, INC.

The lettering looks real sophisticated and all, but what it says is lying some. I'm not exactly incorporated. The guy I hired to paint the sign on my door added that himself. He said that he was trying to make me sound like some big company. Like IBM or AT&T or something. After he went to all that trouble, I didn't have the heart to make him wipe it off.

I couldn't help it. My eyes sort of wandered to the sign on my door before I answered Ruta. "That's right," I said. "I'm Haskell Blevins." I thought about adding, Who did you think I was—the air conditioner repairman? But I decided against it. No use sounding antagonistic to a potential client.

Ruta's eyes traveled to the sign on my door, too. She still made no move to actually open my door and walk on in, though. She just kept on standing out there on the landing, reading my sign real slow. I was pretty sure I saw her lips moving.

There was every possibility that Ruta was *not* a brain trust.

Still looking at my sign, she finally said, "You the guy who solved the chicken murder?"

Skepticism was in every syllable Ruta spoke.

I nodded. The murder she was referring to was the last case I worked on. It was a few weeks ago, and contrary to what Ruta said, it did not actually involve the killing of poultry. It involved the murder of the owner of a huge broiler operation located about thirty miles outside of Pigeon Fork. And I really did solve the thing. Fact is, I was feeling downright proud of myself after the whole thing was over—right up until I heard folks around town calling it "the chicken murder." That sort of takes the wind out of your sails.

Ruta shook her curly head, as if trying to clear it. "You? *You're* the guy?"

I'm getting used to this reaction by now. It seems like everybody who comes up my stairs is expecting to meet up with Mike Hammer or Peter Gunn or somebody like that. Instead, they meet up with me—an ordinary thirty-four-year-old guy with red hair. Ordinary face, ordinary build, ordinary height. About the only thing that isn't ordinary about me is the quantity of freckles I'm carrying around. If freckles weighed anything at all, I figure I'd be hauling around about four tons.

I think it's the four-ton freckles and the red hair that have caused some folks around these parts to suggest that I bear a remarkable resemblance to Howdy Doody. I'm hoping, however, that this isn't really true, and that these folks are just being cruel.

Ruta's mouth was now hanging open a little. *"You're* the great detective I been hearing about?"

Oh yeah, that was disbelief in her tone, all right.

I gave Ruta a big smile anyway. Then I finished putting the philodendron under the air conditioner, went over, and held open my door for her. "What can I do for you?"

Ruta hesitated a little before she walked on in. I thought for a second there that her hesitation might've been because of the current condition of my office. Even when my office doesn't have a big puddle in the middle of it, Melba—the secretary I mentioned earlier—calls my office the "Bermuda Rectangle." Melba says it looks exactly like some mysterious force has sucked in every piece of paper and trash from within a five-mile radius and deposited it on my floor and the top of my desk. Melba is exaggerating.

6

She is.

But even *I* had to admit that the water on my floor had not done the assorted stacks of magazines and newspapers any good. Some of them had been pretty much reduced to sodden lumps. Ruta, however, didn't really seem to notice. She stepped nonchalantly around the puddle, carelessly pushed a couple of *Popular Mechanics* magazines off the chair in front of my desk—narrowly missing the puddle, I might add—and sat down. "I'm Ruta Lippton," she said.

Obviously Ruta's hesitation had nothing whatsoever to do with my office. I think, then, that I could assume that it had a lot to do with me. If I were the sensitive type, I could take this kind of thing personally. I'm not sensitive, though. You can't afford to be if folks keep comparing you to Howdy Doody.

I nodded, waiting for Ruta to go on, but evidently that wasn't a big enough reaction for her. She immediately leaned forward and repeated, "That's *Lippton,* like the tea bag. Only with two *p*'s."

Ruta did look a little like a tea bag, now that she mentioned it. Deeply tanned, she was brown and lumpy. I don't want to sound crass, or whatever, but I couldn't help but notice that Ruta had two particularly large lumps right out in front. One reason I couldn't help but notice these lumps of hers was because Ruta's uniform buttoned down the front. At least, it tried to. The buttons over her ample chest looked as if they were holding on for dear life, and there were a couple of noticeable gaps between them. Evidently, to help out her buttons, Ruta had added two large safety pins to hold the gaps closed. These pins looked as if they, like the buttons, were under an awful lot of pressure. In fact, it looked as if any second those pins might spring loose and shoot across the room. Perhaps, say, putting some-body's eye out.

I'd been intending to mop up my floor while I talked to Ruta, but Ruta was sitting facing the puddle. I decided maybe it would be better to get out of safety pin range. I moved behind my desk, and sat down. "Well, I'm real glad to meet you," I said, smiling. I purposely did not look at Ruta's safety pins.

"I own the Curl Crazee?" Ruta's tone implied that if I didn't already know this, I wasn't the detective I pretended to be.

I nodded again. "The beauty shop," I said.

"The *hair salon*," she corrected. Ruta's heavily mascaraed Spuds eyes said loud and clear that I'd just insulted her.

I didn't know what to say. What Ruta called a *hair salon* was two blocks away, if you turned left at Pop Matheny's Barber Shop. I'd strolled by Ruta's quite a lot, on my way to one place or another. In an old white frame building with long, narrow windows, Ruta's shop was the only shop on her block that had a sagging front porch. The reason her porch sagged so much probably had a lot to do with the Coke machine she had sitting on it, right next to the screen door. I knew for a fact that there were folks around town taking bets on the exact date Ruta's Coke machine was going to drop through her porch. It was sort of like betting on when the Tower of Pisa was going to fall. Ruta's Coke machine was so old, it still said its Cokes were ten cents a bottle. Ruta, or one of her employees, I guess, had taped a sign directly over the coin deposit that said, "45¢, NOT 10¢!"

In addition to the ancient Coke machine, Ruta's shop featured the usual pictures of various hairstyles taped all over her front windows. A couple of these pictures featured the hairdo that is evidently the tried-and-true favorite of a lot of the women here in Pigeon Fork. The beehive. Ruta's shop also had a couple of hand-lettered signs. "Haircut, $5." "Permanent Sale." Which evidently spoke the truth, since that sign never came down.

The hairstyle pictures and the signs were pretty run-of-the-mill. It was several other signs, as I recall, that made Ruta's front windows truly unique. The signs that said: "Ceramic Classes, Twice a Week," and "SIGN UP NOW—Ceramics add that decorator touch!"

This was Ruta's *salon*. The Curl Crazee Hair Salon and Ceramics School.

I gave Ruta a smile that was meant to look apologetic. "Hair *Salon,*" I said. "Of course."

Ruta gave a quick nod of her dark curls, as if to indicate she forgave my stupidity at calling her establishment a beauty shop, and then said, "Well, the reason I'm here is that I've been robbed, and Vergil is not doing a thing about it."

The Vergil Ruta was referring to had to be Pigeon Fork's sheriff, Vergil Minrath. This sure didn't sound like the Vergil I knew, and I knew Vergil pretty well, his having been my dad's best friend back in high school. Vergil, as best as I could tell, always took any crime committed in his jurisdiction as a personal affront.

"Your shop was broken into?"

Ruta shook her curls again. "Oh no," she said. "My home. Somebody busted into my home this morning after I left for work. I only found out about it this quick because I happened to run my hose, and had to go back home and change. I walked in and found out that I've been, what you call, *broken and entered!*"

I just looked at her. I believe the crime Ruta was referring to here was breaking and entering.

"And," Ruta went on, *"Vergil is not doing a thing about it!"*

This last appeared to be a continuing refrain.

"Why not?" It seemed like a reasonable question to ask.

Ruta sniffed and gave her shoulders a shake this time. "Who knows?" Leaning forward, she started fiddling with one of her spit curls, wrapping it round and round a manicured finger. Ruta's fingernails were an even brighter shade of pink than her uniform. "Vergil's just lazy, I guess," she went on. "I called him up, told him I've been robbed, and Vergil didn't do a thing—"

"—about it," I finished for her.

I realized right away that I should've just let her finish for herself, because Ruta threw me a hard stare before she went on. "Oh, Vergil went through all the motions, but you could tell his heart wasn't in it. He didn't even come out to my house hisself." Ruta twirled her spit curl again. "Vergil sent one of them twin deputies of his, instead. As if either one of them could find his own rear end in the dark!"

I didn't say anything, but Ruta was probably right. Finding their rear ends in the daylight might pose some real problems, too.

Around these parts, Vergil's deputies—the Gunterman twins, Jeb and Fred—were definitely better known for brawn than brains. Matter of fact, at the Crayton County Fair two years ago, part of the entertainment had been the Guntermans competing with each other as to who could lift a cow the quickest. I, of course, had still been back in Louisville then, so I'd missed the excitement. I've been told, however, that the contest ended in a tie.

Ruta was now hurrying on, her voice getting tearful. "I just don't know what I'm going to do. I've got somebody breaking into my own house, for God's sake, and all Vergil did was send one of his twin goons to dust for fingerprints! Which, of course, he didn't find any of!" Ruta was really working herself up now. She was fidgeting with her safety pins, crossing and uncrossing her legs, and smoothing out imaginary wrinkles on her pink skirt. "And my husband, Lenard, is a truck driver! With him on the road all the time, I just don't feel safe. Fact is, I'm real scared, I don't mind telling you, and Vergil's no help at all—"

Ruta sounded as if all her fidgeting might be leading up to a crying jag, so I jumped in real quick. I've always been real bad around weeping females. My ex-wife, Claudine—I call her Claudzilla—has told me more than once that I lack interpersonal skills. Maybe she's right. I never do seem to know what to say if somebody starts crying on me, and I never do seem to have a box of Kleenex handy. Like now, for example. For all the papers and stuff all over my desk and floor, there wasn't one Kleenex among them.

Uncertainly, I reached across the desk and patted Ruta's hand. "There, there," I said. Whatever that means. I hoped I sounded soothing. "I'm sure Vergil just doesn't realize—"

Mentioning the sheriff's name probably wasn't my best

idea. Ruta pulled her hand back as if she'd just been stung. "Vergil!" She repeated the name with disgust. "Just because nothing was missing, that man just gave up!"

I just looked at her. This last bit did seem to be a significant part of the story. I leaned forward. "What do you mean—nothing was missing?"

Ruta shrugged. "Well, my three TVs, and my microwave, and my VCR were all still there. And, of course, my camcorder and my—"

It was getting a lot more clear why Vergil might've been less than eager to investigate this case. I interrupted Ruta's List of Things Recently Overlooked By a Burglar. "You mean to tell me that you think your house was broken into, but *nothing* was taken?"

Ruta looked disgusted again. "Well, of course, something was taken," she said. "Something *had* to be taken. They wouldn't have busted in there for nothing." Her tone now implied that she didn't think *I* was a brain trust, either. "It's just that nobody seems to know exactly what they took," Ruta went on. It was her turn to lean forward now. "That's one of the things I need you for," she said. "To tell me what was stolen."

My first response to this, of course, was, "How would I know?" After all, wasn't it generally the job of the robbery *victim* to come up with the list of stolen items? I was pretty sure I'd never heard it working any other way. Not to mention, how in the world was I supposed to figure out what was no longer there if I'd never known what was there in the first place?

I started to say all this, but then, almost immediately, I reconsidered. For what, I admit, was not the most selfless of reasons.

You see, I've been in business for almost a year now, and I might as well admit it—real live clients have been few and far between. This alone wouldn't have been so bad, I guess, except that when I first moved back home, I made this agreement with Elmo downstairs. My brother agreed to let me have this office space over his drugstore rent-free, if—during slow times—I'd help out down there, mopping the floor and running the soda fountain.

It's important to remember that, at the time I made that little agreement, I'd just spent the last eight years in Louisville, working homicide. Being away from Pigeon Fork for that long, I reckon I'd forgotten a few things. Like, for example, I had no idea just how many slow times a private eye could have in this town. So far, in the twelve long months since I opened up my detective agency here, I figure slow times have outnumbered any other times a hundred to one. There are folks in town who actually believe I work for Elmo full time. I myself am one of them.

So if Ruta Lippton wanted to hire me to investigate a robbery that hadn't really happened, who was I to argue with her? There was one other consideration, though. I took a deep breath and said, "I'd be glad to look into this for you, but you need to know that I charge thirty dollars an hour, or two hundred dollars a day—"

Ruta waved her hand at me, like she was batting away a pesky fly. Pulling out a pink ballpoint pen and a pink checkbook from one of the front pockets of her uniform, she started writing real fast. "Here's a day's pay to start you off," she said, handing the check to me with a flourish. "Now, can we get on with this?"

We got on with it. I pocketed that check and didn't even stop to mop up my office floor.

Following Ruta in my Ford pickup, it took only about ten minutes to drive from downtown Pigeon Fork to Ruta's home. It was real easy to follow Ruta, because she was driving a brand-new, bright red Pontiac Firebird. It was like following a stop sign down the road.

The Curl Crazee must've been doing all right, or else Ruta's husband, Lenard, was hauling a gold mine in that truck of his. The house we pulled up to was in Pigeon Fork's newest and most prestigious subdivision, Twelve Oaks.

Actually, to call Twelve Oaks Pigeon Fork's most prestigious subdivision is a little misleading. Twelve Oaks is Pigeon Fork's *only* prestigious subdivision. Up until the new interstate went in a few years back, Pigeon Fork just had your plain, ordinary kind of subdivisions. The kind where all the houses look pretty much alike, and where quite a few of the yards have cars and trucks jacked up, in various states of repair.

I reckon the new interstate got some folks thinking that Pigeon Fork should now have the kind of subdivision where folks' eyes widen a little when you tell them where you live. Just like the big cities. Twelve Oaks qualifies as a genuine eye widener, I reckon. It got its name, so Melba has told me, from one of the plantations in *Gone With the Wind*. Melba said that the developer no doubt called it that so it would sound "real fancy-schmancy." Personally, I'm not so sure. I think this subdivision might be called Twelve Oaks because that appears to be all that's left after the developer finished clearing the land and building the houses.

Ruta's sprawling brick ranch was set on a postage stamp of a lawn, and it didn't have one tree to call its own. Oh, there were two twigs out in her front yard which, in about fifty years, might actually be called trees, but for right now—you can't fool me—those were twigs.

I parked my truck, got out, and took a quick look around. One thing about it. If I were a burglar, I'd certainly pick the most expensive subdivision in the area to do my burgling in.

Ruta also paused when she got out of her Firebird, and glanced over at me. I could see that she was waiting for me to say something, so I tried to look impressed. "Nice place you've got here," I said. I wasn't exactly lying. Her house did look real nice. It had two big bay windows in the front, a big arched window over the door, and two huge double front doors. I do believe I've seen *churches* with smaller doors than Ruta's house.

"It *is* nice, isn't it?" Ruta said, and headed inside. Apparently Ruta felt there was no point in acting modest. I followed her, wondering what I always do whenever I drive through a subdivision around here. Why on earth would a person choose to live in a small, rural town like Pigeon Fork and then buy a home out here in the kind of subdivision that

13

could be located just outside of Louisville? Or Nashville. Or Atlanta. Oh, I realize that all the way out here, you could build yourself a real impressive home for a lot less than you can in a big city. Still, you'd think that folks would choose to live out in the country so they'd have themselves a pretty big parcel of land. Evidently that sure wasn't the case with Ruta. If you stuck your hand out one of her side windows, you could shake hands with her neighbors.

If, of course, they wanted to shake hands.

Ruta's next-door neighbors on both sides—and her neighbor in the back—had tall redwood privacy fences all around their property. It looked as if there was every chance that Ruta's neighbors might not be the hand-shaking sort.

It also looked as if someone could have easily snuck into Ruta's yard without anybody seeing.

Following Ruta into a huge foyer, through a sunken living room, down a long hallway, and finally into a bathroom larger than my dining room, I figured out why Ruta hadn't noticed the general disarray in my Bermuda Rectangle earlier. Apparently Ruta had a few Bermuda Rectangles of her own. There were magazines and books littering every room, clothes lying on the floor in the hall, and over all the obviously expensive cherry furniture was a fine layer of dust.

"Excuse the mess," Ruta said carelessly as she led the way, "but it's all Lenard's fault. That man absolutely refuses to do his share around the house. And he won't let me hire a cleaning lady. Says it's a waste of money to hire somebody to do what we can do for ourselves. Can you beat that?"

I didn't say anything. I hadn't met Lenard yet, but I knew it wasn't a good idea to start taking sides in any kind of marital dispute. Back when I was training to be a cop, I learned that was a real good way to get yourself shot. By either party.

As soon as we reached the bathroom, Ruta stepped aside. "Here," she said, "see for yourself. Have I been robbed, or what?"

The answer to that, in the absence of anything missing,

was probably "what," but I didn't say it. I just moved into Ruta's bathroom and started looking around. As luxury bathrooms go, Ruta's was right up there with the most luxurious. She had a gold marble double sink, a huge oval bathtub with gold fixtures, and a shower off by itself—as if maybe it would be too low class to actually shower in the same thing you bathe in.

Ruta's bathroom even had a bidet. A thing which I might not even have identified otherwise, except that my ex-wife once told me what they were. In a real condescending voice, I might add. A bidet, as best as I can remember, is something like an automatic squirt gun for your rear end. I can't imagine what could possibly be classy about a thing like that, but it must be or else luxury bathrooms like Ruta's wouldn't have one.

While I was looking at her bidet, Ruta was evidently losing patience with me. "Look at my *window*," she said testily. *"That's* where he broke in."

I followed Ruta's instructions. The bathroom window over her tub definitely showed signs of forced entry. The window sill had been badly gouged, and if that wasn't convincing enough, there was a large hole in the glass directly under the lock, big enough for a hand to go through.

"This has already been fingerprinted?" I said.

Ruta shrugged. "Oh sure, that Gunterman goon scattered some dust around, but he said there wasn't a single fingerprint to be found. Can you believe that?"

Actually, I could. Surely a burglar with any sense at all would know to wear gloves. I shook my head, though, to show Ruta how sympathetic I was, and then I started going through her house.

It took a while, being as how her house had ten rooms. Plus three baths, and a full basement. Everything, however, seemed untouched. Literally. This included two portable color televisions, a large console TV, a microwave, a camcorder lying on its side on the living room floor, a 35-mm camera on Ruta's dresser, and a wooden jewelry box lying next to the camera—all the kind of things that it's been my experience that burglars usually touch quite a bit.

You could tell none of these things had been handled at all, because the dust that layered their surfaces had not been disturbed. Dust seemed particularly to collect on the vast quantity of ceramic figurines that Ruta had sitting on end tables, coffee tables, and displayed in wooden shadow boxes on almost every wall. There were ceramic dogs, ceramic cats, and ceramic children, all captured in some cutesy pose, all painted in some of the ugliest and brightest colors I'd ever seen. Ruta apparently took to heart the sign on her shop—"Ceramics add the decorator touch."

In Ruta's home, they also added about a hundred pounds of dust.

Throughout the house, there were cobwebs in most of the corners, and in several of the rooms we actually had to step over laundry in order to get inside. Ruta, however, didn't seem at all perturbed about someone seeing her home in this condition. She followed me, occasionally kicking a pile of socks and shirts out of the way. About halfway through the tour, she pulled a nail file out of one of the pockets of her uniform and began filing her nails.

Since a client was dogging my every footstep, I was even more thorough than I regularly would be. I checked in closets, looked in bureaus, opened drawers. I even checked under Ruta's bed.

I wasn't sure what I was looking for. I certainly wouldn't know if anything was missing, and being as how Ruta's entire house looked as if it had been ransacked, I wasn't sure I'd notice any additional ransacking that hadn't been there before her burglar broke in.

I guess, mainly, what I was looking for was something out of the ordinary.

It was under Ruta's bed that, believe it or not, I found it. A very out-of-the-ordinary thing. For Ruta's house, anyway. Under Ruta's bed, the hardwood floor was gleamingly clean. Everywhere else the floor was uniformly coated with dust and tracked with footprints, but under her bed, it actually looked as if someone had taken a dust mop and swished it around under there.

I asked what I thought was the obvious question. "Have you dusted under here lately?"

Ruta's pink mouth pinched up. "You men are all alike," she said. "That's all you think we women are, isn't it? *Maids.*" Facing me, she jabbed her nail file in my direction. "Well, I've got news for you, mister. I run a hair salon full time, I've got ceramics classes to teach and Lord knows what else to do, so if you really think, after all that, I could possibly have the time to—"

I stared at Ruta. Apparently I had struck a nerve. I could imagine Ruta saying these exact same things to her husband, Lenard. Perhaps saying them, oh, a hundred thousand times or so. I decided to head her off at the pass. "Whoa," I said, holding up my hand. "I was just asking a question, that's all. I didn't mean anything by it."

I wasn't sure if Ruta believed me or not, but she blinked a couple of times and seemed to calm down a little. "Well," she said, twirling her spit curl again, "you men sometimes."

That's exactly what she said. You men sometimes. I just looked at her. Was this some kind of shorthand language I was supposed to know? I decided not to pursue it.

Being as how my last question had gotten such a great response, I sort of hated to ask my next one. "You don't happen to have a dog or a cat, do you?" I hadn't seen either one, but you never knew. Maybe they were out walking around the neighborhood, looking for some nice, clean garbage can to rummage through. After they'd gotten finished crawling around under Ruta's bed.

Ruta gave me the sort of stare she gave me earlier when I was standing in the puddle. "No, we don't have any pets," she said. "Why do you ask?"

"Oh, just wondering," I said. Casual as could be. I then took a deep breath and asked my next question. "Have you or Lenard or anybody else been under your bed lately?"

I believe the look Ruta gave me then was probably identical to the one she'd given the Gunterman twin earlier. "Well, now, what do you think?"

"I guess not," I said, turning away.

Ruta, however, wasn't going to let me go that easily. "Why on earth would anybody be under my bed?" she said.

I just stared back at her. That, of course, was the Question of the Year.

2

I was still going over Ruta's question in my mind as I headed back to my office. Why indeed would somebody have been under her bed? I was driving down Highway 46, bouncing around curves in my Ford pickup, passing large, fenced pastures filled with lazy-eyed cows, passing a couple roadside stands offering quilts and homemade jams and paintings on velvet for sale, but all I was really seeing was the underside of Ruta's bed.

I'd checked around under there pretty carefully before I left, feeling around under the mattress, even looking over the box springs and the frame with a flashlight Ruta got me from her kitchen. I'd kind of hated to look under her bed with Ruta standing right there. For one thing, she kept looking at me as if I were out of my mind. This from a woman with corkscrews all over her head. I tried to act real nonchalant, though. Like maybe it was standard procedure for detectives to do their investigating under their clients' beds.

Other than finding a dust ball in the far corner under there that looked to be about the size of a tumbleweed, I hadn't found anything unusual. Except, of course, for the lack of dust on the left side of the bed that I'd noticed in the first place.

There *had* been a little bit of something sticky on the lower part of Ruta's headboard, just under her mattress, but I'd decided not to ask Ruta if she could hazard a guess as to what this sticky stuff could be. I was pretty sure I didn't want to hear any of her guesses. I myself was hoping that this stuff was just a bit of chewing gum that had dropped down there. I decided, however, that it would probably be a good idea to wash my hands in Ruta's luxury bathroom, right after I left her bedroom.

Ruta stood in the doorway to her bathroom, watching me the whole time I was in there. You might've thought she was worried I might be inclined to do some burgling of my own. Frankly, I couldn't see anything in Ruta's bathroom to steal, unless Ruta was afraid that the brightly painted ceramic animals that she'd arranged in groups on either side of her gold marble sinks might catch my fancy. I didn't want to hurt Ruta's feelings, but there wasn't much chance that I wanted to take home a fuchsia puppy with a daisy in its mouth or an orange rabbit holding an Easter egg. In fact, I probably would've insisted that Ruta pay me to take these pieces off her hands.

I was just drying my hands when Ruta said, "So. What did the burglars steal?"

I gave her a look. Did she really expect me to come up with a list of missing items just by taking a stroll through her house? I was good, but I wasn't that good. I decided I'd better level with her. "To tell you the truth, Ruta," I said, "I think there's every chance that nothing was stolen."

This apparently was not what Ruta wanted to hear. She gave her corkscrews a contemptuous toss and said, "What? Are you kidding? Do you really think that somebody broke in here for no reason?"

I held up my hand, trying to calm her down. Her corkscrews looked as if they might be spinning out of control. "Oh no, somebody did this for a reason, all right," I said. "I'm just not sure what the reason was. *That*, in fact, is what I'm trying to figure out."

Ruta now gave me a hard look of her own. "You're trying to figure this out by crawling around under my bed?"

Oh yeah, that was skepticism in her tone again.

I swallowed, and then, looking Ruta straight in the eye, I said, "That's standard procedure when you're investigating a burglary."

Ruta, believe it or not, actually bought it. She blinked her black eyes a couple of times, and then said, "Oh. Of course." Her tone implied that she already knew this, but that it had slipped her mind.

I gave Ruta a shrug that said, That's OK, we private investigation professionals don't expect mere laymen to know all the intricate ins and outs of our job, anyway.

Ruta was actually looking humble when I left. I'd poked around a little more in her house, but hadn't found anything else worth noticing. Ruta followed me to her front door. "Now, I don't want you thinking I was trying to tell you how to do your job or nothing," she said. "Everybody around town has been telling me what a real good detective you are and all. It's just that it's real upsetting to have your house broken into, even if you can't find nothing missing. Lord, if Lenard wasn't due back home tonight, I'd be a nervous wreck, staying here alone!"

"You know," I said, "it might be a good idea to get yourself some kind of burglar alarm."

Ruta nodded so vigorously, her corkscrews looked as if they were in a wind storm. "Oh, I've already thought of that. I'm not going to have me any more break-ins, you can bet your booty on that!"

I tried to give Ruta the kind of confident smile that said I was sure my booty was in no jeopardy whatsoever.

Ruta smiled back at me. "And I know you're going to get to the bottom of this for me, Haskell." She reached out and gave my arm a quick squeeze. "You're going to find out exactly who it was that broke in here, and you're going to find it out real quick. *I just know it*. Understand?"

I understood. This was Ruta's version of a pep talk.

She stood there in the doorway to her home, both arms now folded across her ample chest, staring at me with those black Spuds eyes.

I don't recall, however, ever seeing Spuds look that rattled.

I was real tempted to tell Ruta about the lack of dust that I'd noticed under her bed, but like I said before, I didn't want to scare her any more than she already was. I was pretty sure the possibility of somebody hiding under her bed—perhaps while Ruta herself was also in the house—probably wouldn't set any too well with her.

Then again, I could be wrong about somebody being under Ruta's bed. No use scaring Ruta with the idea if it wasn't even so. Maybe there was a perfectly good explanation for there being no dust under there.

That's what I kept trying to come up with all the way back to my office. A perfectly good explanation. If someone had not crawled under Ruta's bed, how could the dust have gotten disturbed? Was it possible that all the dust in Ruta's house had whipped itself into one of those sandstorms you see out on the desert, and that the resulting whirlwind had blown the dust away?

I don't know, but that seemed a tad farfetched.

Unfortunately, that was the closest to a perfectly good explanation I could come up with. By the time I'd finished passing cows and roadside stands and had made a right turn off Highway 46 onto Main Street, I was convinced that somebody *must've* been under Ruta's bed. But why? Had an intruder been surprised in the act of robbing Ruta's house, and hidden under there? That would certainly explain why nothing had been taken. Maybe Ruta's early return had interrupted the burglar right after he'd broken into her house, and he hadn't had time to steal anything yet. Once Ruta walked in, the intruder could've quickly hidden under her bed, waiting for a chance to leave the way he'd come in.

That sure sounded like the most plausible explanation. And yet, was it likely that somebody could lie under Ruta's bed for very long without Ruta knowing they were there? Since Ruta had apparently noticed the break-in right after she'd returned home, a burglar might've had to wait under her bed for quite some time. While Ruta called up Vergil. Maybe even until after the Gunterman twin showed up, and Ruta went out front to answer the door. The burglar would've had to lie under Ruta's bed the whole time, without making a sound. In all that dust. It was a mind-boggling thought. I wasn't sure a human being could stay under Ruta's bed for any length of time without sneezing his head off and giving himself away.

If somebody could've managed such a feat, however, the idea of poor Ruta alone in her house with an intruder hiding under her bed *was* an unnerving thought. In the years I spent working homicide in Louisville, there were quite a few homicides I could recall that had started out as simple burglaries. They'd turned into homicides right about the time the burglar had been surprised in the act. Ruta might've been a lot luckier than she knew.

Just thinking about this made me real glad that Ruta's husband was due back in town this evening. It also made me real anxious to find out who Ruta's intruder was before her husband went off on another road trip. Just in case her burglar decided to give it the old college try one more time.

I parked my truck in back of Elmo's, as usual, but instead of going on up the stairs to my office, I headed into the drugstore. I had several reasons for going in there. Number one, it was a little after two by now, and my stomach was starting to make some real threatening noises. Like maybe if I didn't put some food in it soon, it was going to start trying to digest the nearest major organ. Fortunately—as I mentioned earlier—Elmo has himself a soda fountain along the left wall of his store. It's one of them old-fashioned soda fountains, the kind you don't much see anymore, with a lot of stainless steel and a gray linoleum counter and red plastic-topped swivel stools.

Walking in Elmo's front door, I made up my mind that the perfect lunch for today would be a large cherry Coke, a big bag of barbecue potato chips, and a banana split, heavy on the hot fudge sauce. My ex-wife, Claudzilla, had me on a health food diet just before we got ourselves divorced, and now every once in a while it gives me real pleasure to eat a meal that would make Claudzilla's eyes bug out.

I headed toward the soda fountain. On the way I spotted Elmo over in the antacids section. He wasn't hard to spot. Like me, Elmo has red hair. It makes an orangy-red border around his ears and the back of his head. The top of Elmo's head is another story, though. There Elmo has almost no hair, red or otherwise. These days he keeps what hair he does have cropped real close to his head. Elmo used to let it grow kind of long and shaggy around his ears—no doubt trying to compensate for his lack of hair elsewhere—but he doesn't do that anymore. Not since the folks around town who compare *me* to Howdy Doody started comparing *him* to Clarabell.

From what I could tell, Elmo was right in the middle of helping a customer choose the most effective laxative. This is the kind of nonstop excitement you come to expect in the drugstore business. Ever since I've been back in town, Elmo has been after me to join him in the wonderful world of drugstore management, but I keep telling him, no, thanks. I don't think my heart could take it.

Elmo saw me just about the same time as I saw him. He gave me a quick nod and turned back to his customer. I returned his nod and started looking around for Melba. Melba, you see, was the other reason I headed into Elmo's. I was real anxious to do some talking to her.

Of course, there was a distinct possibility I wouldn't find her in. It *was* only two. Melba's lunch hour, of course, is supposed to be the same as just about everybody else's in Pigeon Fork—noon to one. It's only the first of those times, however, that Melba pays close attention to. At twelve on the dot you can bet your firstborn that she is heading out the door. What time Melba heads back in, however, is anybody's guess.

Sure enough, a glance toward the back of the drugstore told me Melba wasn't at her desk. This, however, didn't necessarily mean that Melba had not yet returned from lunch. Melba has this game she plays. It's called If You've Got a Job for Me, You'll Have to Find Me First. It's a game I myself used to play with my mom when I was a kid. Melba is better at it than I ever was, though. There was every chance Melba had started playing this game the minute she saw me walk through the door.

Melba's game playing and her long lunch taking might make you wonder why Elmo and I keep her on. The answer to that one is simple. Ever since Otis Hawley saw fit to have himself a heart attack three years ago, Melba has been the sole support of five children. Ranging in age from four to fifteen.

Melba keeps ten or twelve framed pictures of her assorted kids on her desk, too. I used to think it was on account of her missing them so much during the day. After meeting her five hellions, though, I've decided that there's no way even a mother could miss them. Melba's kids are probably the only kids in America who could make Cosby want to smack them. No, I've decided that the pictures on Melba's desk are mainly there for mine and Elmo's benefit—to remind us that, no matter what, Melba's got job security.

Don't get me wrong. Melba does have her useful moments. Like, for example, the reason I wanted to talk to her was to ask her what she'd heard about Ruta's break-in. Mind you, it wasn't that I wanted to ask Melba *if* she'd heard anything. I wanted to ask her *what* she'd heard. Because there wasn't a doubt in my mind that Melba would've heard something. After all, Ruta's home had been broken into this *morning*, for crying out loud. Hell, there was every chance Melba already knew the name of the burglar. And maybe his Social Security number.

Since I couldn't see Melba anywhere, I considered for a second going over and asking Elmo if he knew where Melba was, but I thought better of it. Saying the words "Where is

Melba?" to Elmo is a lot like lighting a match during a gas leak.

Instead, I made my way over to the soda fountain, filled a large glass with ice and Coke, added a little cherry flavoring, and then picked me out what looked to be the plumpest bag of barbecue potato chips. I'd just gotten out the banana split dish and was peeling a banana when Melba appeared at my side.

"You want me to do that for you, Haskell?" she said.

Really. She actually said that.

Melba, I was pretty sure, had never volunteered for a job in her life. So for a second I just stared at her, like maybe she was some kind of ghost. Except, of course, Melba was wearing an outfit that I was pretty sure no ghost would be caught dead in. No pun intended.

Her hair in a brown beehive, Melba had on what used to be called a muumuu back in the sixties. It's a real loose, brightly flowered, tentlike thing that I think comes from Hawaii. I also think that muumuus are supposed to be real good camouflage for women who are a little overweight, and that's why Melba wears them so much. Unfortunately, however, poor Melba is not a little overweight—she's a *lot* overweight. I'd guess about a hundred pounds worth. This fact has led some folks around town—the same, oddly enough, who compare me with Howdy and Elmo with Clarabell—to suggest that on Melba, this particular dress ought to be called a moo-moo.

Continuing the Hawaiian look, Melba had stuck three red plastic chrysanthemums in her beehive, real close to her left ear. Unfortunately, she had apparently misjudged the length of the green plastic stems on the chrysanthemums. At least two inches of all three stems protruded from her beehive in the back. If you didn't notice the chrysanthemums in front right away, you might think Melba's hair had been harpooned.

I was staring at her green harpoons, and I guess I didn't answer Melba fast enough, because she reached over and took the partially peeled banana right out of my hand.

"Haskell, *I said* I'd do that," Melba said. Her voice had this real odd lilt.

"Oh. Sure," I said uncertainly, no longer staring at the harpoons but staring at Melba herself. She did look kind of strange. Her round face was flushed, and her small, heavily mascaraed blue eyes looked as if each one had a tiny flashlight inside it.

"I'm feeling in such a good mood today that I want to be all the help I can be," Melba said. "I just want to *do* for my fellow man. Make somebody else's life a little easier. Make the world a better place to live. You know?"

This seemed a lot to ask of a banana split, but who was I to object? Melba was giving me a rapturous smile, so I smiled weakly back at her.

"I'm just so-o-o happy," Melba said. She was slicing the banana lengthwise now, lining the banana split dish with the slices. Her smile had turned smugly secretive. "It really is a beautiful, beautiful, beautiful world, isn't it, Haskell, honey?"

The "beautiful, beautiful, beautiful" was a bit much, but it was the "honey" that really perked up my ears. Melba had never called me anything even close to "honey." A couple times I'd heard her mutter "asshole" as I walked away, but never "honey." I started feeling chilled, staring at her. Lord. This was serious. Either Melba had undergone a major personality transplant on her lunch hour, or the Body Snatchers were in town.

Or there was, of course, another possibility.

"You're not taking any medications, are you?" I asked. Real nonchalant, I thought. I even ate a few barbecue potato chips, real casual-like, right after I asked.

Melba actually giggled. "Nope," she said. Her voice had that unnatural lilt again, and that odd little smile of hers was back. "Oh yeah, I meant to tell you—you don't have any messages."

My mouth almost dropped open, nearly losing the chips I was chewing. Melba, telling me about my messages *before* I asked? The woman really must be having some kind of breakdown. Maybe her hellions had finally pushed her over the edge. I peered at her a little closer. "Melba, are you feeling OK?"

Melba beamed at me. She was plopping large scoops of vanilla ice cream on top of my bananas. "I have never *ever* been better," she said. Her small, round eyes gave me a significant look.

I knew a cue when I saw it. So I asked, just like I was supposed to, "OK, Melba, what exactly are you so all-fired happy about?"

Melba looked positively delighted that I'd asked. Her little smug smile turned into one so big, you could see her back teeth. "Oh, Haskell," she cooed, clasping her plump hands together, nearly knocking over the banana split dish in the process, "I think I've finally found him!"

She had lost *me*. "Who?"

"Him!" Melba said again. Her tone was rapturous. *"Him!"*

I was in no mood to play guessing games. Besides, with Melba, I'd found, she could've been talking about anything. Hell, she could've found Jimmy Hoffa, for all I knew. "Great," I said. "Terrific." And then, after what I thought was a polite pause, I said, "So tell me, have you heard anything about the break-in at Ruta Lippton's?"

My pause evidently wasn't polite enough. Melba's smile dimmed a little. "Nope," she said. "I ain't heard a thing."

My mouth almost dropped open again. Lord. This was every bit as startling as Melba volunteering for a job. "You haven't heard—"

Melba interrupted me, her tone a tad bit testy now. "Haskell, *I said* I ain't heard nothing, didn't I?"

I continued to stare. Melba wasn't even acting *interested* in the break-in. Maybe the Body Snatchers *had* come through town.

Melba hurried on, giving the plastic chrysanthemums in her hair a little, self-satisfied pat. "I'll have you know, Haskell Blevins, that I have other things to do these days than just sitting around and gossiping—"

Now, *this* was definitely news. This time I not only stared, I was pretty sure my eyes bugged out some.

Melba leaned closer, and lowered her voice. Her secret smile was back. "Maybe you didn't hear me, Haskell," she said. *"I said* I've found HIM. The Man of My Dreams."

Oh dear. Melba, you see, has been dreaming for some time now. Ever since poor Otis had his heart attack, she's been casting dreamy-eyed glances at every eligible man in town—and at quite a few of the men who are clearly *not* eligible. She's even cast a few glances my way. Which I've pretended not to see.

"Dalton Hunter is the most wonderful man in the world," Melba was going on. "He just told me today that he's been looking for a woman like me all his life."

I didn't say a word, but before I could stop myself, I thought, All his life? Hell, he didn't have to look hard. He could've spotted you a mile away.

I know. I know. I'm mean. I felt guilty the second I thought it.

Melba was gushing now. "He's new in town, Haskell, and I want you to meet him. I know you'll think Dalton's every bit as wonderful as I do."

I nodded, trying to smile, but to tell you the truth, I couldn't help getting a quick mental picture of Otis, the first Man of Melba's Dreams. Otis, who'd given Melba five juvenile delinquents to remember him by. Otis, with his pockmarked face and huge beer belly. Otis, the man Melba had referred to many times as "The Cutest Man Ever to Walk God's Green Earth."

I wasn't sure, but there seemed to be a real good chance that I wouldn't quite see the same thing in this Dalton character as Melba did.

"I'm real happy for you, Melba," I said. I meant it, too.

Melba giggled again. She actually stood there, squirting my banana split with whipped cream, giggling like a schoolgirl. I'd never seen her like this. Fact is, I started hoping right then and there that Dalton was everything she said he was.

I did have one tiny, little selfish thought. I also hoped that

Melba finding her true love was not going to, in any way, hinder her gossiping abilities. I leaned closer to her. "I was serious about asking you about the break-in at the Lipptons', Melba. I really would like you to keep your eyes and ears open the next few days, and see what you can come up with. OK?"

I stood there, hardly daring to believe that I was actually having to encourage Melba, of all people, to tune in to Gossip Central. It was like reminding a fox not to forget to chase chickens.

Melba, however, obviously needed the encouragement. She gave me a glazed look, still smiling that secret smile, and nodded vaguely. "Oh, sure, Haskell, sure," she said, waving a plump hand distractedly. She was dropping maraschino cherries on top of the whipped cream. "If I hear anything," she said, "I'll, um, be sure to tell you."

You could tell she couldn't care less. She put the last cherry on my banana split, gave me another glazed smile, and wandered off toward her desk. I sat down at the soda fountain, ate my chips and banana split, and finished off my Coke. The whole time, though, I kept glancing over at Melba across the way. As usual, she was spending most of her time staring out the window. The only difference was that you could tell that whatever she was looking at, she wasn't really seeing. Goodness. The last time I'd seen Melba look this dazed with joy, Elmo had just announced a week-long sale on hot fudge sundaes.

It looked like Melba was going to be even more useless to me than usual. And that was saying a lot. Fact is, I wouldn't have believed it possible.

As soon as I finished my lunch, I left Melba continuing to stare dazedly into space, and went to take care of the last and final reason I'd gone into Elmo's in the first place. With a puddle still waiting for me upstairs, I needed to get a bucket and a mop.

As I said before, thanks to my agreement with Elmo, this mop and I have gotten to be real close in the last year. I didn't have any trouble at all finding it. The mop was exactly where I'd left it yesterday afternoon, leaning against the back wall of the storeroom.

It only took me about thirty seconds to get back to my office. It took, however, the next hour and a half to mop up my puddle. The puddle had shrunk some while I was gone, but it was still pretty good-sized. I would've finished earlier, but the magazines that had gotten soaked were now stuck to the floor. I actually had to scrape off a couple *Popular Mechanics* and a *Motor Trend* with my fingernails. Not the most fun job in the world, let me tell you.

I'd just finished peeling off the last magazine and was wringing the mop into my bucket for the very last time when a figure appeared once again out on my landing. Unlike Ruta, this figure knocked.

He not only knocked, he actually opened the door and walked in. In his early thirties, with thick, shaggy blond hair and a full beard, he stood there, staring at me, a toothy grin on his boyish face. Wearing a blue oxford cloth shirt with a button-down collar, khaki twill slacks, hard-soled moccasins, and a gold chain with a peace symbol dangling from it, the guy looked like he couldn't make up his mind whether he wanted to be a hippie or a yuppie. His face was vaguely familiar. I stared at him, mop still in hand, trying to place him.

"Spatterface!" he said. "How in the world are you?"

The answer to his question was, of course: Fine, right up until you called me Spatterface.

Lord. I hadn't heard that one in years. In fact, I'd almost forgotten that's what the guys back in my ninth grade phys. ed. class had once called me.

That's the down side to coming back to live in your hometown. Everybody still remembers stuff about you that you'd just as soon they'd forget.

Like this here nickname thing. Back in the ninth grade, some sadist had started calling me that. On account of my freckles, of course. And the name had stuck. Naturally. Names like that always do. I mean, if they'd started calling me something like, say, "God's Gift To Women," that wouldn't have stood the test of time. "Spatterface," though, now, *that's* a name folks remember.

The guy standing in front of me had to be somebody from Pigeon Fork High, or he wouldn't know the nickname. But he sure didn't have a face I remembered. Of course, it was probably real likely that he didn't have the beard back in high school. I must've looked as puzzled as I felt, because he said, "It's me—Winslow! Winslow Reed. Remember?"

I immediately nodded, shook his hand, and said, "Well, how about that? It's good to see you," and stuff like that, but all the time I was thinking, Good Lord, how this guy has changed. The Winslow Reed I remembered from high school had been a runt. He'd been no taller than five seven, and had weighed in at no more than 130 pounds—and that was just on days he wore heavy clothes. Apparently Winslow had undergone a major growth spurt in the years since we'd graduated. He was now about an inch taller than my own six foot height and he probably had ten pounds on me. Not to mention, judging from the way he shook hands, Winslow must be working out pretty regular at a gym somewhere.

Winslow was now looking at the mop in my hand. "I see you're doing your spring cleaning," he said. The glance he gave my office told me he thought this might be a real good idea on my part.

I nodded, as if to say, Yep, that's what I was doing, all right. No use boring him with my air conditioner problems. I scooted the bucket off to one side, leaned the mop against my desk, and gave Winslow my undivided attention.

"Well, I heard you were back in town, and I've been meaning to come up and say hello before now," Winslow said, still grinning at me. His grin could've been painted on. I remembered that back in high school, Winslow had almost never smiled. No wonder I hadn't recognized him. He was the guy who always sat in the back of the class and didn't say a word. Apparently, in addition to growing some, he'd also learned to talk. "I'm an English teacher now, you know," he said, "at Pigeon Fork High."

I tried not to look as surprised as I felt. Shy Winslow

standing up in front of a class without turning red in the face? Of course, maybe he still did turn red. You just couldn't see it for the beard.

"No kidding," I said.

"And *you're* a detective," he said. As Winslow said the words, his blue eyes got kind of intense, and I suddenly realized that this was not, after all, a purely social call. "Well, believe it or not, that's one of the reasons I came by," Winslow went on. "My house was broken into today, and I don't think the sheriff is taking it seriously enough."

I just looked at him. This was beginning to sound familiar.

"Oh? What was stolen?" I said. I already had a pretty good guess as to what Winslow was going to say next.

Winslow said it, all right. He scratched his shaggy blond head and said, "That's just it. Not a thing was taken. I've looked through the entire house—I even went through the wife's jewelry box—and I haven't been able to find anything missing."

Uh-oh. Where had I heard this before?

3

I don't know which surprised me more. Winslow having the exact same story as Ruta's, or his being married. The Winslow I knew back in high school had not exactly been a lady killer. In fact, I couldn't remember him ever actually going out on a date. Come to think of it, I'd always been real glad to know him back then. The one guy in high school who'd had a less active social life than I did.

"I tried reporting the break-in to Vergil," Winslow was saying, "but you could tell the sheriff stopped listening the second I told him nothing was stolen. He just took the report over the phone, and then sent over one of his deputies to dust for fingerprints."

I just stared at him. Winslow sounded as if he were reading from the same script Ruta had read from earlier. It was weird. By the time Winslow had finished telling me that the Gunterman twin had found no fingerprints during his search, just like Ruta, and he'd written me a check to cover a day's pay, just like Ruta, I was going through déjà vu in a big way.

It even took me just about the same time to follow Winslow's gray Toyota Camry over to his house as it had for me to follow Ruta's Firebird over to hers. This had a lot to do, however, with the fact that Winslow also lived in Twelve Oaks. Winslow's backyard butted up to a wooded area, but it was only three streets over from Ruta's.

Like Ruta's, Winslow's home was a huge structure on a postage-stamp lawn. Unlike Ruta's, however, Winslow's house was a white Spanish-style stucco, with arched windows and arched doors and black wrought-iron trim. Winslow's place looked every bit as expensive as Ruta's, all right, but I can't say it was the kind of architecture I particularly like. Houses like Winslow's always make me want to drive up to a side window and order a taco.

Winslow himself drove around to the side, but he didn't stop at any windows. He pulled up his Camry in front of the attached stucco garage, and got out. I parked my pickup right in back of the Camry, and followed Winslow up the pebbled sidewalk.

On the way, I couldn't help but notice that in front of each of the five upstairs windows facing the street was a small wrought-iron balcony. None of these balconies looked sturdy enough or big enough to hold human beings. They were apparently, then, little wrought-iron *bird* balconies. In fact, at that very moment, a couple of blackbirds were perched on the wrought-iron balcony directly above the door. As I headed up the sidewalk, I also noticed something else. These birds—or maybe a flock of other ones—had evidently been there quite a while. They'd left little mementos of their visit on Winslow's front porch.

Now, I don't want to sound picky or anything, but this here seemed like a real design flaw to me.

Winslow, however, didn't seem to notice the bird leavings. He unlocked his huge oak front door, stepped aside to let me go in first, and I—ever mindful of the birds overhead —went through so fast, you might've thought I was eager to see if the Spanish theme had been continued inside.

It had been, but I can't say I was eager to see it. *Amazed* was more like it. Looking around me, I was pretty sure there were people in Mexico whose houses looked less Spanish than this. There were red, green, and yellow straw hats hanging all over the walls, red, green, and yellow straw baskets in almost every corner, and huge cactus plants sitting all over the place in—you guessed it—red, green, and yellow pottery containers. The couch in the living room was upholstered in what looked to be a Mexican blanket, and on each end table there were ceramic bullfighters with red capes dramatically swirling around them. In my opinion, the dramatic effect was somewhat spoiled by the red lampshade on each bullfighter's head, but maybe I was being picky again.

Standing out in Winslow's foyer, there was even what looked to be an actual conquistador. It startled me for a second—I actually thought for a second that maybe Winslow had hired this guy to stand there. Maybe paid him by the hour. On closer examination, however, I realized that this was a genuine life-sized wooden statue. Like one of them cigar store Indians, only in a different outfit. This conquistador had the same look of distaste on its wooden face, though, that you always see on the wooden Indians. In fact, this conquistador statue looked downright embarrassed to be there.

I can't say I blamed it.

My own amazement at all this must've shown on my face, because Winslow nodded as if I'd said something. "The wife did the decorating. She's got a real flair for it."

Flair is not what I would've called it. Obsession, maybe. This entire house could've been carted into a psychiatrist's office as a symptom.

I gave Winslow an insincere smile. "Nice," I said.

Winslow nodded. "The wife and I went to Cancun for our honeymoon, and she wanted our home to be a constant reminder."

I glanced around again. This ought to do it, all right. If this entire house wasn't one big souvenir, I didn't know what was.

I followed Winslow out to the family room, where there were still more Mexican hats and baskets and blankets, and where, sure enough, it was obvious that the sliding glass door had been jimmied. It looked as if somebody had taken a screwdriver to it. The aluminum frame was badly scarred, and one sliding panel was now leaning off the track.

Winslow frowned, looking at it. "When the wife gets home and finds out about this, she's going to be really upset. The wife takes a lot of pride in her home."

I nodded, but to tell you the truth, it was beginning to make me feel kind of uneasy the way Winslow kept referring to the woman he married as "the wife." Maybe it was because I could hear echoes of my ex, Claudzilla, going on and on the one time a friend of mine had referred to *his* wife this way. Claudzilla had said that it was just as if this guy's wife were some kind of object, and not a person at all. As I recall, Claudzilla had also told me that if I ever referred to *her* as "the wife," she'd start referring to me as "the jackass."

I started going through Winslow's house the same way I did Ruta's. Checking in closets, looking in bureaus, that sort of thing. It was here, however, that my feelings of déjà vu came to an abrupt halt. Mainly because where Ruta's house had been a collection of Bermuda Rectangles, Winslow's house looked like a museum. A Mexican museum, but a museum nevertheless. None of the hats or the baskets or the bullfighters showed the slightest trace of dust. In fact, in every room, the carpet looked freshly vacuumed.

"The wife is a stickler for neatness," Winslow said as he followed me through the house. "She vacuums every day when she gets home from work."

I glanced over at him. For a second there, I wasn't sure if he was bragging or complaining. Winslow must've taken my glance for a question, because he went on, "The wife is church secretary at the First Baptist, you know."

Matter of fact, I didn't know. Moreover, it suddenly occurred to me that I also didn't know Winslow's wife's name. Winslow hadn't yet called his wife by name once. It made you wonder if this was just an oversight, or if his was a marriage not made in heaven.

Or even, say, Mexico.

We were walking into the master bedroom about then. Here I checked in the two double closets, looked in the drawers of the nightstand and the two dressers, and, yes, looked under the bed. When I did that, Winslow gave me a look that could've been the twin to Ruta's earlier.

"Standard procedure," I said. Real casual.

Winslow's look didn't change.

Unfortunately, being as how Winslow's bedroom was carpeted, you couldn't tell if anybody had been under his bed or not. I'd brought along a little penlight from out of my glove compartment, and I flashed it around under there. There was pretty much nothing to see, though. There might've been a little bit of something sticky on the lower part of the headboard, but I couldn't be sure. I sure didn't want to make a big deal of fooling around under his bed—particularly while Winslow was standing right there, looking at me as if he were trying to figure out how big a padded room he should reserve for me—so I stood up as quickly as I could and gave Winslow a smile that was meant to be reassuring.

Winslow, of course, was still giving me the intense look he'd been giving me earlier.

It took something to keep my smile from wavering. "You've got to be real thorough when you're investigating a burglary," I said, by way of explanation. And I moved quickly out of the room.

Winslow followed me. His footsteps now seemed a tad on the uncertain side.

"Well, you're right, there sure doesn't seem to be anything taken," I said. My thinking here was primarily to get Winslow on another subject other than what in hell I was doing under his bed, and yet what I said was true. I could understand why a burglar might've passed on the hats and baskets and Mexican paraphernalia. There was every chance that even a burglar could've had good taste. However, there were still quite a few other things throughout the house that even a real discriminating burglar would not have overlooked. Things like a microwave, two color televisions, an expensive stereo system, a gold necklace just lying out on the dresser in the master bedroom. Some of the things, I'd noticed, had not been the most prestigious brand names, but in my experience, no self-respecting burglar has ever been *that* particular.

Which left pretty much the same situation that I'd found at Ruta's. An obvious break-in, with a lot of stealable stuff lying around, and yet, nothing apparently touched. Was it possible that the burglar had once again been surprised right after he'd broken in? Had the intruder *again* found it necessary to run before he could get his hands on anything? If so, this had to be some kind of world's record for bad timing. This kind of luck could possibly make a burglar turn to another line of work.

Or else it could make him that much more determined.

Winslow and I were heading back into the living room now. I stopped and turned back to Winslow. "Did you hear anything unusual right after you returned home?"

Winslow shook his head. "Not a thing."

"Nobody running away, or—"

Winslow shook his head again. "Nothing." Apparently the possibility of surprising a burglar in the act had already occurred to him. "Breaking in that door would've made some noise, don't you think?" he said. "And yet, I heard *nothing*. No footsteps. No movement of any kind. Absolutely nothing."

Winslow seemed pretty positive about this. And yet, if Winslow had not scared off a burglar, then the obvious question remained—why in the world would anybody go to all the trouble of breaking into somebody's house and then not take anything? "You don't know of anybody who might want to pull a prank on you, do you?"

Something flickered in Winslow's eyes, but he blinked and looked away, shaking his head. "No, not really." He shrugged and added, "Of course, one of my students could've been trying to get back at me for a bad grade, I guess."

I stared at him. That made sense. Breaking into a teacher's house sounded like just the kind of prank a disgruntled teenager might pull. It was even possible that this very same teenager could've also been paying Ruta back for, say, a bad hair-styling job. Come to think of it, this last theory was lent additional credence by Ruta's own remarkable hairdo. And yet, looking at Winslow, who was now shifting his weight uneasily from one boot to another, I wasn't so sure.

Winslow was not meeting my eyes. If I didn't know better, I'd say my old school chum here wasn't telling me everything he knew.

So much for the old school spirit.

I took a deep breath. "You know, Winslow," I said, "if you've got any guesses as to who could've done this, I'd sure be glad to hear them."

Winslow immediately started fingering the peace symbol on his gold necklace, but he shook his head just like before. "No, no," he said, "I have no idea. None at all." He gave me a quick grin. "That's why I'm hiring you."

I nodded. Hm-mm. Right. There sure didn't seem any way to get Winslow to tell me anything if he didn't want to, so I finished up looking around his house and headed toward the front door. I wasn't about to stand outside on the porch under Winslow's bird balconies saying my good-byes, so when I got to the conquistador in the foyer, I stopped and turned to shake Winslow's hand. "I'll be asking some questions around town, and I'll get back to you as soon as I find out anything, OK?"

Winslow's handshake was real firm, but not so strong that you felt like he was testing your endurance. We'd no sooner finished doing our handshaking when the front door in back of me opened, and someone walked in. I realized it was Winslow's wife even before I turned around. Mainly because Winslow said, "Oh. Here's the wife." That was sort of a tip-off.

Judging purely on her decorating, I reckon I was expecting Winslow's wife to be either (a) somebody on the order of Carmen Miranda, with ropes and ropes and ropes of brightly colored beads hanging around her neck and wrists, and maybe clicking a pair of castanets for good measure, or, at the very least, (b) a woman wearing one of them peasant-style dresses and balancing a pile of fruit on her head.

Mrs. Winslow Reed, however, was none of the above.

Petite and graceful, wearing a full-skirted navy blue dress with a white lace collar, navy low-heeled pumps, and carrying a navy blue shoulder bag, she was already beginning to smile when I turned around.

I recognized her right away. June Jacoby. Captain of the Pigeon Fork cheerleading squad, secretary of the senior class, and the girl voted Miss Pigeon Fork High the year we graduated. My God. Winslow Reed had not only managed to get himself married, he'd gotten himself married to one of the most popular girls back in high school. I swallowed, trying not to stare.

With glossy short brown hair, enormous brown eyes, and cheekbones that made you think of Meryl Streep, June Jacoby had been one of a group of girls that I'd secretly called The Untouchables. Either cheerleaders or officers in the student council or just plain gorgeous, The Untouchables were all girls so far ahead of me on the social ladder that back then I felt lucky they let me breathe the same air.

June hadn't been uppity about her social status, though. Back then she'd always had a smile for everybody. Even lowlifes like me. As I recall, a smile from June Jacoby as she sashayed down the hall after a pep rally, her short cheerleader skirt swaying to and fro, had been enough to render me light-headed for the rest of the day.

From what I could see, June hadn't changed much over the years. Oh, she might've put on a couple pounds, but for the most part, she looked as I remembered her. Cute. Petite. With the deepest dimples I'd ever seen. June demonstrated them for me as she came toward me.

"Well, Haskell Blevins," she said, extending her hand, "as I live and breathe." June's voice was just as I remembered. It had always sounded like lotion. Warm and soothing.

For a split second there, I wondered if I was supposed to

kiss June's hand or something, the way she'd presented it to me with a little flourish, as if it were some kind of gift. To tell you the truth, I was actually tempted. That's how ridiculously pleased I was that one of the cutest girls in high school had actually remembered my name after all these years.

"Well, isn't it great to see you after all this time," June said. Her grip on my hand was as light as a feather. She was not, however, looking my way when she said this. Her large brown eyes were on her husband, clearly questioning what I was doing there.

Winslow answered the question June hadn't asked.

"Haskell's a—uh—private detective now, you know, and he's—uh—here, looking into an incident that—uh— happened today." For an English teacher, Winslow was not real articulate all of a sudden.

Not surprisingly, after that little statement, the question in June's eyes did not go away. She dropped my hand and said to Winslow, "What do you mean? *Incident?*"

I had looked over at Winslow while he was being inarticulate, but something in June's tone now made me glance back toward her. She was standing pretty close to me by then, and I could see that my first impression had been wrong. Something *had* changed about June. Between her brows there were now two very deep vertical lines.

"What's happened, Winslow?" she asked. The two lines between her brows deepened. "Tell me right this minute." Was I imagining it, or had June's voice changed some? It sounded as if maybe the lotion had been left in the refrigerator awhile.

Winslow must've heard it, too, because he shuffled his feet a little, swallowed once, and then turned to me. "You've got all you need here, Haskell, haven't you?"

Which was, of course, the same as saying, Isn't it about time you left? I didn't need to be asked twice. I pick up real quick on this kind of subtle nuance. I told June it was real nice seeing her again, told Winslow once again that I'd be getting back to him soon with what I found out, and I headed out the door.

Winslow looked downright relieved to see me go. Apparently he wasn't at all inclined to explain to "the wife" what all had happened to their patio door with me standing right there, taking it all in.

It made you wonder just how upset Winslow expected "the wife" to get over the news.

I didn't have the chance to find out, though, because Winslow firmly shut the front door in back of me as soon as I cleared the doorway. I would've liked to stand out there on the porch and listen in on June and Winslow's conversation, but it would've been real awkward. I don't know what I would've said if one of Winslow's neighbors spotted me hanging around out there, or if, say, Winslow himself happened to see me. Then again, there *were* the bird balconies overhead. That right there was enough of a reason to go ahead and leave.

I probably made it off that porch and out to my truck in record time. It was about six-fifteen by then, so I decided to head on home, instead of going back into the office. Melba would've been long gone by now, anyway, and I figured that since Melba when she's not love-stricken rarely leaves me any messages, the chances of my finding any messages on my desk today were zero to none.

It took me almost twenty minutes to drive home. During that time I reckon if I were truly the private investigation professional that I'd acted like I was with Ruta Lippton earlier, I should've been going over and over the details of the two cases I was working on. Trying to figure out what in hell was going on. Trying to come up with a reason that two houses in the same neighborhood had been broken into without the intruder taking anything.

That's what I should've been thinking about. Instead, I was wondering about something else entirely. Something that boggled my mind even more.

How in the world had one of the least popular guys in my high school ended up with one of the most popular girls?

I know I should've been real happy for Winslow and all, but the fact was, I felt kind of bad. Back in high school, there hadn't been a dime's worth of difference between me and Winslow. In fact, I might've been a rung up on him on the social ladder. At least I dated every once in a while. It might've taken considerable whining and pleading on my part, but I did actually get a girl to go out with me. Occasionally. Winslow, as I recall, had not dated at all.

And yet, now—a mere sixteen years down the road— Winslow Reed had ended up living with the cute and dimpled June Jacoby, and I, on the other hand, had ended up living with a creature that was considerably less than cute and not at all dimpled.

My dog, Rip.

It was enough to make you depressed. Even realizing that June did not seem to have quite the sunny cheerleader disposition she had once had didn't make me feel any better.

Rip doesn't have all that great a disposition, either.

He was demonstrating just how great his disposition was several minutes later, as I turned in to the driveway to my house. Even over the noise of my truck's motor, I could hear Rip barking his head off, as usual, up at the top of my hill.

Rip's bark is pretty impressive, I reckon. Half German shepherd, half big black dog, Rip is sort of like E. F. Hutton. When he speaks, you listen. Even though I was only about halfway up my driveway, I could hear him real clear up there, snarling and carrying on.

The house Rip and I share is a small cedar A-frame situated on five wooded acres up a real steep gravel drive- way. My driveway is not only steep, it's real long, too— about a quarter mile—so that even with four-wheel drive, it slows me down some. I think Rip is real happy about the length of the driveway, because it gives him that much longer to bark.

I'm pretty sure Rip is not all that happy, though, about where it is we live. About seven miles from Pigeon Fork's city limits, Rip's and my house is real secluded. This is great for me, being as how I like the privacy and all. It's not so great for Rip. Being as how he doesn't get much chance to bark at anybody.

I think that's why Rip apparently made up his mind a long time ago to put in his barking time whenever I show up. He makes quite a show of it, too, howling and carrying on, like maybe he's mistaken me for Al Capone.

I had two other dogs before Rip, and neither one of them ever barked at me. Of course, neither of them lived past a year old either. For a while there, I was having some real bad luck with dogs. It seemed like every time I got myself one, it would up and die. I got them all their shots, took them regularly to the vet, and still they died. When I got my third pup, I was so discouraged, I just wrote R.I.P. on his doghouse.

That was almost seven years ago, though. It looks like Rip is going to live.

Unless, of course, I kill him myself. Even after I parked my truck and was walking toward the house, Rip kept right on barking. Snarling and slobbering and growling under his breath. Doing his impression of Cujo in the last few minutes of the movie. Rip's Cujo impression is real irritating because you know damn well that he's got to have recognized you by this time. So he's just doing this for fun.

Or, maybe, because he was desperate by now. It *had* been a long day.

This, of course, is the other reason why Rip is probably not any too crazy about where we live. Other than offering a distinct lack of barking opportunities, my house is completely surrounded by a large redwood deck. With a lot of steps to the ground. And Rip, unfortunately, has this slight psychological condition.

He's afraid to go up and down stairs.

Rip's been like this since he was a puppy. According to the vet, poor Rip has been traumatized on a permanent basis. How in the world it happened, I can only guess. Maybe his mom dragged him up and down stairs, bumping him on every step. Or maybe he's like Jimmy Stewart in *Vertigo*. Whenever Rip gets up high, the world starts spinning around. I've actually tried coaxing that fool dog downstairs with steak—thick, juicy porterhouses—and Rip refuses to budge. He just sits there, on the top of the deck, cocking his head to one side and giving me a brown-eyed stare. I finally decided that, like Jimmy Stewart, Rip was probably waiting for Kim Novak to show up and do the coaxing. Until then, Rip wasn't about to move.

I was almost to the top of the deck by now, so Rip dropped his Cujo impression and started doing a scene from *Lassie Come Home.* You would've thought that fool dog hadn't seen me in years, the way he carried on, wriggling all over and dancing back and forth and occasionally leaping in the air with joy. If I had not known that Rip goes through this same routine whether I've been gone for a day, or just five minutes down to the grocery store, I might've been more touched.

"Good boy, Rip, good boy," I said. This is what I always say, but it's evidently something Rip can't hear enough of. He seemed to go wild, wriggling all over and leaping back and forth in hysterical frenzy.

When I was almost to the top step, Rip abruptly cut the hysterics and scooted over as far as he dared to the edge of the deck. There, as usual, he waited. For me to, yes, pick up all of Rip's sixty squirming pounds and lug them down to my side yard.

This could possibly be a reason why I myself could be less than crazy about where we live. Because every night and every morning I have to carry Rip up and down stairs. So Rip, of course, can do his business in my yard, rather than on my deck. This is something that, no doubt, should've occurred to me before I bought this place. Rip's been pretty good, though. He hasn't made a mistake the entire time we've been here. I figure Rip either has one huge bladder, or he ought to be giving seminars on self-control.

As soon as I reached for him, Rip sprang into my arms. So he *was* desperate. Unfortunately, Rip's leap nearly knocked me over backwards, so I stumbled halfway back downstairs before I regained my balance. I let out a yell, and then I said, "Rip, never, never, *never* jump on me! OK, boy? NEVER." I don't know why I was telling him this. The dog obviously does not speak my language. He just kept right on squirming and trying to lick my face until I put him down on the grass.

When Rip was through decorating my side yard, I picked him up again and carried him back up on the deck. Rip this time gave up on my face and tried to lick my ears. I think he does this because my ears are easier to get to. Or maybe because he knows I hate it. "No, boy, no, boy, no, no, NO! NO! NO!"

"No" is, I think, the word I use most often with Rip, and yet, after seven years, it's a word he still hasn't seemed to grasp. He kept right on aiming his wet, sloppy tongue in the direction of my ears until I got him up on the deck. A couple of times he connected. Ugh.

I couldn't help thinking, as I carried Rip squirming and licking away, that it was probably real unlikely that Winslow at this very moment was carrying June out to the yard.

And that, if he was, and if indeed she was trying to lick his ears, he probably wasn't spending his time yelling "No!"

Oh yeah. I was depressed. I started in making dinner. Since I'd eaten a sugar coma for lunch, I thought I'd better fix myself a nice rib eye and a salad. To achieve some kind of nutritional balance. While I was shredding lettuce, I forced myself to stop thinking about June licking Winslow's ears and start thinking instead about something a little more cheerful—at least, to my way of thinking. I started thinking about Ruta's and Winslow's break-ins.

Was it possible that their would-be burglar really was just a victim of bad timing? What do you suppose were the odds that a burglar could break into two homes at the exact same moment that *both* owners were returning? I didn't know, but it didn't seem any too likely. What did seem likely was that this turkey was either a disgrace to the burgling profession —or he was up to something else. And yet, what could that something else be?

The phone rang just as I was starting to cut up tomatoes.

"Haskell?" I recognized the voice right away. Immediately I could picture the bright cheerleader smile. "Look, I'm not sure if Winslow made himself clear earlier," June said.

June's voice did not, after all, sound any too cheerful. In fact, what she sounded like was angry. I mentally erased the cheerleader smile.

"What do you mean?" I said.

"What I mean is—" and now I could hear her voice real clear; it sounded as if the lotion had been left in the deep freeze this time "—Winslow should've told you that we want this case cleared up immediately. We need to know who did this, understand? *Right away.*"

I wished I could tell her that it was going to be a snap, but that wasn't exactly the truth. I took a deep breath. I hate telling folks something they don't want to hear. "You realize," I said, "that it's going to be tough connecting somebody with the break-in if there are no fingerprints and nothing stolen that anybody could find in the culprit's possession."

June evidently wasn't hearing me. "Look," she said, "I want you to find out who did this! I take a lot of pride in my home, and I won't have it violated! You have to catch whoever did this! Understand?"

I understood, all right. I also wondered what exactly she wanted me to do for an encore. Walk on water? "I'll certainly try," I said.

There was a sharp intake of breath. "We're not paying you to *try*," June snapped. "We're paying you to catch who did this."

Old June was definitely losing popularity with me. What did she want from me? A guarantee? I sure couldn't give her one. "Look," I said, "all I can tell you is that I'll do the best I can. I can't promise anything."

I reckon my own tone was sounding a little strained by then, because June paused, gave a nervous little laugh, and said, "Well, Haskell, of course. I understand that. I just wanted you to know how important this is to me. That's all." Her voice was back to warm, soothing lotion again. "Oh, and there's one other thing," June added. "Make sure you tell *me* what you find out as well as Winslow, OK?

Winslow is so busy, he sometimes forgets to keep me informed."

I took a minute, thinking that one over. Because this sure put me in a sticky situation. Winslow, after all, was the one who hired me. Wasn't his and my business confidential? I didn't even know if Winslow knew that June was calling me.

June must've realized what I was thinking, because she said, her voice getting refrigerated again, "Do I need to put Winslow on the phone? So you can get his OK?" The cheerleader smile could definitely be erased by now. No question about it.

"I reckon I would like to speak to Winslow, yes," I said.

June exhaled audibly, and then after about a second, Winslow's voice came abruptly on the line. "Uh—Haskell," he said, "uh—" the inarticulaté English teacher again "—the wife and I don't have any—uh—secrets. So whatever you tell me, you can—uh—tell her, too, OK?"

"OK," I said. I would follow his directions—I sure didn't have any problem with that—but I'd bet money that what Winslow had just told me wasn't true. If the Reeds had never had any secrets from each other, why was June insisting that I also report back to her? I may have been leaping to conclusions here, but it sure sounded as if somebody didn't trust somebody.

June got back on the phone. "So. When will you know something?" Her tone now was brisk. And irritated.

I tried to make my voice real calm. To sort of short-circuit her fuse. "Well, I'll be asking questions around town tomorrow, and I'll call you as soon as I hear anything."

I was telling her the truth. I fully intended to talk to Melba again, and to Vergil himself, and to anybody else I could think of who might know something.

You might've thought I was lying, from June's reaction, though. "I expect to hear from you tomorrow," she said. "EARLY." And she hung up.

I stood there, looking at the dead receiver in my hand. One thing was clear. I'd spent way too much time envying

Winslow. It sounded as if June had not been leading any cheers in an awful long time. It could very well be that Rip was the better bargain.

Across the room, Rip lifted his head and gave me a tongue-lolling grin. Sometimes, I swear, that dog can read my mind.

4

The next morning, true to my word, I dropped by Elmo's to talk to Melba before I even went up to my office. It had now been almost twenty-four hours since the two break-ins, so I figured the Pigeon Fork rumor mill had to be humming by now.

Melba, surprisingly enough, was at her desk, writing something on a steno pad.

That right there was a bad sign. It wasn't like Melba to be seated calmly at her desk at eight-thirty. Just like she was supposed to be. You might get the wrong idea. Like maybe she was conscientious or something.

And it certainly wasn't like her to be actually *writing* on a steno pad. The last time I'd seen a steno notebook in Melba's hand, she'd been fanning herself with it.

Another bad sign was the outfit she was wearing. Melba had apparently chucked the muumuu look for something a little more provocative. A black knit jumpsuit with a real low-cut V neckline. On a skinny model type, the outfit might've been alluring. On Melba, to put it as kindly as I can, it was frightening.

When I walked up to her desk, I found myself staring into several inches of cleavage. Lord. It looked as if a small child could fall into Melba's chest and never be seen nor heard from again.

With that cavern to stare at, it was difficult to raise my eyes to Melba's face. When I did, though, I realized she was wearing more makeup than I'd ever seen her wear. Her round cheeks were splashed with red, her eyebrows were bold streaks of black, and her heavily mascaraed eyelashes looked as if they might require a real effort to lift. Melba's mouth had also not been spared. It looked unnaturally red and very shiny.

Melba must've noticed my eyes on her mouth right away, because she gave her brown beehive a quick pat, pursed her lips, and said, "Nice, huh? It looks just like real expensive lip gloss, doesn't it?"

I allowed as how it did.

Melba nodded happily. "Well, it's not." She leaned forward, causing her cavern to grow. It looked as if an earthquake were taking place right before my eyes. I looked away. "It's not lip gloss at all. It's petroleum jelly!"

I sort of wished Melba had not shared that with me. "No kidding," I said.

Melba smiled even wider. "No kidding," she said.

I could only think that Melba's beloved Dalton was in for a real treat if he happened to plant one on her any time soon. He'd probably slide into the cavern. I decided that this was probably an ideal time to change the subject. "Have you heard anything about the break-ins at Ruta Lippton's or Winslow Reed's?"

Melba shook her brown beehive. "Nope," she said. "Have there been *two* break-ins? Goodness gracious." Melba's tone was that of a sleepwalker.

I resisted an impulse to shake Melba awake. "Melba," I said, "remember my telling you yesterday to ask around and see what you could find out for me?"

"Huh?" It was obvious that Melba was not paying attention. Even while I was speaking, her small blue eyes had traveled back to what she'd been writing when I walked up. I could see now that she'd been doodling. She'd been drawing large, curlicued hearts with the words "Melba + Dalton" penciled in the center.

Oh yeah. Melba was useless, all right.

I took a deep breath. "Melba, did I have any messages from yesterday?"

I don't think Melba even heard me this time. She'd started drawing another heart, this one bigger than any of the others. I gave up. It was pretty clear that even if I did have messages, Melba was in no condition to remember them. I started to turn to leave, but Melba's voice abruptly stopped me. "Haskell, did I tell you? Dalton's taking me to lunch today." She said it the same way you might say someone was taking you to Paris.

I gave her an insincere smile. "Really," I said. My voice was flat.

Melba's voice had that funny lilt again. "Really," she said, her eyes dancing with excitement. "Dalton's going to pay for it and everything!" Melba's tone implied that this was something that happened about as often as Halley's Comet went by. And that maybe it deserved as much media attention.

I gave Melba another smile. This one not so insincere. Poor Melba obviously didn't get out enough if just having someone take her to lunch got her all this excited. "You enjoy yourself, Melba," I said. "You deserve it."

She beamed at me, and I immediately felt guilty for every unkind thing I'd ever thought about her. Melba was, after all, not a bad sort, in spite of her secretarial shortcomings. And, let us not forget, she *was* the sole support of five kids. At the very least, she had a tough row to hoe. Which reminded me. I couldn't help but wonder if the illustrious Dalton had met Melba's brood yet.

If he hadn't, he was in for an even bigger treat than petroleum-jellied lips. The first time I'd met all five of Melba's kids at once, they'd done the cutest thing. While the two youngest diverted my attention by kicking me in the ankles, the other three had gone to work on my truck with a crowbar. When I'd finally turned around, all three of Melba's oldest were starting to play Frisbee with my hubcaps, laughing to beat the band.

I sure hoped Dalton had a sense of humor.

I left Melba drawing still more hearts, and headed on up to my office. At that point I'd pretty much given up on Melba being any help whatsoever on the break-ins. I intended to open up my office, check my mail, and then mosey on down to Vergil's office to talk over the break-ins with him.

Hopefully Vergil wouldn't have fallen in love any time lately.

No sooner had I finished unlocking my front door, though, when somebody started climbing my stairs right behind me. She was wearing the kind of dress you expect to see on square dancers—an old-fashioned-looking green gingham check with green rickrack around the collar, a real full skirt, and a lot of green ruffles around the sleeves and hem.

The Square Dancer started talking to me about halfway up, as soon as she got within hearing range. "I don't know if you remember me or not, but we used to go to Pigeon Fork High, and I was a year behind you? Phyllis Mayhew was my maiden name, and I guess I've changed some since high school, but maybe you remember me—we were in the same Algebra class my sophomore year. Of course, you *were* a junior then and you might not remember, but I just thought—"

I *did* remember her. Back in high school Phyllis Mayhew had been well known for her amazing ability to talk a blue streak. Unfortunately, however, that wasn't the only reason I remembered her so well. Poor Phyllis had the sort of face you don't easily forget, even if you wanted to real bad. And, contrary to what she'd just said, she had not changed much over the years. Now, just like in high school, she still looked a whole lot like Mr. Ed, her brown eyes small and close set, her face long and thin, her front teeth too prominent. It didn't help any that Phyllis was still wearing her thin brown hair in the same style she'd worn it in back in high school. A ponytail, appropriately enough.

Even if I hadn't remembered her face, I would've found it difficult to forget her voice. Phyllis always talked as if she had a clothespin on her nose. "—my last name's Carver now," she was saying, her mouth going a little faster than her thin legs as she continued to climb my stairs. "Back in high school, like I said, my last name was Mayhew, but that was before I got married, you know, and anyway, I got me a problem I need you to look into, and I been hearing around town what a good job you did on the chicken murder, so I thought, well, here's the guy to talk to, and so here I am."

Apparently Phyllis finally ran out of air here, because she actually paused for a split second, giving me a chance to say, "What can I do for you?" as I held my door open for her.

Phyllis swept through, nearly hitting me in the stomach with the large white patent leather purse she was hauling around with her. I jumped out of the way just in time, but Phyllis didn't seem to notice. She was too busy dropping her purse with a loud *thunk* on the floor beside her, and taking a seat in the large overstuffed chair I've got right next to my desk. "You can find out who broke into my house, that's what you can do," she said, crossing her legs. "They didn't take nothing, but they did bust in my back door—I don't know what they used, maybe a screwdriver—and they must've done it right after my husband, Orval, left for work this morning, because I always go right back to bed after he leaves, and I didn't hear anything—"

I just stared at her. Another burglary that wasn't a burglary. Just like the other two. What the hell was going on?

"—I just woke up around seven-thirty or so, went into the kitchen, and saw my door all busted," Phyllis was going on. And on. "My husband is a repairman, you know, he works on electronic equipment—televisions, radios, that kinda thing—and he leaves every morning around seven, and today wasn't any different, so that must've been when it happened, you know? Right when I was sleeping in my bedroom. Like I said, I didn't hear a thing, but of course, I was asleep, so naturally, I wouldn't have—"

As best as I could tell, Phyllis had yet to take a breath. The woman must have one powerful set of lungs, or else she was carrying around oxygen equipment in that shiny white purse. Maybe that was why it was so big. And heavy.

"—and I didn't get a look at them or anything, so I couldn't identify anybody, but I just thought that maybe you could look into this thing for me and find out who coulda done such a thing—"

I decided that if I was ever going to shut off the word flow, I would have to interrupt. "What did the sheriff say?"

I was all ready to hear the exact same thing I'd heard from Ruta and Winslow, but I was wrong. Phyllis looked affronted. She reached down, put her large purse smack in the middle of her gingham lap—like maybe she thought she might be needing it for protection—and began kicking her leg. She was wearing pointy white patent leather flats, too. A couple of times I was sure she was going to ram her patent leather point into the edge of my desk, but each time she managed to miss it. "Oh, I didn't call the sheriff," she said. Her little brown horse eyes now looked agitated. "Nothing was taken, like I said, so I knew the sheriff wouldn't do anything about it, and besides, you're the one everybody's been talking about, so I just thought—"

Vergil would, no doubt, love to hear this little vote of confidence. He's had his nose a tad out of joint ever since I moved back to town. As I mentioned before, Vergil and my dad were best friends all through high school and, in fact, right up until my dad died of a heart attack a little over nine years ago. So Vergil and I go back a long way. Vergil stood right there by my side at my dad's funeral, just like he'd stood there the year before when my mom died of cancer. Vergil's practically family. And yet, he has made it real clear that he does not believe that crime investigation within a fifty-mile radius of Pigeon Fork should be a family undertaking. My solving what the entire town seems to call "the chicken murder" hasn't helped.

"You didn't call the sheriff?" That's all I said, but Phyllis must've heard something entirely different.

She gave her brown ponytail an indignant toss, and put her kicking leg into overdrive. "Well, now, just a cotton-picking minute, if you're implying that I'm stupid or something for not calling the sheriff, then you've got another think coming. I'll have you know that just because a person is a housewife doesn't mean she's dumb or anything," she said. "Besides, I am not just a housewife. I'll have you know I *do* work outside the home. I take dictation and do typing for the McAfee brothers. *Two* days a week."

The McAfees own the only full-service garage in Pigeon Fork. Frankly, I couldn't imagine what kind of dictation and typing there would be to do for the McAfee brothers—unless it would be answering complaints. As one of Pigeon Fork's monopolies, the McAfees might need Phyllis to tell their customers in writing to put their complaints where the sun doesn't shine.

Come to think of it, if *that* was Phyllis's job, she was right. It could be a real career.

Phyllis's outrage had actually left her speechless for a moment, so I jumped in, holding up my hand. "Hey, look, I didn't mean anything by what I said." It seemed as if I was saying things like this a lot here lately. First to Ruta about her housekeeping, and now to Phyllis. Either these women were awful touchy, or my ex-wife, Claudzilla, was right. She always said I didn't know the first thing about women. More and more, I was beginning to believe her. "I was just thinking that maybe you'd want the sheriff to look into this so he could dust for fingerprints, that sort of—"

Phyllis's eyes grew even more agitated. "Oh, no," she said. "I wouldn't want to bother the sheriff with this. There ain't nothing missing, and I just wanted you to take a look and see what you think. I mean, you're the guy who knows about stuff like this. Not the sheriff."

I stared at her. I would have to make sure that Vergil never heard Phyllis say anything even approximating this.

Amazingly enough, Phyllis actually took a breath after

that last statement. She leaned forward a little, and added, "I've heard, you know, that there have been some other break-ins like this in town. Is that so?"

For a second, I didn't say anything. It isn't a real good idea to give folks the notion that, as a private detective, you're not all that private. And yet, here Phyllis was, telling me that she'd already heard about the break-ins. It didn't seem like it would do any harm to confirm what she'd already heard. "As a matter of fact, there have been a couple," I finally said.

Phyllis must not have actually believed the rumors she'd heard, because for a split second she looked startled. Her horse face went a little pale, and her foot stopped swinging in midair. "Really?" she said. She drew her white purse a little closer to her and said, "Whose house was broken into?"

Here I drew the line. "Well, now, that's confidential," I said. "I don't reckon I can tell you that."

Phyllis just stared at me for a minute. Then she gave her ponytail another toss. "I know who it is, anyway," she said. "I heard it was Winslow Reed's and Ruta Lippton's." Her eyes were glued to my face.

This time I didn't say a thing—not a word—but I reckon my not denying it told Phyllis everything she needed to know. She gave a quick nod of her head, and then she started kicking her foot again. "I know the Reeds and the Lipptons, you know. We all go to the same church—the First Baptist Church of Pigeon Fork? My husband, Orval, is a deacon there. This makes me wonder if maybe there's a connection, that is, I mean, maybe whoever's doing this might even go to our church, you know, I mean, that could be a possibility, don't you think?"

I just looked at her. Phyllis could use more words to get a thought out than anybody I ever saw. And yet, she had a point. It *was* odd that all three folks whose houses were broken into happened to go to the same church. Still, Pigeon Fork was a small town. There weren't all that many churches around these parts. It might've been just coincidence that the Reeds, the Lipptons, and now the Carvers all went to the

First Baptist. Nevertheless, it was something worth bearing in mind.

Phyllis, however, was looking like she'd just cracked the case or something. "It could be, don't you think? That the guy who did this goes to our church?"

"It could be," I said.

Phyllis was nodding vigorously, her ponytail flopping up and down. "To my way of thinking," she said, her brown eyes getting agitated all over again, "there's a lot of hypocrites going to that church, folks acting so good and virtuous, and yet, well, you know—why, the other day I caught one of the kids in the *choir* writing in the hymnal! Really! He was just scribbling away, like it was nothing! It just goes to show you, that church ain't teaching the right Christian values!"

It seemed to me to be a real leap from hymnal writing to breaking into people's houses, and an even larger leap to blame all these transgressions on the church a person happened to attend, but I wasn't about to argue with her.

It took a while for Phyllis to get back on the subject of her house being broken into, what with all she had to tell me about how many of the folks who regularly attend the First Baptist were living lives of sin. According to Phyllis, the choir director was an outrageous flirt, most of the women's auxiliary were outrageous flirts, and she had it on good authority that the minister himself was, you guessed it, an outrageous flirt. I just sat there, and shook my head sympathetically, until Phyllis finally seemed to remember why it was she'd dropped by. "Well," she said, clutching at her purse again, "I guess this is going to be expensive, having you look into this for me, and, well, I might as well tell you right off that I don't have a lot of money—me and Orval are just regular folks, you know, not like some here in town—so's I want you to bear that in mind, because I'm sure not wealthy or anything—"

I had to interrupt again. It looked as if she might be going on in this vein for the next few days if I didn't. "My fee is thirty dollars an hour or two hundred dollars a day."

Apparently I'd stumbled upon a way to shut Phyllis up. For a long moment she just stared at her purse, clutching it a little tighter, her horse eyes genuinely alarmed. "Well, my goodness, that *is* expensive, it really is," she finally said, "my goodness, yes, and I don't suppose you take Master-Card or Visa—" Her eyes darted to mine hopefully.

I shook my head.

"No, no, of course not, well, maybe you could just take a tiny down payment, just to get you started, maybe twenty dollars, it's all I've got, you know, and I'd be taking it out of my grocery money this week, but I reckon Orval and I could just eat macaroni for a couple of days—"

I was starting to feel like a banker foreclosing on somebody's homestead. Before I could stop myself, my mouth had said, "How about if I just bill you?"

I know. I know. This is something you're never supposed to do if you're a private detective. You're always supposed to get some cash up front. Mainly because, in the detecting business, there's always the chance that you could find out something that your client doesn't want to hear—and then, after that, your client might not be any too glad to pay you to have told it.

Phyllis's face lit up. "Oh, would you, Haskell, would you just bill me? Why, that would be wonderful, it really would, I would so appreciate it, and you don't have to worry, I'm good for every nickel, I really am, and, well, I guess you'll be needing to take a look at my house now, won't you? You can follow me, I'm parked right out front, so maybe we ought to—"

I followed Phyllis down my stairs. I was real glad we were going to be driving separate cars, because my ears were more than ready for a break.

I half expected Phyllis to drive toward Twelve Oaks, but instead of turning left on Highway 46 off of Main, she turned in the opposite direction. Her means of transportation was considerably different from Ruta's or Winslow's, too. Phyllis was driving a Toyota Corolla that had to be at least ten years old, its faded green finish streaked with rust around the doors and wheels.

I followed Phyllis down Highway 46 for at least ten miles. It took a lot longer than you might think, because the speed limit on this narrow two-lane blacktop is only forty-five. It's real easy to figure out why the speed limit is so low, though. Anybody who'd go any faster than that on all the hairpin curves and roller coaster dips is just plain suicidal.

For all the dips and curves, there are quite a few houses and businesses located on Highway 46, particularly within the first five miles or so outside of town. We passed Guenther's Used Cars, the Crayton County District #2 Firehouse, the First Baptist Church, and Calvert's Wrecker Service, among others. Finally, though, we passed the Pentecostal Church of the Holy Scriptures Campground.

I've been down Highway 46 lots of times, and I've always figured that the Scriptures Campground is a sure sign that you've just arrived in God's country. After the campground, there's just trees, and fields, and more trees, and more fields.

And only a very occasional house.

With regard to houses, I reckon Highway 46 is no different from any other country road around these parts. On this road you'll find huge homes that look just like they might be featured in *House and Garden* next month. They'll have Tara-type lawns, an in-ground pool out back, and a satellite dish out front. These opulent homes, however, will be right across the street from a tiny frame farmhouse badly in need of paint, with an ancient washing machine sitting out on its front porch.

I think this is one of the reasons I like these winding country roads. They keep folks humble.

I'd been driving along with my windows down, enjoying the sweet smell of honeysuckle, but when Phyllis and I passed the nine-mile marker, I started rolling up my windows. Having been down this road before, like I said, I knew what was coming. Highway 46, you see, runs right by one of the largest pig farms in Crayton County. Which means that you'll be passing what has to be one of the largest mudholes in the world, and more pigs than you ever wanted to see in a lifetime.

It also means something else.

Even with the windows rolled up, I could still smell it. Pig farms always seem to smell as if every one of the pigs has very recently been sick to its stomach. Of course, I wouldn't doubt that they had, being as how the pigs also have to smell that smell themselves.

About a hundred yards after the pigpen, Phyllis abruptly turned right onto a small, one-lane blacktop road that had no sign. This isn't unusual around these parts. A good proportion of the roads don't have street signs. I reckon the sign makers figure that, if you're driving this far out in God's country, you probably already know where you're going. And if you don't, you'll need God's help, because you're sure not going to be getting any from them.

The nameless blacktop road that Phyllis and I turned onto almost immediately became a small, one-lane dirt road. I say "dirt road" instead of "gravel road," because it looked as if all the gravel that had ever been on this road had long ago slid off. I was immediately glad the pigs had made me close my windows, because Phyllis's Toyota kicked up so much dust ahead of me, it looked as if I were heading into a scene from *Lawrence of Arabia.* A couple of times I couldn't even see her ahead of me.

I did see, however, when she made another right turn onto yet another nameless dirt road, and then finally, about a quarter mile later, a left turn into a dirt driveway. A minute or so later, we were pulling up in front of a small, white frame house that on its best day could only be described as a cracker box. A couple of dried-up shrubs were growing on either side of the tiny porch, and Phyllis's grass wasn't doing any too well in the shade of several large maple trees that towered above the house.

I got out of my truck and looked around. I thought my own house was secluded, but this one took the cake. It looked as if the Carvers' closest neighbors were squirrels.

Houses like this one always make me wonder how in the world did the owners ever find them to buy in the first place? Did they walk into a real estate office and ask for a house that you'd need a map to get to?

Which made me wonder about something else. How had the burglar found this place? Even more important, why had he bothered? If the exterior of this place was any indication, the Carvers didn't even come close to enjoying the kind of lifestyle the Lipptons and the Reeds enjoyed.

Either the burglar's taste had taken a real nose-dive, or he had now decided to break into houses so far off the beaten path that even the house's owners might not be able to find their way home. Maybe the burglar figured that this would be a good way to ensure that he wouldn't be interrupted again during the crime.

Phyllis, no surprise, started talking the second she got out of her car. "Well, here we are, home sweet home, as they say, Orval and I have been out here almost five years, you know, we rented for a while and then we saved up the down payment and we moved out here, so now we've got three acres around us, you know, and—"

She went on and on, heading for the house. I might as well admit it; after a while, I wasn't paying a whole lot of attention to her. It got to be sort of like listening to a radio that's on in another room. You can hear it going, but you're not hanging on every word.

I did notice, however, that Phyllis seemed to be even more agitated here in her own home than she'd been back in my office, oddly enough. Her hand was actually shaking as she opened her front door. Once I got a look inside, though, I was pretty sure I knew the reason Phyllis was so uneasy. Her house was pretty threadbare. The living room floor was covered in a shaggy beige carpet so worn that in several places you could see the dark padding underneath. These bare spots made the rug look as if it had mange.

Phyllis's carpet, unfortunately, went real well with her furniture. Backing up against the right wall and upholstered in a faded floral print, her living room sofa sagged real bad in the middle. Either a giant had sat on it once, or regular-sized folks had sat on it about a million times.

Across from the sofa, against the opposite wall, Phyllis had two light blue wing-back chairs covered in what I believe they call crushed velvet. Both these chairs looked as if maybe the velvet had been crushed *after* it was put on the chairs. They both leaned a little. In between the chairs was an ancient black-and-white console TV.

Across from the TV and directly in front of Phyllis's sofa was an Early American coffee table which apparently doubled as a telephone stand. The coffee table, with its scarred maple veneer, had clearly seen its best day about thirty years ago. Even the phone was an old model—dark brown with a rotary dial.

Phyllis was not meeting my eyes. "It's not a palace, of course, me and Orval are just regular folks like I told you, but I try to keep it nice, I really do—"

That I didn't doubt. The place looked well tended. The faded print pillows on the couch looked freshly plumped, and on the coffee table Phyllis had carefully placed a neat stack of memo paper and a pencil right next to the phone.

Phyllis followed my gaze. "That's right, I keep paper and pencil next to the phone for Orval, you know, he gets real mad if he don't have something to write on when a customer calls, so I always—" The Phyllis Carver Talk Show continued as she led the way out to her kitchen.

The kitchen wasn't any better than the rest of the house. The beige linoleum on the floor looked faded from too many washings, and Phyllis's copper-tone appliances had to be twenty years old, if they were a day. There was no dishwasher. No microwave.

It definitely made you wonder why a burglar would've bothered breaking into this place. And yet, sure enough, just like Phyllis said, her back door had obviously been pried open with some tool or another. The wood all around the lock was splintered. "—see, ain't that awful?" Phyllis said. "Orval's not going to be happy about having to replace that doorframe, I tell you, Lord, it's hard enough to get him to do anything around this place, and now I'm going to have to add this to his list—"

I started going through the house much the same way I'd done at Ruta's and Winslow's. The only difference was that this time I was doing this as much to get away from the constant drone of Phyllis's nasal voice as anything else.

Unfortunately, Phyllis followed me into every room, keeping up a running commentary. The woman had a real talent for saying a great deal about absolutely nothing. After a while she started reminding me of all those folks on TV who do the commentary on the Thanksgiving parade every year. Maybe Phyllis was cut out for another career other than being the McAfees' secretary.

"—and here's the bedroom, Haskell. I told Imogene, my sister, that I was going to paint my bedroom pink, you know, but Orval said no way, so I ended up painting it blue—of course, I shopped around until I found the paint on sale, but I do think it turned out real nice. What do you think, Haskell?"

What I was thinking was that I should've brought along a couple of earplugs. There didn't seem to be any way to shut her up. That is, there didn't seem to be any way until I pulled out my trusty penlight, got down on my knees, and flashed the light around under her bed.

That pretty much did the trick. Phyllis actually stopped in midsentence.

I was, of course, peering under her bed by this time, so for a second, I thought maybe my hearing had blown a fuse. Perhaps from an overload.

If I'd known this would shut Phyllis up, I would've looked under her bed first thing. Except, of course, I really didn't expect to see anything under there. Like Ruta's, Phyllis's bedroom floor was hardwood. Unlike Ruta's, however, Phyllis's floor had been dusted. So there was no way of telling if anybody had been under her bed any time recently.

I flashed around the penlight under there, but it didn't take long to figure out it was pointless. There wasn't even a trace of something sticky on Phyllis's headboard.

The only thing that looking under Phyllis's bed had accomplished was that it had closed her mouth for a spell. Which, come to think of it, made it worth the effort.

Phyllis didn't speak again until I'd already finished taking my look and was getting to my feet. When she finally spoke, her nasal voice had a distinct tremor. "Why did you do that?"

"Standard procedure," I said. I was getting used to saying this by now, and this time I think I said it with more assurance than I ever had before.

Phyllis did not look impressed. She just stared at me for a good minute. Not saying a word.

Which was pretty amazing, all by itself.

I was fairly certain that I could include Phyllis's name on a list of folks who think I should be in a mental institution. She didn't question me, though, like Ruta and Winslow. She just stared at me, no doubt mentally fitting me for a straitjacket.

After that, I may have been imagining it, but Phyllis seemed real anxious to send me on my way. Her chatter seemed a tad more feverish, and she repeated more than once, "Are you going to be much longer? Because I really do have to get to the grocery, you know. This burglary thing has really messed up my day, I was going to pick me up some milk, and some bread, and—uh, let me see—some eggs, and some—"

While Phyllis was going over her grocery list, I finished going through her house. It didn't take all that long, because Phyllis's house only had five rooms, if you counted the bathroom. Before I knew it, I was telling Phyllis exactly what I'd told Ruta and Winslow earlier. About how I'd ask around town and I'd get back to her as soon as I found out anything. I also advised her to report her break-in to Vergil.

Phyllis immediately nodded. "Well, if you say so, I will, I surely will, don't you worry about it, Haskell, I'll call the sheriff as soon as, well, as soon as I get back from the grocery. Although I don't like to worry him none, especially since nothing's missing, but if you say so, I'll give him a call—"

I couldn't be sure, but I think Phyllis was still talking as I pulled out of her driveway.

It seemed strangely quiet during the twenty minutes it took to drive back to my office. Sort of like the way things seem after somebody's just turned off a jackhammer.

On the way I made up my mind that I needed to talk to Vergil as soon as possible. It was pretty clear by now that something mighty strange was going on. You could possibly believe that a burglar had been interrupted in the middle of a burglary two times in a row, but *three?* Surely there couldn't be any burglars with luck that bad. And as far as Phyllis's house was concerned, there had been nothing that I could see that had been worth stealing. So that left just one question. What was this so-called burglar really up to?

It was a question I intended to put to Vergil as soon as I checked back in at my office. Checking back in was probably a waste of time, of course, but there was always the chance that Melba had had a lucid moment during her love-struck trance and had actually taken some messages for me.

I'd just gotten my office door open when my phone began to ring. It took some fast moving on my part, but I got it on the fourth ring. Like a fool, I actually expected to hear Melba's voice.

"Haskell?" the voice said. "This is Ruta. I, um, just called to let you know that I've been doing some thinking, and I've decided to, um, forget about investigating this break-in thing. You can keep the day's pay. OK?"

I was so surprised for a second, I couldn't speak. "But, Ruta, I thought you were real scared, what with your husband being—"

That was all I got out before Ruta interrupted me. "Nope, I've decided I was just being silly. I mean, nothing was stolen or anything. I've decided I was just making a mountain out of molehill."

This was the woman who was almost crying in my office?

The woman who'd been so irate because Vergil wasn't doing anything about her break-in? And now this very same woman was asking *me* not to do anything, either?

"But," Ruta was going on, "thanks, anyway."

What could I say? "You're welcome."

I was so stunned that for a long moment after Ruta hung up, I just held the receiver in my hand, staring at it. I'd just been fired. *Fired.*

When I finally replaced the receiver, it immediately rang. So fast it startled me. I actually jumped before I picked it up.

This time the voice on the line was as cool and soothing as lotion. "Haskell, this is June. I just wanted to let you know that Winslow and I *do* appreciate your help, but we've decided not to pursue this break-in thing after all."

Uh-oh. Déjà vu was kicking in again. In a most unpleasant way.

"I mean, it's not as if something had actually been stolen," June was saying. "No, Winslow and I have decided that we've just been making a mountain out of a molehill."

I swallowed. Was it me, or was it odd that both June *and* Ruta would use the exact same phrase to fire me? Was this just a coincidence? Or did something stink worse than the pigs I'd passed on Highway 46?

5

Psychologists tell you that you're supposed to look at being fired as a positive thing. It's supposed to be an opportunity for growth, giving you the chance to reexamine your goals in life, chart a new course for the future, all sorts of good stuff.

I think I reacted to being fired in a way that would've, no doubt, made all those psychologists proud. I sat at my desk, stared at the opposite wall, and tried to come up with something to blame it on. Something other than myself, of course.

My motivation here was real simple. If I didn't come up with some other reason, I might actually have to conclude that my being fired might have something to do with the way that I—like a total goon—had crawled around with a flashlight under both my ex-clients' beds, right in front of both my ex-clients' appalled faces.

Instead of focusing on this as a possible explanation, I preferred—oddly enough—to consider the possibility that something strange was going on. It *was* weird, wasn't it, that both Ruta and June had called me up within minutes of each other to give me the ax? Sure it was. It did make you wonder.

It could even make you think that maybe both these women had been encouraged in some way to do it. Maybe they'd even been threatened. Was that why they'd both fired me only a day after hiring me?

Having heard from both Ruta and June, I halfway expected to hear from Phyllis, too, any minute. Of course, Phyllis *had* told me that she was going out to the grocery. Maybe she hadn't been home, and whoever might've contacted Ruta and June hadn't been able to get in touch with Phyllis yet.

As I considered this, I glanced over at my phone. If this particular theory was correct, my phone should be ringing real soon after Phyllis got back from stocking up on milk, bread, eggs, and the rest of the stuff she'd rattled off while I was looking through her house.

My phone, however, continued not to ring.

While I stared at it, I couldn't help thinking that the worst thing about all this was that it sort of left me in limbo. I'd been intending to head on down to the sheriff's office to discuss Ruta's and Winslow's break-ins—and maybe Phyllis's break-in, too, if she'd already reported it. But now I wasn't even working for Ruta and Winslow anymore. I couldn't very well tell Vergil that I was doing some investigating for them, when all he had to do was pick up the phone to find out that I was lying.

And maybe I was being a little sensitive here, but I sure hated to mosey into Vergil's office and tell him that I'd like some information on the Lippton and the Reed break-ins even though I'd just been fired. Twice. Old Vergil was liable to pop a vein laughing.

So that just left Phyllis's near-burglary. The problem with that one, though, was that if Phyllis had not yet reported it, it was going to be real hard to discuss that particular violation of the law with Vergil. I knew without even thinking about it that the very idea that folks might be reporting crimes to *me* before they got around to telling Vergil would not do his out-of-joint nose problem any good.

The only thing left for me to do seemed to be to quit waiting around and go ahead and give Phyllis a call myself. To find out for sure whether she'd called Vergil yet. Phyllis hadn't said how long she'd be grocery shopping, so there was a chance she'd already be back.

It was not, of course, a good chance. Which I immediately found out as Phyllis's phone rang and rang and rang.

The phone was on its sixth ring when I heard a tap at my door. I looked up, fully expecting to see Phyllis standing there, no doubt intent on firing me in person. Instead, I stared into the love-glazed eyes of Melba Hawley.

"Haskell?" she said, opening my door and then just standing there, letting my air-conditioning blow past her. Melba evidently was anxious to prove that you really could cool a neighborhood with just one room air conditioner. "Well, I told you I wanted you to meet HIM." Hands on meaty hips, Melba put a heavy emphasis on that last word. "So I brought him up here to do just that." There was an unmistakable giggle in Melba's voice as she said this.

Since I'd seen her early this morning, Melba had evidently decided that the perfect thing to set off her black knit jumpsuit was a few fresh flowers. She'd stuck five pink and purple pansies where the V-neck of her jumpsuit came to a point. Melba had, no doubt, shown real restraint here. You might've thought that she had enough room at this particular location to provide bedding ground for a large bouquet and maybe a rosebush or two.

I squinted at Melba's pansies. They looked suspiciously like the ones Elmo had planted in the two flower boxes out in front of his drugstore.

While I was trying to decide if she was guilty of pansy theft, Melba was continuing to giggle as she stepped into my office and said with a flourish, "He-e-ere's Dalton." Melba sounded a little like Ed McMahon, but I decided this wouldn't be a good time to mention it.

A tall man with dark brown hair and even darker brown eyes followed Melba in. "So glad to meet you, Haskell," he said, extending his hand. "Melba has told me so much about you."

For a second, I couldn't move. I couldn't even talk, looking at him. Tall and slim, Dalton Hunter was the spitting image of Cary Grant, right down to the dimple in his perfect chin. Dalton, however, looked like Cary when Cary was in his early thirties. No distinguished graying temples here. In fact, you got the impression that if Dalton should ever happen to have graying temples, he'd immediately do something to correct the condition. Dalton's dark, wavy hair looked professionally styled, the hand he extended in my direction looked professionally manicured, and the designer suit he was wearing looked as if it might possibly cost more than I had paid for my Ford pickup.

Let's face it. If a vote was taken that minute, Dalton Hunter could easily have won Handsomest Guy in Town.

As a matter of fact, Melba must've been showing off Dalton all over town, because Dalton looked as if he was accustomed to the kind of reaction he was now getting from me. He just stood there, giving me an indulgent smile, obviously waiting for me to collect myself enough to actually be able to talk.

Melba's smile, however, was a lot more than indulgent. Clearly overwhelmed at her tremendous good fortune at being Dalton's chosen companion, Melba's smile looked as if it might wrap around her face a couple of times.

I finally found my voice. "Glad to meet you, Dalton," I said, gripping his hand. I hoped, for Melba's sake, that I was telling the truth.

Dalton's handshake was firm and vigorous. "Any friend of Melba's is a friend of mine," he said.

Dalton had the instant warmth of a used-car salesman. I gave him an uncertain smile.

"We're here to take you to lunch," Melba said, beaming at me. "And we're not taking no for an answer, neither. I'm real anxious for you two to get acquainted. My best guy and my favorite boss."

I wasn't sure whether to look flattered at that or not. Melba's only other candidate for favorite boss was, of course, Elmo, and I knew for a fact that Melba referred to Elmo as "Shithead" at least once a day. It didn't seem all that hard to beat out my competition.

Dalton, on the other hand, looked tickled pink to be designated Melba's best guy. He gave her a tender smile, reached over, and squeezed her hand. Then, turning to me, he said, "Isn't she the cutest thing you ever saw?"

For a second, I thought this might be a trick question. Melba, though, was standing there in her pansy-bedecked black jumpsuit, patting her beehive and looking at me expectantly, so I had to answer. "She sure is," I lied.

Dalton nodded, slapping me on the back. Apparently I'd come up with the right answer. "Come on, Haskell, I've been looking forward to getting to know the man my Melba talks about so much. According to Melba, you're the best detective in Crayton County."

I was fairly certain I was the *only* detective in Crayton County, but there didn't seem anything else to do but smile a little wider and accept their invitation. I followed them both out to the landing. After coming up with an answer to Dalton's question, I was now pretty much at a loss for words. It didn't seem to matter, though. Melba and Dalton were lost in each other's eyes. I probably could've mentioned that my clothes had just caught fire, and neither one of them would've turned around.

To tell you the truth, seeing Dalton stare lovingly at Melba made me feel a little suspicious. I know. I know. Men and women aren't supposed to judge each other on the basis of looks, but let's face it, they do. It's a known fact that men who look like Dalton do not generally choose to hang around with women who look like Melba. Not that Melba isn't a real nice person and all, but she is not exactly easy on the eyes. I was probably being a real cynic here, but I couldn't help wondering if Dalton was for real. He was actually looking at Melba as if she were Michelle Pfeiffer.

Then again, they do say that love is blind. In Dalton's case, love was evidently walking into walls.

"Haskell, you'll never guess where we met," Melba was now saying. She had started climbing down the stairs first, and she paused to throw Dalton, who was right in back of her, an adoring look before she continued. "At the Crayton County Supermarket! Can you believe it?"

Actually, I could. I had no doubt that Melba spent a significant portion of her life selecting foodstuffs. If you wanted to run into her at all, the grocery seemed a good bet.

"That's right," Dalton chuckled. "I found my little tomato in the produce section."

Melba roared with laughter. Really. You might've thought that Dalton had said the wittiest thing in the world, the way she hooted and slapped his arm. "Oh, Dalton," she cooed, "you are a caution." She then looked over at me. "Isn't he a caution, Haskell?"

I nodded. I wasn't all that sure exactly what a caution was, but I decided to trust Melba's judgment on this.

The two lovebirds were now staring into each other's eyes again, Dalton's handsome dark ones riveted to Melba's small blue ones.

It looked like it was shaping up to be a real long lunch.

"You know," I said, "I'm waiting for a phone call so I really can't be gone for very—"

This little ploy was doomed to failure. Melba waved a chubby hand in the air. Her fingers looked like five Vienna sausages. "Never you mind about that, Haskell," she said. "I let Elmo know that Dalton and I were taking you to lunch, and I told him to get your phone."

I almost choked. She'd told *Elmo* to answer my phone? As if she were the boss, and Elmo were the secretary? I could only imagine how well that one went over. No wonder I'd won "favorite boss."

I opened my mouth to tell Melba never to do such a thing again, but we were at the bottom of the stairs by then. And my attention was diverted by something else.

Dalton's car, parked not two steps away.

My mouth stayed open, but no sound came out. Because Dalton's car was a brand-new, ketchup-red Cadillac de Ville. With tinted windows, enough sun-catching chrome to blind the nearest pedestrian, and one of them curly antennas stuck on the back window that proclaims to the world that the driver inside has himself a car telephone.

Dalton evidently also had himself an alarm system, because he didn't do anything so mundane as actually unlocking his car with a key. Oh no, he whipped out a tiny black box from his left front pocket, pointed it at the car, and with a shrill beep-beep, the car unlocked itself.

When Dalton did that, Melba threw me a look. It was a look that said, How's that for class?

I had to admit it. Dalton was clearly doing all right. At whatever it was he did.

"What kind of business are you in, Dalton?" I asked as I got into a red leather backseat which might possibly have held all my living-room furniture.

The range of things that Dalton could possibly be doing seemed pretty much unlimited, as far as I could tell. It could be anything from oil well drilling to, say, Cary Grant impersonations. Both of which could make the man, I'm sure, a hell of a lot of money.

Dalton had already held Melba's door for her—something, I might add, that made her break into giggles again—and he was getting into the driver's seat. Dalton took a deep breath, and sort of snorted through his nose. I'm pretty sure Cary had never done such a thing in his entire life, but Dalton made the snort sound real smug. "Well, Haskell, real estate's my game," he said, as he started up the Cadillac. "I buy up property and I develop it. You might say I do the same thing as Donald Trump."

I stared at the back of his Cary Grant head. Did this mean from now on, I should call him "The Dalton"?

We drove out of town real slow. Of course, we didn't have much choice. The speed limit in downtown Pigeon Fork is twenty-five miles per hour. Folks who come to visit generally assume that the reason the speed limit is so low is for money-making purposes. They think the town has set up a speed trap to catch unwitting out-of-towners. I'm pretty sure these folks are wrong. The reason the speed limit was made this low has got to be so that everybody in Pigeon Fork can get a good look at you when you drive by.

As Dalton, Melba, and I headed out of town, I noticed we turned the heads of all the old guys who, in warm weather, spend the majority of their day sitting on the benches out in front of the Crayton County Courthouse. We also turned the heads of every customer at Pop's Barber Shop, including that of Pop himself. *And* the heads of pretty much every man, woman, child, and dog on the street.

I thought Melba would burst from the sheer thrill of it all before we even got to the turn onto the interstate. She kept giggling and patting at her beehive. You might've thought she was being seen riding out of town with the president. Why, she even rolled her tinted window down so folks could see her better.

It didn't take long to figure out where we were headed. There's only one real nice restaurant around these parts. It's not exactly what you'd call a four-star establishment or anything like that, but in Pigeon Fork about all that's required to be designated "a real nice restaurant" is that your dishes be clean and your food tasty.

The other two eating places in town—Frank's Bar and Grill and Lassiter's—both meet the "tasty" requirement. It's that other one that seems to give them trouble. Only Gentry's Family Restaurant, located about ten miles outside of town, if you keep traveling north on the interstate, meets both stringent requirements.

In fact, the only problem with Gentry's is that the restaurant itself is just a sideline. Mainly what the Gentry family does is run the U-Pick-Em Farm, getting folks to come from as far as Louisville to stand in their fields, perspire heavily, and pick their own tomatoes and corn and beans. It's sort of like running a migrant worker camp, only in this case, the Gentry's don't pay the migrant workers. The workers pay them.

Sometimes I think even the Gentrys themselves are amazed that they can get folks to actually do this.

The problem with running the migrant worker camp is that the Gentrys are clearly not concentrating on the restaurant end of the business during the summer months. That's why I pretty much avoid Gentry's Restaurant while the crops are being planted and harvested. To my mind, it's sort of like that rule about eating oysters. The one about avoiding oysters except in months ending in *r?* The rule for the Gentry's Family Restaurant is: Avoid during months ending in May, June, July, and August.

Otherwise, you have to put up with Mama Gentry glaring at you when you walk in the front door. Like maybe you've just interrupted her day. Mama Gentry is one of them big-boned, heavyset farm women, too. She looks as if any minute she might take after you with a hoe.

I was a little surprised that Melba hadn't told The Dalton about the Gentry Rule, being as how everybody in Pigeon Fork pretty much knows it. When we got to the restaurant, though, I found out why.

In The Dalton's case, the Gentry Rule didn't apply.

Dalton held the front door of Gentry's open for Melba, then sailed right up to Mama Gentry, who was standing at her usual post, right outside the dining room, scowling. "Lovely lady," Dalton said, "how wonderful to see you again. I have been looking forward all morning to lunching here at your elegant establishment."

At this point I gave Dalton a glance. He was making Gentry's sound as if it were the Four Seasons or something. Now, don't get me wrong, Gentry's *is* real nice, what with its cheery red and white checked tablecloths and its red plastic carnations in white vases on every table. But the Four Seasons, it ain't.

Not that I've ever been to the Four Seasons to find out. I

think this is an assumption, though, that I'm pretty safe in making.

"I expect that lunch will be every bit as wonderful as the sumptuous dinner you prepared for Melba and me last night," The Dalton was going on.

There was a moment of silence, during which I fully expected that Mama Gentry was deciding that what Dalton had just said could fertilize every one of her fields. I took a step backward, afraid that Mama was about to reach for that hoe I'd mentioned earlier, but amazingly enough, Mama's scowl immediately faded. She wiped her huge, weathered hands on her red calico apron and gave out with a distinctively Melba-like giggle. "Oh, Mr. Hunter, how you do go on," she said. I couldn't be sure, but I thought that beneath her deep farmer's tan, Mama Gentry was actually blushing.

Up to that moment, I think I had been fairly open-minded about The Dalton. After all, if Melba liked him, that was all I needed to know. Watching Dalton, however, turn Mama Gentry, of all people, into a simpering idiot did sort of harden my heart against him.

Of course, if that hadn't done the trick, what all Dalton had to say over lunch definitely would've.

Gentry's serves their meals family-style, which means they bring a bunch of bowls of food right to your table, and you help yourself. Its lunch menu is real simple—you can go with either the fried chicken or the hamburger patty. Both choices are printed on the red and white paper place mat, right under your red plastic plate. Most folks from out of town lift their plates to read the menu, but Dalton was too cool for that. He sat down, put his paper napkin in his lap, and turned to me. "So, Haskell, what do you recommend?" he said.

For a second there, I thought he was talking about his relationship with Melba. I was wondering if I should tell him that he probably ought to get out of town while the getting was good, when—thank God—I realized he was talking about *lunch*. "The fried chicken is real good," I said.

No matter what you choose as your main course, what you're going to get with it is creamed corn, green beans swimming in bacon drippings, hash browns, homemade apple butter and grape jam, and biscuits fresh from the Gentry oven. Melba, The Dalton, and I all went with the fried chicken.

The Dalton was slathering apple butter all over his biscuit when he said, "So, Haskell, Melba tells me you used to live in Louisville. What brought you back to a burg like this?"

I stopped right in the middle of taking a bite off my chicken drumstick. "Burg" is a word that a lot of small-town folks like me don't really like to hear. There are quite a few words like this, most of them spoken by folks who apparently feel, having lived their entire lives in a larger city, that that alone gives them some kind of superiority. Personally, I don't get their logic.

"I came back here because I love it here," I said. I tried not to sound as irritated as I felt, since Melba was now looking over at me, her eyes getting a little worried. "I was born here, I lived all but eight years of my life here, and when I was in Louisville, I missed it here."

The Dalton raised one perfectly arched eyebrow. "Really?" There was disbelief in his tone.

"Really. Pigeon Fork is a great place to live. The air is clean, there's no traffic problems, and the folks here are friendly, unpretentious, and wave at you on the street." I tried not to emphasize the word "unpretentious."

The whole time I was talking, The Dalton kept nodding his head, as if he'd heard all this before and he'd agreed with it the first time. "You're right, Haskell, Pigeon Fork *is* a great little town," he said. "I've been telling Melba here that I've got some ideas for this place that will really put this little hick town on the map."

You know those other words I mentioned before that we small-town folks find offensive? "Hick" is another one. I've never been able to figure out where this particular word came from. The only other time I've ever heard "hic" was when it was connected with "cup," and since folks in small towns don't walk around hiccuping all the time, I'm sure stumped as to how we ever got to be called this one.

I wanted to tell The Dalton what I was thinking, but Melba must've known it already. She was really fidgeting now. She was fussing with her pansies, fluffing them up nervously, and giving me sidelong looks.

I gave The Dalton a look of my own. "On the map, you say," I repeated.

Dalton nodded his handsome head eagerly. "I've got a vision, I tell you—"

I took a sip of tea. The last guy with a vision in Pigeon Fork had been one of the parishioners of the Pentecostal Church of the Holy Scriptures. He'd sworn that he'd seen all twelve apostles setting up tents in the middle of the church campgrounds. On the whole, I was pretty sure that I would probably lean further toward believing in the camping disciples than in any vision that The Dalton might have.

Dalton was leaning forward now, pointing at me with his biscuit. "I've got an idea that's going to make this place grow. Why, folks will be coming from miles around. *Miles.*" Dalton's movie star eyes were glittering with excitement. "That's why I came here, Haskell. Pigeon Fork is not going to be a small town much longer!"

I just looked at him. About every year or so, somebody seems to come up with a new idea for turning Pigeon Fork into a big city. Right after I moved back to town, Cyrus Lassiter and Pop Matheny and a couple of the other movers and shakers in town decided that Pigeon Fork ought to be trying to attract all the tourists that go right by us on the interstate on their way to Florida. As Pop told me in his barber shop, "Whoever heard of Orlando before they started going after tourists?" The answer to that one had been, of course, *Walt Disney,* but at the time I hadn't said a word. Because I think I knew even then that the idea of Pigeon Fork as a tourist mecca wasn't what you'd call an easy sell.

In fact, the idea lasted right up until folks actually started trying to come up with a list of tourist attractions around here. The only thing they could think of was the one-room schoolhouse up by the Shell station. That old schoolhouse does have history—it's got to be over two hundred years old—but even Pop had to admit, the thing was falling down. If a tourist ever actually walked into the place, there was a good chance he might not walk out.

It was generally agreed that rumors of missing tourists probably wouldn't do the town any good.

With the schoolhouse eliminated from the attractions list, the only thing anybody could think of after that was the Wal-Mart. Which was halfway to Louisville. That pretty much put the tourist idea on permanent hold.

With all this going through my mind, it was hard to keep a straight face. "I don't know, Dalton," I said. "Pigeon Fork has been a small town a long time."

Dalton made another one of them snorting noises Cary Grant would never have made. "What I'm thinking of is going to change all that," he said. "I'm going to open up a shopping center here, Haskell! With a movie theater, and restaurants, and a Saks Fifth Avenue, and a Toys R Us—"

Melba evidently had heard The Dalton's vision before, because she was nodding now, too, her brown beehive beating time with his words.

I didn't know what to say. About six months after the tourist talk had died down, there had been talk that they were going to open up a McDonald's in Pigeon Fork. It had been big news for a while. In fact, some folks had actually started calling the town McPigeon Fork. The excitement had lasted right up until the folks at McDonald's got through running what they called a market study. This market study thing is something evidently that they run all the time to find out whether a community would have enough business to keep a McDonald's going. The answer, in Pigeon Fork's case, was no.

We couldn't support a fast-food restaurant, and The Dalton here thought that he could make an entire shopping center work? I didn't want to bust his balloon or anything, but he had to be kidding. "You know, Dalton, there's not a whole lot of folks living near here—"

The Dalton interrupted me. "I know what you're thinking, but I tell you, I've done this a hundred times all over the United States," he said, leaning back in his chair and beaming at Melba. "I've gone into towns where you'd think a shopping center would never be successful, and I've done it. I've gone in, laid the groundwork, gotten the funding, and I've made it happen. All over the United States. *All over.*"

He made himself sound like Johnny Shopping-Center-Seed.

The Dalton's words had obviously whipped up Melba into a frenzy. Her head was now nodding to beat the band, and she actually fanned herself with one sausage-fingered hand, as if all these wonderful ideas had heated her up to a fever pitch. "Isn't he something, Haskell?" Melba said. "Isn't he something?"

"He sure is," I said. What that something was, though, was probably Total Fool.

I was real glad when the lunch finally came to an end. During the rest of the meal, Dalton mentioned the "hick" word five more times, and the "burg" word twice. If Melba had not been sitting between us, her eyes focused adoringly on Dalton's perfect features, I think I would've asked to borrow Mama Gentry's hoe.

As glad as I was that the lunch was over, I was even more glad when The Dalton's Cadillac de Ville pulled up in front of Elmo's drugstore, and I could get out. Now that I'd spent some time in the backseat, I'd decided that I really didn't like red leather upholstery in red cars. It was too much like getting in and out of a roast.

Dalton pumped my hand vigorously as he and Melba left me. "I'm so glad we had this chance to talk," he said.

Melba was looking at me expectantly, so I had to lie. Again. "Me, too," I said.

I was rewarded with a smile from Melba that showed the fillings in her back teeth.

"You've got a great girl here," I told Dalton. I immediately wished I'd said "wonderful" instead of "great," but Dalton didn't seem to notice.

"You're telling me," he said, giving Melba a wink that, you guessed it, made her giggle almost as much as Mama Gentry had earlier.

I escaped inside the drugstore to look for Elmo and find out if I had any messages.

I found him behind the soda fountain, dishing up a hot fudge sundae. His response was short, but not at all sweet. "Nope," he said. At least, that's what he said with his mouth. His eyes said, Get out of my store and don't ever ask me to take messages for you again.

I got out of his store.

Back in my office, I dialed Phyllis's telephone number. This time, instead of the thing ringing and ringing like before, I got a recording. It was one of them computer voices that say each word as if it's a sentence in itself. The. Number. You. Have. Reached. Is. Out. Of. Order. I called Phyllis's number twice just to make sure I hadn't dialed wrong, but the computer message remained the same.

That was odd, but I didn't think too much about it. After all, it wasn't all that farfetched to think that someone with Phyllis's amazing gift of gab could possibly break a telephone. Maybe she'd just worn the thing plumb out.

I decided to hop in the truck and take a trip out there, though. I really did need to find out if Phyllis had called Vergil yet, and her phone being on the blink pretty much left me no choice.

I think it was while I was driving around all the curves and up and down all the hills on Highway 46 that I started feeling uneasy. Of course, at the time I put it down to being a tad carsick.

When I pulled up in front of Phyllis's little cracker box, the first thing I saw was Phyllis's rusty Toyota parked in her driveway. I barely glanced at it, though. I was too busy feeling more and more uneasy. For one thing, Phyllis's front door was standing wide open. It *was* a hot day, sure, but Phyllis's living room had an air conditioner sticking out of one of the side windows. When I got out of my truck, I could hear it humming away. So Phyllis didn't need to leave her door open to catch a breeze.

Other than the air conditioner going, there wasn't a sound. I reckon I'd been a cop too long not to notice the odd stillness. Working homicide, I'd walked into quite a few houses that felt like this one.

My stomach started knotting up real bad.

I didn't really want to, but I kept right on walking toward the open front door, real slow, looking all around for any movement. And wishing, of course, that I'd brought my gun with me. I don't carry it unless I absolutely have to, as a rule.

It was a rule that at that moment I was seriously rethinking.

As soon as I got to the door, I saw her. Still wearing the green ruffled square dance dress she'd worn in my office earlier, Phyllis was lying facedown on her living-room floor, at an angle to the coffee table in front of the couch, her head pointed toward me, her face turned to the right, both her arms bent at the elbow. There were two ugly red smears in the center of her back. In the middle of each smear was a small, dark circle.

Those small circles sure looked like gunshot wounds to me.

I don't know. I guess for all my years working homicide, I am never going to get used to seeing folks in the condition Phyllis was in. My heart started pounding, and my mouth went so dry, I could hardly swallow. When I rushed to Phyllis's side, it was as if I were running on feet that had suddenly fallen asleep. They felt numb and heavy. I couldn't seem to move fast enough.

As it turned out, it didn't matter how fast I moved. As soon as I grabbed Phyllis's right wrist to feel for a pulse, I knew. Her eyes were fixed and staring, and she felt as if she'd been standing right next to her air conditioner for a long, long time.

Somebody had closed poor Phyllis's mouth for good.

When I lifted her wrist, I saw the dark red puddle that had pooled beneath her body. I also saw something else.

Lying on the floor next to Phyllis's right hand were a pencil and a small piece of memo paper.

Before I moved to take a closer look at that paper, I carefully placed Phyllis's hand back down on the floor as gently as I could. I reckon that sounds real dumb, being as how Phyllis was certainly beyond knowing whether I was being gentle with her or not. It seemed important, though, to be extra kind to her now.

Maybe because whoever it was that had seen Phyllis last certainly had not been.

Squatting Indian-style and getting as close as I could, so that I could take a real good look without touching the thing, I stared at the small piece of paper. There wasn't a whole lot to see. On the paper was a single pencil mark. A mark that looked like the number seven.

I swallowed, peering at it. Lord. It looked as if poor Phyllis, realizing that she was dying, had tried to leave a clue as to who had done this to her.

And *I* didn't have a clue as to what it meant.

6

I squatted on the floor beside Phyllis's body, and stared at that note a long, long time. This was a real uncomfortable thing to do, not so much because of the way I was squatting, but because poor Phyllis's head was also turned in the direction of the note. Her brown ponytail was all fanned out, partially covering her face, but you could still see her eyes. With them being wide open the way they were, it made you feel like Phyllis was looking at the note, too. Studying it, just like I was.

I reckon the look on Phyllis's face wasn't any more blank than the one on mine.

I moved a little closer to the note on the floor. What on earth could Phyllis have been trying to say? The mark on the paper looked real wiggly. As if Phyllis's strength had been fading fast, even as she wrote.

I blinked, resolutely putting the picture of Phyllis's pitiful last moments right out of my mind. Then I went into Homicide Mode. Homicide Mode is a state of mind I pretty much perfected while I was working on the police force in Louisville. It's where you put all your emotions on hold, and you don't do anything but record what you see.

I'd already recorded poor Phyllis, lying there, so I didn't look over at her again. Instead, I started taking mental pictures of things that I hadn't noticed in the first awful moments of discovering Phyllis's body. The long smear of blood staining the worn beige carpet to the left of her body, for instance. And the receiver of the brown rotary phone, lying next to Phyllis's hand.

The base of the phone had been pulled right to the edge of the coffee table. I got up from my Indian-squat and followed the telephone wire to where it should've connected into the wall jack. It didn't. Mainly because, about a foot from the wall, the wire had been cleanly cut in two.

Still in Homicide Mode, I mentally recorded several other things. How the other pieces of memo paper on top of the coffee table were no longer in a neat stack, but now scattered all over the tabletop. How some of these papers had been pulled, like the phone, toward the edge of the coffee table where Phyllis now lay. And how the top of the ancient coffee table was smudged here and there with red. Much like the fingers on Phyllis's right hand. And much like the pencil that now lay on the floor.

Looking at all that, I could pretty much guess what all had happened during the final moments of poor Phyllis's life. Her assailant gone, Phyllis had apparently dragged herself over to the coffee table, trying to get to her phone. She must've realized as soon as she put the receiver to her ear that the line was dead.

I sort of hoped that it didn't occur to Phyllis at the time that she and her phone were about to have a lot in common.

But I'm afraid it did.

Phyllis must've realized that she wasn't going to be around to tell us in person who'd done this to her, because she'd reached for the small stack of memo paper and the pencil she kept by her phone. Unable to write legibly on the soft surface of the carpet, she must've propped herself up against the coffee table, using it as a sort of desk, because there was a particularly ugly smear of blood on its edge.

I blinked and swallowed. Phyllis had evidently used up

her last ounces of strength to leave this message, and then she'd collapsed, carrying both paper and pencil with her when she fell.

Obviously the poor woman had gone to a lot of trouble to leave this note behind. And yet, what did it mean? A seven? A *lucky* seven? It obviously was not very lucky for Phyllis.

Then what had she been trying to say?

I didn't take a whole lot of time to think this over, though, because I knew very well that Vergil wouldn't look any too kindly on my taking my time before I got around to telling him that a murder had been committed in his jurisdiction. If he was a mite persnickety about my horning in on *his* criminal investigations, he'd be downright pissed if he thought for a moment I was trying to conduct one on my own. There was no way to call Vergil from Phyllis's, so I got back in my truck and set off in search of Phyllis's nearest neighbor.

Phyllis's nearest neighbor turned out to be the pig farm I'd passed on Highway 46. Wouldn't you know it?

The pigs had evidently just had a major bout with the flu, or maybe they'd all been morning sick. And maybe afternoon sick, too. Whatever the cause, when I got out of my truck and got a whiff of that smell on top of what I'd just seen at Phyllis's house, it was enough to make my stomach lurch a couple of times before I got to the porch.

The guy who opened the front door looked as if his own stomach lurched when he saw me standing there. I put it down, though, to his not being accustomed to having company drop by any too often. For obvious reasons.

For a moment we both just stood there, staring at each other. I was staring at him in sheer amazement. You know how a lot of folks sort of look like their pets? This guy bore more than a passing resemblance to the animals he raised. Short and squat and bald, with tiny brown eyes, round pink cheeks, and a gray stubble on his chin, he was wearing a pair of faded overalls stretched tight across his massive stomach, no shoes, and a brown-stained white T-shirt. I didn't particularly want to hazard a guess as to what those T-shirt stains could be, but as it turned out, I didn't have to.

Piggy continued to stare at me for a few seconds more, then abruptly turned his head, and spit. From where I stood, I couldn't be sure if he had a spittoon next to his door or not, but I sure hoped so.

"Hello, I'm—"

That was all I got out before Piggy interrupted with— what else?—a grunt. "I know who you are. You're Elmo Blevins's brother, ain't ya? You're the—the—" His tiny pig eyes all but closed as he squinted at me and tried to remember.

I was already nodding before he finished, because you get used to this kind of thing around these parts. I couldn't ever recall seeing this guy around town—and I was pretty sure I would've remembered *him*—and yet, apparently he knew me. Or so I thought until Piggy finished with, "—you're the *criminal!*"

I abruptly stopped nodding.

This is another thing you get used to around these parts. Folks know you—sort of. They've talked to somebody who knows somebody else who might possibly have actually met another somebody who's actually met *you*. Only it's sort of like that game you used to play back in elementary school where a message was whispered from one person to another until finally it came out so garbled, it wasn't even close to what it started out being. Here in Pigeon Fork, folks end up with a vague idea about you that's sort of connected to the truth. Like in this case, Piggy obviously remembered that I had something to do with the law. Only apparently he'd picked the wrong side for me to be on.

No wonder he'd looked so startled when he opened the door.

I gave him a tolerant smile. "I'm Elmo's brother, all right—Haskell Blevins. But I'm a private detective." I paused here, giving Piggy a chance to introduce himself. After a second or two of Piggy continuing to squint silently in my direction, I realized that Piggy evidently had no intention of getting acquainted with someone he expected to see pretty soon on "America's Most Wanted."

I smiled a little wider and hurried on. "I need to use your phone. OK?"

As I spoke, Piggy was taking a step away from the door. Obviously so that, if he got the notion, he'd be able to slam it right in my face. His small pig eyes were getting smaller by the minute as he stared at me, so I half expected him to say something like, "Not by the hair on my chinny-chin-chin." Instead, he shook his head and said, "You ain't no detective. That's not what I heard."

He already had his hand on the door, so I smiled as wide as I could. "I used to be a cop. Back in Louisville. *That's* probably what you heard."

Piggy was still shaking his head, still staring. "Nope, nope," he said, "that wasn't it." He pronounced "wasn't" as if it were spelled with a *d*. Wuddent. "I think they tole me you'd just got outta prison."

Well now, I *had* been feeling a trifle burned-out working homicide back in Louisville—and I had experienced a sort of release when I finally hightailed it back home, where I belonged—but I don't think I'd ever describe my former occupation as *prison*. My smile was starting to hurt. "Look, I really did used to be a cop, and now I really am a private detective, and I really do need to call the sheriff. There's been a—" Here I realized that if I told Piggy that there had been a murder, he would no doubt decide that *I* was the one who'd committed it. Hell, he'd probably think I was now going door to door, getting rid of anyone who'd seen my car going down the road. I changed what I was going to say in midsentence. "There's been an *accident*. And I need to report it."

For an answer, Piggy switched his chewing lump from his right cheek to his left cheek. And spit again.

It occurred to me that, generally, when folks spit into a spittoon, you hear a kind of metallic *ping*. A faint bell-like sound. I heard nothing. And I was listening. *Real* hard.

My smile probably looked insincere after that. Maybe that was one of the reasons why Piggy decided that he'd let me use his phone only on one condition. His phone evidently had a real long cord, because Piggy said he'd bring it to me and I could make my call *only* if I remained out on his porch.

After not hearing any spittoon sounds, I can't say I minded a bit.

Vergil, on the other hand, *did* seem to mind hearing from me. Oddly enough. "What? What do you mean *a sort of* accident?"

I didn't want to spell the whole thing out for Vergil while Piggy was standing right there, squinting and spitting behind his front door, so I just repeated what I'd just said. "Vergil, there's been a sort of accident at Phyllis Carver's place. I need you to get over here RIGHT NOW."

Vergil apparently is not one for subtleties. He repeated what *he'd* just said. "What do you mean *a sort of* accident?"

Piggy was now peering at me from around the edge of the door, so I wasn't about to tell Vergil that what had recently happened to Phyllis had hardly been an accident. That, in fact, what had happened to her had clearly been done on purpose.

I took a deep breath, moved as far away from Piggy's front door as the telephone cord would allow me to go, and lowered my voice. "Vergil, Phyllis has had the sort of accident that you and I looked into about six weeks ago. On the poultry farm? Remember?"

Maybe I shouldn't have been that graphic. Vergil let out a scream so loud, you might've thought he'd been shot instead of Phyllis. "NO-O-O-O! Oh my God! You don't mean that she's been—"

"Yes, she has," I said as gently as I could, knowing full well just how bad Vergil was going to take this.

He took it worse than I thought. I think I mentioned earlier that Vergil takes any crime committed in Crayton County real personal. I do believe he actually thinks folks are doing these things just to get his goat.

"Oh God, oh God, oh God. Lordy, Lordy, Lordy!" Vergil went on like this for a while. "This is awful, oh yeah it is, it's awful, Lordy, Lordy, Lordy—"

I had to call his name five times before he finally stopped. "Vergil. Vergil. Vergil. VERgil. VERGIL!"

What Vergil had to say when he stopped almost made me wish I'd just let him keep on with his Lordys. "My God, Haskell, everywhere you go, somebody dies!"

Now, this was a slight exaggeration. I'd been in town almost a year, and I'd only run into two people who'd gotten themselves murdered. Vergil was making me sound as if any minute, the town was going to start calling me Typhoid Haskell. If I had any doubt about that, what he said next removed it. "Why, folks are going to start avoiding you like the plague!"

I thought that was a little less than kind. "Vergil, it wasn't my fault. I wasn't even there. I barely knew the woman—"

Piggy was at that moment staring fixedly at me, switching his tobacco nervously from one cheek to the other. So I decided that this probably wasn't the best time to try to convince Vergil I was not the human equivalent of the Kiss of Death. "Vergil, can you get on out here?"

I gave Vergil directions to Phyllis's house—no easy task—and I hung up.

Piggy's tiny brown eyes looked real suspicious when I handed him the phone.

"Thanks for your help," I said, giving him another insincere smile.

Piggy didn't even blink. "Uh, did you say Phyllis Carver down the road has had herself an accident?" he asked. He pronounced the word *ak-see-dent*. "What kinda accident has she had?" Piggy apparently saw no reason to even pretend that he hadn't been eavesdropping.

I got the feeling that good manners weren't a big priority with him.

I also got the feeling that there was no use lying. By evening the news of Phyllis's death would be all over Pigeon

Fork. "Actually, it wasn't an accident," I said. "Phyllis was murd—"

That was all I got out before Piggy slammed the door in my face.

I sighed, turned, and walked back to my truck. I tried to walk with distinctly uncriminal-like steps, being as how I was pretty sure Piggy was still watching me from behind the curtains in the window next to his front door. It was an almost certainty that old Piggy had himself a shotgun in there. For hog killing and, no doubt, throwing a good scare into folks who came knocking at his door.

It was with something real close to relief that I hurriedly got back in my truck, and headed on back to Phyllis's. No doubt if Vergil ever talked to Piggy about the probability of folks dying every time I happened to be in the vicinity, Piggy would vote with Vergil.

While I waited for Vergil and the rest of his entourage to show up, I decided to go through Phyllis's house again, much like what I'd already done earlier that morning. For one thing, it gave me something else to do besides sitting in the living room, looking at poor Phyllis's body. For another, I knew without a doubt that once Vergil got here, he was not going to let me do much looking around. If he let me do any. He was going to put up his yellow caution tape, and pretty much fence me out.

Like I said, Vergil's been in a kind of snit ever since I moved back to town. It's like crime solving is a game he doesn't want to share. Working on cases here in town, I've had folks try to kill me a couple of times, I've had my tires slashed, my dog nearly poisoned, and once I even ended up in the hospital. Each time Vergil's been outraged. He thought I was hogging all the fun. For a while there I was afraid I might actually have to make a couple of attempts on his life just to even things up.

I took my time going through Phyllis's house this second time, looking through drawers and closets a lot more thoroughly than I had before. I'd pulled on a pair of work gloves that I keep in the glove compartment of my truck, so Vergil wouldn't find my fingerprints all over everything.

After a while, I found myself almost tiptoeing through Phyllis's house, it seemed that unnaturally quiet without the Phyllis Carver Talk Show going on in the background.

My search seemed to take forever. In fact, I'd worked my way through almost the entire house before I found anything worth mentioning. Everything I saw pretty much confirmed the impression that I'd gotten at the start. The Carvers were not even close to being well-to-do. I was sure I'd seen furniture in far better condition in a Salvation Army secondhand store. Also, Phyllis's clothes closets were not exactly packed with dresses and shoes and doodads, either. It actually looked as if her *husband* had more clothes than she did. Which, to somebody like me who'd been married to a serious contender for the heavyweight shopping championship, was a startling surprise. My ex-wife, Claudzilla, could've given Phyllis lessons in credit card abuse.

Near the end of my search, while going through a small desk that Phyllis had in her bedroom, I found a small brown address book. Covered in the stuff they call "leatherette"— which, as best as I can tell, is another word for brown plastic—the book was real easy to find. It was lying on top of a bunch of papers in the lower right-hand drawer. Remembering Phyllis's note still lying next to her out there in the living room, I flipped to page seven. The heading at the top of the page said "L/M." There was only one name listed on the page: Ruta Lippton. Along with her address and telephone number.

I might as well admit it, I wasn't sure what to make of this. Was this just a coincidence? Or was it really possible that Phyllis, having just been shot twice, could actually remember on what exact page a certain name had been written in her address book? I don't know, but it sure didn't seem likely. I myself—without so much as a hangnail, let alone a couple of bullet wounds—could not have told you on what page any of the names in my own address book were listed. In fact, I wasn't even sure the pages were numbered.

I went through the rest of Phyllis's address book just to see who else was listed. June and Winslow Reed were in there. And Vergil, on the R/S page, under the heading "Sheriff." In fact, it looked as if half of Pigeon Fork was listed in there. On the A/B page I even found my own name, with my office address and phone number.

If being in Phyllis's address book was incriminating, both Vergil and I were in trouble.

Now that I thought about it, though, I wondered if maybe the number seven on Phyllis's note could've been the beginning of a telephone number. Or maybe even an address. Even as I considered it, however, I was already getting skeptical. Because why on earth would Phyllis write someone's phone number—or their address—instead of their name? If you're in the process of dying, it did seem like real good planning to keep your messages as short as possible. Of course, Phyllis had not exactly been known for saying things quickly. Maybe the poor thing had underestimated how long it would take her to write out somebody's address. Maybe she'd run out of time before she finished.

I put the address book back where I'd found it and moved on.

There was another leatherette-covered book in the upper left drawer of Phyllis's desk. Small gold letters on the front said, "Appointments." I reached for the book, my heart speeding up a little. Maybe this was the significance of the seven. Maybe Phyllis had been killed by whoever she was supposed to meet today at seven o'clock. This theory had a few holes, of course, being as how it was now only a little before four, but maybe whoever it was had dropped by early. If you had a murder to commit, you might get a tad anxious to get it over with. I turned to today's date, and my heart slowed right back down.

The page was blank.

As was every other page in the book. Either Phyllis didn't have all that many appointments to remember, or she didn't bother writing them down.

I put the book back in Phyllis's desk, and headed for her

kitchen. There, in the drawer next to the stove, I found about a hundred grocery coupons that Phyllis had carefully saved. They were all stacked neatly and alphabetized. I closed the drawer, feeling a wave of sadness. All that work, and all those coupons, and poor Phyllis would never get to use them.

I was trying to dredge up Homicide Mode again, trying to push what I was feeling to the background, as I moved around the rest of the kitchen. In the cabinet over the refrigerator, I found something a lot more interesting than grocery coupons. It was, in fact, even more interesting than Phyllis's address book. On the very top shelf, in back of a box of confectioner's sugar, I found three small voice-activated tape recorders.

All, curiously enough, with something sticky on the back. Glue, maybe.

Two of the three recorders were empty. The third, however, still had a tape in it, partially rewound. I pressed "play," and immediately heard what I thought at first was a man and a woman suffering from real bad asthma. After about a half second, though, I realized that these folks were not suffering at all. Quite the contrary.

This tape, in fact, could've been the soundtrack to a porno movie.

About a minute into it, the woman on the tape started repeating the name "Orval" over and over and over. In between little squeals. And giggles. And kissing sounds.

At that point I did what I believe any private eye would've done under similar circumstances. I rewound the tape, turned up the volume, and put the recorder closer to my ear. Phyllis had told me her husband's name was Orval. And yet, the female voice on this tape clearly did not belong to Phyllis. It was higher-pitched, breathy, and not a bit nasal.

After the woman got through calling Orval by name, she started calling him "Loverbug." In between the little squeals I mentioned before. And the giggles. And the kissing sounds.

Listening to all that, I was now not only feeling sad, I was feeling *depressed*. I can't rightly say that my love life has been a thrill a minute since I got back in town. It seems like every time I find somebody halfway interesting, I find out real quick she doesn't find the Howdy Doody type all that appealing.

Listening to that tape, I also couldn't help remembering that it was only toward the very end of our marriage that Claudzilla had called *me* names. And they were not anything at all like "Loverbug."

I was almost glad that I heard wheels crunch onto the gravel driveway out front right then, and I had to stop listening to the folks on the tape having fun. Moving as fast as I could, I put all three tape recorders back on the top shelf over the refrigerator, and I hurried out front.

Vergil was just opening the door of his patrol car.

7

In the past, whenever I've seen Vergil show up at a crime scene, he's always come barreling in with enough sirens going full-blast to maybe do permanent damage to your eardrums. It's always sounded as if his *car* were just as loudly angry about what had happened as Vergil himself.

This time, though, I noticed the sheriff had pulled up in front of Phyllis's without so much as a honk of the horn. None of the folks he had with him were running their sirens, either. The county coroner, the guys from the crime lab, and Vergil's deputies all quietly parked their cars beside Vergil's. It was almost as if they were trying to *sneak* in here to do their job. I swallowed uneasily. Vergil must be taking this one real hard. This time, having a murder happen in his jurisdiction wasn't just an outrage. It was even worse. It was an *embarrassment*.

Vergil's face, as he got out of his car, did look slightly pink beneath his deep farmer's tan. In his late fifties, with thinning salt-and-pepper hair and a stomach that probably should have the word "Michelin" written across it, you can tell Vergil tries real hard to look dapper in his crisply pressed tan uniform. He might succeed if he didn't run his hands through his hair so much when he gets upset.

Sticking out around his ears at odd angles, Vergil's hair today could've gotten him to the finals of an Einstein Look-Alike contest. Vergil probably would've lost in the end, though, because he doesn't have one of them whisk-broom mustaches. In fact, he doesn't have a mustache at all. I think one reason for this is that a mustache would probably cover up his frown. Vergil, I am sure, wants the whole world to know just how unhappy he is.

"Haskell," Vergil said. His voice was mournful.

"Vergil," I said. Around these parts, we don't generally waste time with hellos. We just say the other person's name, more or less acknowledging that "yep, I know who you are, all right," and we get down to business.

Evidently, business at that moment for Vergil was getting one of the Gunterman twins to put up a yellow caution tape, having the other Gunterman twin escort me over to the front yard, and disappearing himself inside Phyllis's house for a while. I believe I mentioned earlier that this is what would happen. Maybe the next time the private eye business gets slow, I could find work as a clairvoyant.

Vergil was in Phyllis's house an awful long time. Of course, it might've just seemed like that on account of my having to spend all that time standing next to the Gunterman twin. I can't tell the twins apart, but whichever one this one was, he kept eyeing me sideways. Like maybe he couldn't decide whether I was a witness or a suspect.

When Vergil finally appeared in Phyllis's front door, I don't mind saying I was right glad to see him. Vergil stepped carefully over the yellow caution tape, and walked over to where the Gunterman twin and I were standing. We'd picked ourselves a spot in the shade, under a large maple tree about fifteen feet or so from Phyllis's front door.

"Well, Jeb, it looks like we don't have a murder weapon. The assailant must've taken it with him," Vergil said. He sounded grief-stricken at the thought. "And, judging from a quick look around, the place seems to have been wiped clean of fingerprints."

Vergil said all this looking directly at Jeb Gunterman, but it was pretty clear that this was his way of giving me the information. Because telling it to Jeb was pretty much like shouting it into the wind.

Even Jeb himself looked surprised that Vergil was actually talking to him. Jeb's eyes got about two sizes larger, and he shifted his weight uneasily from one foot to another. Jeb and his brother are real big guys, about six foot three and 240 pounds apiece, so this weight shifting took quite a bit of effort. Maybe that's why it took so long for Jeb to respond to what Vergil had just told him.

It's their size that's earned the Guntermans the nickname "Two-Ton Twins" around town. It's a nickname, of course, that nobody says to their faces. On account of both their faces looking so mean. The twins have got beefy jaws, short pug noses, and they've apparently copied their mutual hairstyle from that of a famous person they both probably look up to. Curly, of the Three Stooges.

Jeb cocked his close-cropped head to one side the way a dog does when he doesn't understand the instructions you've just given him, and finally said real slow to Vergil, "Uh, you mean, there wasn't no weapon and, uh, no fingerprints? Uh, *gosh.*"

After that in-depth summing up of the facts known so far, Vergil gave Jeb a sad stare for a full five seconds, and then turned to me.

Vergil gave me a sad stare, too, but not quite as long as the one he'd given Jeb. "Haskell, Haskell, Haskell," Vergil said when he finished staring at me. Really, that's what he said. Vergil's brown eyes, as always, seemed to be looking at all the misery in the world.

I had no idea what to say back. "Vergil," I said again, a tad uncertainly this time. Even though Vergil had felt moved to repeat *my* name a couple times, I decided that just saying his name once would be plenty.

"Another homicide," Vergil said. *"Another* one. It's only been six weeks." Vergil always sounds as if he's delivering a eulogy, but this time his eulogy sounded faintly accusing. "What in hell happened?"

I ignored the accusation in his tone, and gave him a brief rundown of how I'd come to find Phyllis's body. I told him pretty much everything I knew—how Phyllis had hired me this morning, how I couldn't get in touch with her, and how I'd finally ended up out here. The only thing I left out, of course, was the part where I'd searched Phyllis's house and found her address book and the tape recorders. No use causing Vergil any more grief than he already had. Besides, I was sure that Vergil and his entourage were perfectly capable of finding these things without any help at all from me.

I'd no doubt told Vergil more than I needed to, because apparently he'd only heard one thing. "You mean to tell me," he said when I'd finished, "that this one was a client of yours, *too?*"

I believe Vergil's point was that the last homicide we investigated—the one at the poultry farm—had also been one of my clients. I just looked at him. What exactly did that have to do with anything?

Vergil made the connection abundantly clear. "Lord, they're dropping like flies, aren't they, Haskell?" His tanned face is crisscrossed all over by tiny lines like spiderwebs, and the lines get even deeper when he gets upset. The ones on either side of his mouth right now looked like ravines. "This cain't be good for business." Vergil's funereal tone sounded sympathetic, but I was pretty sure I detected a faint glimmer of amusement in Vergil's sad eyes. "It just doesn't look good. Having all your clients die on you."

Now, Vergil was exaggerating again. He does this a lot. "Vergil," I said, trying to sound a lot more patient than I felt, "there *are* clients of mine who are still walking around breathing."

In fact, only two of my clients have met an untimely end

while I was in their employ. The poultry tycoon and Phyllis. I reckon, though, that I *was* feeling kind of defensive about all this. On account of my feeling so bad about what had happened to Phyllis and all. Not to mention Jeb Gunterman standing right there next to me under that maple tree. The big deputy was now looking at me with eyes that showed the whites all around, like maybe he'd just discovered I was the private eye version of Bluebeard. So, of course, like an idiot, I started naming, in a real loud voice, all those folks who'd somehow managed to survive hiring me.

Let me see, there was Toomey, my first case. He'd hired me to find out who stole the feed sacks in front of his hardware store. Toomey was still breathing. And Cyrus Lassiter. After his brother died of a heart attack, I'd helped him locate his brother's stepdaughter to give her the sad news. Cyrus was still alive and kicking. And, of course, Cordelia Turley, who'd hired me to investigate the murder I mentioned before—of her grandmother and her grandmother's pets. Cordelia had actually lived to return to Nashville, where she was from. And various and sundry folks around town. All still walking around. Not even sick.

I probably would also have mentioned Ruta and Winslow except, of course, I might've had to admit to Vergil that I was no longer currently an employee of theirs. Vergil probably would've viewed this as real good judgment on their part. He'd think they'd fired me just in time to save their lives.

I was still naming off client survivors when Vergil interrupted me with a sigh. He's real good at sighing. Fact is, if they ever give blue ribbons for it at the Crayton County Fair, Vergil's a sure winner. "All I'm saying is that it seems real odd that it's only *your* clients who seem to be getting themselves murdered here lately."

Vergil, in spite of his tragic tone, was obviously enjoying himself. He knew very well that the murder of the poultry tycoon had been solved for some time now, and that it had had nothing whatsoever to do with the guy being a client of mine. It wasn't as if there could actually be a serial killer running around loose, preying on folks who happened to hire me. What was Vergil's point then? Was he implying that folks with a death wish should drop by my office?

"I also ran down a couple of lost books for the Crayton County Library, and *both* the librarians there are still alive," I found myself saying. Have I already mentioned that I was an idiot?

Vergil looked as if he agreed. His glance was now pitying. I guess he'd started feeling like he was picking on the disadvantaged or something, because he abruptly changed the subject. "I noticed back in the kitchen that the door's been busted in. You think Phyllis interrupted a burglary?"

I just stared at him for a second. I hated to tell him, but there didn't seem to be any way to get around it. "Actually, Vergil, that door was broken in this morning. When I was here last. That's why Phyllis hired me in the first place."

Vergil's sad eyes suddenly looked a lot sadder. "Phyllis didn't tell *me* anything about a break-in." His tone was injured.

"She was going to call you," I said. "Phyllis told me she was going to call you right after she got back from the grocery. In fact, I'm sure if she were still alive, you would've heard from her by now."

This didn't seem to make Vergil feel any better. He heaved a sigh this time that probably would've won him Best of Show at the fair, and once again changed the subject. "So, what do you think she meant by this?"

I knew before Vergil pulled it out of his back pocket what he was about to show me. The note Phyllis had left. He'd put it in one of them clear plastic evidence bags that he always seems to be carrying around with him.

I looked at it and fervently wished that I could tell Vergil right off exactly what it was that Phyllis had been trying to say. I would've loved to stand there and spell it out for old Vergil in a real offhand sort of way.

And then watch his mouth drop open.

Unfortunately, I didn't even have a good guess. "I'm still working on it," I said.

Vergil, oddly enough, did not look all that upset to hear it. He peered at the note through the plastic himself and drawled, "Well, could be she was just starting to write a phone number." His voice was again infinitely sad. "Of course, just one seven isn't going to be much help, is it?"

I got his point. The telephone exchange for almost everybody who lives in Pigeon Fork is 733, the only exception, of course, being folks like me. While I have a Pigeon Fork address and I only live seven miles from downtown, I have a Dawesville phone. With an 843 exchange. Dawesville is the next small town down the road. In actuality, my house is about a mile closer to Pigeon Fork than it is to Dawesville, but apparently the two small phone companies competing with each other for business around these parts don't much care. If I want to call Pigeon Fork from my home, it's going to be long distance. Actually, I have a sneaking suspicion that the possibility of collecting a whole lot of long-distance charges might've been the major motivating factor for the phone companies to draw up their boundaries this way. Call me cynical.

Vergil was still studying Phyllis's note. "Then again, maybe she wasn't writing a phone number a-tall. Maybe she was starting to write an address. And she ran out of time." It sounded as if Vergil was pretty much coming up with the same ideas that I'd had earlier. Which can kind of make you understand why Vergil's so persnickety about my horning in on his crime solving. I reckon Vergil just feels real insulted that anybody might get the idea that he could possibly need some young whippersnapper from the Big City telling him how to do his job. He does pretty well all by himself.

I also think Vergil could be a mite worried that I not only want to help him, I might actually have designs on his job. Which, to put it as delicately as I can, is about as likely as my deciding to be a terrorist. Nope, I had about all the fun I could stand in the law enforcement field when I was back in

Louisville. I'd broken up enough family fights, been punched by enough drunks, and arrested enough teenage prostitutes to last me a lifetime. Vergil was welcome to it.

Vergil and I didn't have time to talk about Phyllis's note anymore, because at that moment, a black late-model Toyota pickup pulled into the driveway. Since the driveway was pretty much full of vehicles, the driver of the pickup had to park his truck fairly far away. In fact, right next to the crime lab van. The driver got out and started walking toward us.

That is, his feet were walking toward us. His eyes, however, were traveling real fast from the crime lab van to the car clearly marked "Coroner" and then over to Vergil's patrol car. As his eyes moved from one vehicle to the other, they got bigger and bigger.

Vergil put Phyllis's note back in his pocket, and he and I stopped talking and watched the new arrival. Tall and muscular, wearing a denim coverall, a cowboy hat, and what looked to be pretty expensive alligator boots, he walked toward us, carrying a toolbox. In spite of what his eyes were doing, he was walking real slow. Almost nonchalant. I reckon that's what made Fred, the other Gunterman twin, who was still putting up yellow caution tape around the side yard, think that this guy must not be one of Phyllis's next of kin. Or maybe Fred wasn't thinking at all. As I believe I've made real clear, thinking is not the twins' strong suit. It could've been taking all of Fred's concentration just to get the tape in position. Whatever the cause, when the driver of the pickup passed the deputy and asked, "What's happened here?" Fred didn't even hesitate.

"Phyllis Somebody got herself killed," he said.

The driver stopped walking.

He also dropped his toolbox.

And let go with a scream of anguish.

I couldn't help staring at him. This, no doubt about it, had to be Orval Carver, Cowboy Repairman and Porno Tape Star.

Right away I started wondering exactly how many smarts old Orval had here. You'd think if you were married to a woman with a horse-face, the last thing you'd dress like would be a cowboy.

Orval must've felt that it was all right for cowboys to give free rein to their emotions, because he sobbed out loud for a solid five minutes after Fred broke the news to him. Orval did some more major sobbing after he saw poor Phyllis's body.

It was, of course, Orval's big idea to see Phyllis for himself. Vergil and both Gunterman twins tried to keep him from it, but Orval insisted, dodging around them all and charging headfirst through the living-room door.

Once Orval got a good look at Phyllis, it was clear he sincerely regretted having been so insistent. He went ramrod-stiff just inside the open doorway, doing a fairly good impression of somebody who's just been struck by lightning. There was a split second of total silence, and then I could've sworn Orval's sobs rattled all the windows in the house.

Orval's sobs also rattled Vergil. In the face of Orval's unashamed weeping, Vergil's already pink undertones went even pinker. He looked as if he were having to stand and listen to somebody's embarrassing family secrets. Vergil grabbed Orval's arm, turned him around, and guided him right back out the front door. And over to the shade of the maple tree where I was still standing, watching all the goings-on.

Apparently Vergil's thinking here was that if Orval wasn't actually looking at Phyllis anymore, Orval might manage to get himself under control.

I'd say Vergil was being a little optimistic. Standing there under that tree, he and I pretty much did nothing for the next ten minutes except watch Orval dab at his eyes and sob. Vergil kept staring at Orval mournfully and fidgeting with something in his back pocket.

I knew what Vergil was fidgeting with, of course. The note

Phyllis left. Obviously Vergil had decided it would be real rude to interrupt Orval's weeping to ask him about it. So he was just biding his time, waiting for Orval's sobs to die down.

I hated to say so, but the prospects didn't look good. The way things were going, we could be standing there watching Orval grieve all night.

The Gunterman twins were also standing and watching, except from a slightly more distant vantage point. After he got Orval out of there, Vergil had stationed Jeb and Fred in front of the living room door. Apparently to keep folks like Orval from doing what he'd just done.

Orval clearly could've kicked himself, the way he was weeping and wailing and carrying on.

I myself probably would've bought Orval's grief hook, line, and sinker if I hadn't known about the porno tape. And, of course, the Unknown Giggler whose high-pitched voice was on the tape along with Orval's. As it was, I couldn't help viewing Orval's sobs with some skepticism.

Vergil, however, hadn't heard the tape yet, and he looked almost as upset as Orval. When Orval's sobs diminished enough so that you could actually hear somebody talk, Vergil cleared his throat and said, "Real sorry about your wife." At the time he said this, Vergil was staring fixedly at the patchy, dried-up grass on Orval's lawn. Being as how nobody else in the vicinity had recently lost a spouse, however, Orval seemed to realize immediately that Vergil was talking to him. He gave Vergil a quick nod.

For a split second there, Orval actually seemed between sobs.

Vergil must've realized he'd better get Orval's reaction to the note while the getting was good, because he whipped that note out of his pocket so fast, it was almost a blur. "I got something here I need you to look at," Vergil said. "Your wife wrote it just before she died. Do you have any idea what she was trying to say?"

Orval blinked, peered at the note, wiped his eyes, and

swallowed. All before he finally answered. "Why, that looks like a seven." Orval's tone implied that Vergil ought to be able to recognize numbers without any help from him.

Vergil stared at him, his eyes getting sadder by the minute. "It does look like a seven, doesn't it?" I believe Vergil was showing remarkable patience here. "Do you know why she wrote it?"

Orval's answer was real helpful. "No, why?"

Vergil's eyes looked plumb grief-stricken now.

"Why would Phyllis leave a piece of paper with a seven on it?" Orval seemed to be asking the world at large. Which was a good thing, because clearly nobody around him knew the answer. Vergil looked like he might want to ask Orval a little more about the note, but his window of opportunity slammed shut right about then. Orval teared up real good again. "Oh my Lord, I'm going to miss her so much," Orval said, whimpering. "I don't rightly know what I'm going to do without her."

It seemed to me, from the tape I'd heard, that old Orval might be able to think of *something*, but I didn't say a word. I just nodded sympathetically, along with Vergil, both our heads going in unison. Even if I'd wanted to say something, I wouldn't have had the chance to anyway. Just about the time Orval's sobs once again died down enough for someone else to be heard, another car pulled up in the driveway.

This car was a vintage sixties red Mustang, and judging from the condition it was in, it had been well cared for. The woman who got out of the Mustang, oddly enough, didn't look quite as well cared for as her car. Her shoulder-length, wavy brown hair looked as if it could stand a good brushing, and although she was wearing a real nice navy blue tailored suit with a fluffy red bow at the collar, her slip was showing a good half inch in the back.

I watched her as she headed toward the house. She was not beautiful by any means. Big-boned and shapely, she was attractive, though, in a farm-fresh sort of way. The woman must not have noticed Vergil, Orval, and me standing under the maple tree, because she didn't even glance our way. Instead, she walked straight up to the Gunterman twins and said, "I'm Imogene Mayhew, Phyllis's sister, let me pass."

Just like that. All in one breath. Fred, the deputy closest to her, immediately started shaking his massive head no, and his brother stepped over to back him up. "Uh, you don't wanna go in there," Jeb said, "uh, you—"

You had to kind of admire Imogene. She didn't even let Jeb finish before she said, "Look, you big goons, I'm going inside, and you can't stop me."

Jeb and Fred evidently felt otherwise, because they both moved closer together, forming a human wall in front of her. A particularly ugly human wall, I might add.

"*Move*, you idiots!" Imogene yelled. "This is my sister's house, and I want to see her!" She gave emphasis to what she was saying by giving Fred a stinging slap on his arm. Which, I believe, took a considerable amount of courage to do. It was, as far as I was concerned, right up there with poking a tiger.

"Just a minute, little lady," Vergil said at this point. "Hold on a second." Vergil must've decided that the Gunterman twins needed some help in explaining the situation.

I'm pretty sure, however, that Imogene didn't hear a word Vergil said. She was now yelling, "Look, goons, get out of the way!" And trying to kick both Jeb and Fred in the ankle.

After being referred to as goons and idiots, not to mention having their ankles assaulted, the twins must've decided that Imogene deserved what she got, because—sure enough —they exchanged a look and then simultaneously stepped aside. And Imogene at that moment got a real good view of the guy from the crime lab as he finished drawing a chalk outline around poor Phyllis.

Watching Imogene's reaction was a real painful thing to see. For a second she didn't make a sound. She just stood there in the doorway, with the stunned look of somebody who's just been hit right between the eyes with a mallet.

"Oh God," she said. In a very small voice. As she spoke, she swayed just the slightest bit.

Vergil and I had started moving toward Imogene at the same instant, but I beat him to her. I grabbed Imogene's arm just as she was swaying forward, and I steadied her some. Then I led her as gently as I could out to the maple tree, while Vergil followed. Imogene went with me without resistance, moving woodenly, like somebody in a trance.

When we got to the shade, and it seemed safe to let go of her arm, I asked, "You OK?"

I reckon I already knew the answer to that one, but under the pressure of the moment, I couldn't think of anything else to say.

Imogene gave me a look that said I should've tried harder. She took a real deep, shaky breath. "I've been better," she said.

Standing this close to her, I realized that Imogene and I had quite a bit in common. Quite a bit of freckles, that is. Unfortunately, Imogene's freckles were at that moment starting to get streaked with tears. She swiped at her tears with the back of her hand, as if embarrassed to be caught crying in public.

If crying in public embarrassed her, she probably didn't want to stand any too close to Orval. He had moved to stand on the other side of the tree now, still dabbing away at his eyes, and occasionally moaning under his breath.

In times like these, it's been my experience that folks who knew the dearly departed usually kiss and hug, trying to offer each other some kind of comfort. As I recall, even Vergil gave me an awkward hug at my dad's funeral. Here, however, I couldn't help noticing that Imogene made not one move toward Orval.

For a moment I thought maybe she hadn't yet noticed he was over there. After a while, though, and as Orval's moans continued, I knew Imogene *had* to know Orval was there. You'd have had to be deaf to miss the sounds he was making. And yet, Imogene acted as if Orval were invisible. She just stood there next to me, staring straight ahead and listening to what Vergil was telling her about what had happened.

Vergil told her pretty much everything, even mentioning, with a nod in my direction, that the guy who was standing next to her was the one who'd discovered her sister's body. Imogene's eyes darted toward me when Vergil told her that. They did not, however, dart even once in Orval's direction. Not even during those frequent times when what Vergil was saying was punctuated by Orval's loud sobs.

I stared at Imogene. Maybe she was still in a trance or something. Suffering from shock and all.

Then again, there was always the distinct possibility that she didn't buy Orval's loud, moist grief any more than I did.

"I—I just can't believe it," Imogene said to no one in particular. Her voice was a monotone. For a moment I thought Imogene might be talking about Orval's performance, but then she went on, "I just talked to Phyllis this morning. She called me at work and she sounded so happy." Here Imogene pretty much gave up trying to wipe away her tears. Instead, she just pretended she wasn't crying at all. Tears made tiny rivulets down her face, and she kept right on talking. In that odd monotone. "I'm a real estate agent, you know. My office is in town. Phyllis called me this morning right after I got to work. God, she sounded so happy."

Imogene was repeating herself, but nobody pointed this out to her. With her tearing up the way she was, I reckon Vergil decided he'd better jump in while he had the chance.

"Phyllis left this here note," he said, extending the plastic bag containing the note toward Imogene. "Does this mean anything to you?"

Imogene stared at the small sheet of paper for a long moment. "A seven?" she said. "Phyllis wrote a seven?"

Orval stopped in midsob to say, "Yeah, don't that beat all?"

From Imogene's reaction, you wouldn't even have known that Orval had made a sound. Of course, that made sense. If she couldn't hear his weeping and wailing, she sure wouldn't be able to make out a little thing like his talking.

Imogene continued to stare fixedly at Vergil. "What does this note mean?" Imogene must've known we weren't going to give her an answer, because she went right on. "I can't imagine what she was trying to say." Imogene's eyes looked troubled as she ran her hand through her brown hair.

Vergil sighed and put the note back in his pocket. His voice infinitely sad, he said, "Did Phyllis say anything in particular when you talked to her earlier?"

Imogene swallowed once before she answered. "Phyllis asked me to stop by and see her after my office closed tonight." Here Imogene drew a ragged breath. "She said she was going to have a big surprise to show me."

I was pretty sure that all this was not what Phyllis had had in mind.

Vergil looked as if he agreed. He nodded sadly and turned to me. "Haskell, when she came by your office this morning, did Phyllis mention some kind of 'surprise' to you?"

I opened my mouth to answer, but I didn't get the chance. No sooner had Vergil said my name than Orval wheeled around, staring at me, his eyes wild. He seemed to be looking at me for the first time since he'd gotten here. "Haskell? Haskell Blevins?" he said. "Are you Haskell BLEVINS?"

I made the mistake of nodding my head.

And Orval lunged for me.

"You did this! YOU killed her!"

To give everybody the benefit of the doubt, I do believe Vergil and the Gunterman twins were all caught off guard. Much like me. No doubt that was why none of them were able to grab Orval in time. As it was, Orval seemed to have all the time in the world to punch me a good one in the stomach.

I immediately doubled over, making a sound that I believe sounded a whole lot like the one Rip makes when somebody is headed up our driveway.

WOOOOF!

That, of course, was the last sound I was able to make for quite a few minutes.

8

Orval probably would've hit me again, while I was still doubled over trying to get my breath back, except that Jeb and Fred ran over and grabbed Orval's arms. I must say, it was the first time I fully appreciated the twin deputies' unique abilities. I particularly appreciated the way, for a second there, it looked like the twins were going to play "Make a Wish" with Orval, gleefully snapping him in two like a wishbone.

In pain the way I was, my vote was for them to go ahead. Vergil, however, apparently thought that this was not the most appropriate way to treat the recently bereaved. "That's enough, boys," Vergil said.

Jeb and Fred both looked real disappointed, releasing Orval only when Vergil glared at them.

Orval immediately moved out of the twins' reach, eyeing them both uneasily while he tried to explain himself. "Haskell deserved it! Hell, he deserves a lot worse!" As Orval said this, he threw me a vicious look. "Phyllis told me last night that them two had been having an affair!"

My mouth actually dropped open. What a bald-faced lie!

"It was an awful shock! Awful!" Orval went on.

If Orval thought it was a shock to *him*, he could only imagine what a shock it was to *me*.

Orval's voice appeared to be rising in direct proportion to his outrage. "Them two had been sneaking around while I was at work!"

I was still doubled over, unable to speak, so I just looked at him, trying to decide who exactly was doing the lying here. Orval? Or had it been Phyllis?

"To find out that your own wife was carrying on behind your back! It was just so—so" Orval seemed to be searching for just the right word. He came up with, "—so *sordid!*"

This, from a guy who made porno tapes with a woman who wasn't his wife. Apparently old Orval believed that what was good for the gander was not at all good for the goose. Even if what he was saying *was* a lie, Orval had to be the hypocrite of all hypocrites. If I'd been able to make a sound at that particular moment, I probably would've blurted out all I knew about the tape then and there.

"Phyllis also told me last night that she was going to break it off with Haskell." Here Orval wheeled around and jabbed his finger dramatically in my direction. "That's why you killed her! If you couldn't have her, you didn't want nobody else to!" At this point, Orval must've temporarily lost his mind, because he actually lunged for me again.

Either the Gunterman twins really like me a lot, or else they really like manhandling somebody. I leaned toward believing the latter once I saw how tickled pink they both looked when they got to rush forward and grab Orval again. This time they held him squirming and grunting between them, Orval's feet at least two inches off the floor, his cowboy hat knocked a tad crooked.

Still not quite able to speak, I could only glare back at Orval. Let's face it, the idea of me and Phyllis carrying on was ludicrous. The woman, mind you, did look like Mr. Ed. Of course, I wasn't about to point this out to anybody. It didn't seem like good form to say anything derogatory about the recently departed. Particularly in front of the recently departed's next of kin. I satisfied myself with just shaking my head. Which, doubled over the way I was, made me feel a little sick to my stomach.

Orval looked sicker than me, dangling the way he was, like a rag doll, between Jeb and Fred.

Vergil looked quite a bit less sympathetic toward Orval this time. "Are you going to behave yourself, Orval?" he said.

Orval nodded, his crooked cowboy hat bobbing up and down vigorously, but he was still glaring in my direction.

Vergil heaved another one of his blue-ribbon sighs. "Put him down, boys." Vergil made it sound as if this were a tragic thing to do.

Judging from the way their faces fell, I was pretty sure the twins thought so, too.

I got my voice back just about the time Orval's feet were hitting the ground. "Orval's making all this up," I said. "Nothing whatsoever was going on between Phyllis and me. I barely knew her." My stomach was still hurting pretty good, so maybe the pain clouded my judgment some. Before I could stop it, my mouth had added, "Besides, Orval, it's common knowledge around town that you were having a little something on the side yourself. Weren't you, *Loverbug?*"

Orval's face went white.

Oddly enough, Imogene's face also went real pale. She gave me a sharp look, blinked, and then quickly glanced over at Orval. For what was probably the first time since she got here.

I might really be clairvoyant after all. Because it was plain to me from the expression on Imogene's face that it was not the first time she'd heard the nickname "Loverbug." Could she have also listened to that tape? My guess was yes, because Imogene didn't just look startled. She looked disgusted.

Maybe this was why she hadn't been any too eager to comfort Orval in his hour of need.

Orval, on the other hand, looked as if he were once again seriously considering popping me one in the stomach. I took a couple of unsteady steps away from him. "OK, OK," Orval said, "maybe I did run around on Phyllis a little. That don't mean we weren't happily married."

I just looked at him. This was a fresh approach to wedded bliss. I wondered if Phyllis would've backed him up on this.

Somehow, I doubted it.

Looking around at the others, I realized that everybody else looked as if they doubted it, too. Even Jeb and Fred were looking at Orval like he had to be kidding.

Orval must've realized his credibility here was in the minus, because he started talking real fast. "Look, I'm telling you all the truth. Phyllis and I were real happy. She understood about my—my—" Here Orval again seemed stuck for a word. What he came up with this time was, "—my *recreation*. She knew it didn't mean nothing. That it was just, uh, exercise, is all. Just exercise."

Was Orval trying to convince us that what I'd heard on the tape was just another way of working out? This sure could revolutionize the aerobics industry.

Nobody seemed to be buying Orval's exercise theory, either. Faced with four skeptical faces staring at him, including my own, Orval took a long, exasperated breath. "Look, didn't Phyllis promise to give Haskell up? Didn't she? Would she have done that if our marriage was on the rocks?"

To my way of thinking, it didn't take any effort at all to give up what she'd never had, but Orval didn't seem to be asking me. He was staring straight at Vergil.

Vergil cleared his throat. "Orval," he said solemnly, kicking at the dirt at his feet, "I don't reckon I've ever heard of a wife who really didn't mind if her husband wandered. And I don't believe for a second that Phyllis and Haskell here were carrying on."

Jeb and Fred both nodded when Vergil spoke. They looked like twin metronomes, beating time to Vergil's voice.

I reckon I should've been feeling kind of relieved that nobody appeared to be giving any credence to what Orval was saying. And yet, standing in the shade of that maple tree with the rest of them, I started to feel real uneasy. Was the idea of some woman having an affair with me all that farfetched? Maybe I was being insulted here. It wasn't like I particularly wanted to be added to the list of suspects, but I could've sworn that when Orval first mentioned that Phyllis and I could've been having an affair, Vergil had choked back an outright chuckle.

Apparently old Orval had just made first-string of the suspects team, and I wasn't even a bench warmer. On account of it being so absolutely unbelievable that a woman who looked like Mr. Ed would find *me* irresistible. A thing like this could really hurt a guy's feelings.

Vergil's sad face still looked as if it were halfway leaning toward amused as he started quizzing Orval real hard about his whereabouts during the day.

Before Orval answered, he took off his cowboy hat and started fiddling real nervous-like with the brim, twisting it round and round in this hands. When he took off his hat, I realized why Orval wore that Stetson so much. Why, in fact, he even wore it on hot days like this one.

It looked like Orval had less hair on his head than my brother Elmo. And that was going some. Elmo has just nineteen hairs left on top. I counted them once when he fell asleep on my couch watching TV. Orval, however, made Elmo look like Rod Stewart in the hair department. Orval had no hair at all on top, and just a faint shadow of brown above each ear.

Why, Orval could've gotten himself a white robe, kicked off his socks and boots, and given Sinéad O'Connor a run for her money.

Apparently, being questioned by Vergil had rattled Orval so much that he'd forgotten he was exposing his bare head for all to see. "Look, I wasn't even near here," he said, still twisting and turning his hat brim. "I was all the way on the other side of Crayton County, repairing a console TV in one house and a stereo in another house and a microwave in another one."

Vergil pulled a little notebook out of his pocket and started writing to beat the band.

Orval's eyes widened when he saw the notebook. He drew himself up and said, his voice shaking with righteous indignation, "Sheriff, I'll have you know you're welcome to check on my story. If I have to, I'll give you the name and address of every one of the customers I saw today."

Vergil fixed him with a sad look. "You have to," he said.

Orval looked as if Vergil had slapped him, and immediately started tearing up again. "How you can think that I would do anything to my sweet Phyllis, my darling, darling, darling wife, well, I——" For the next few minutes you couldn't hear anything again except Orval's blubbering.

This scene, of course, was where I came in, so I started to move across the lawn, heading toward the front door of Phyllis's house. I was intending to talk to the guys from the crime lab as soon as I saw my chance. Just to see if they'd come across anything particularly interesting.

I hadn't taken five steps away from Vergil and Orval when Imogene appeared at my side. "Haskell, can I talk to you a minute?" As she spoke, I noticed that she'd positioned herself so that her back was to Phyllis's house. So that even if she tried, Imogene couldn't get a clear view of the open doorway. I reckon Imogene had seen all of poor Phyllis in her present condition that Imogene ever wanted to.

I can't say I blamed her.

Imogene ran her hand through her brown hair. "Look, I just—um—wanted you to know that I don't believe for a second what Orval just said about you and Phyllis. The very idea is idiotic."

I just looked at her. What was I supposed to say to that? *Gosh, thanks?* Once again, I couldn't help wondering if I was being insulted. I mean, I know I haven't been exactly lucky with women and all, but I don't think that believing a woman would actually go to bed with me is up there with believing in UFOs, Bigfoot, and the Loch Ness monster.

Imogene was shrugging her shoulders. "For one thing,

Phyllis and I were very close—" here Imogene's voice got a little ragged, but she swallowed once and hurried on "—and if such a thing were true, I know Phyllis would've told me about it. We told each other everything." Imogene blinked, drew a deep breath, and said, her voice cracking a little, "God, I—I'm going to miss her so much."

I nodded, trying to look as sympathetic as I could. I'm real bad in situations like this. I never do know how to act around a person who's just lost somebody they loved. Particularly when that somebody's been murdered. All the usual things you say to the bereaved to try to be comforting just don't seem right in a case like this. Like, "She's gone to a better place," that sort of thing. It seems to me that if you say that, you're pretty much ignoring the particularly cruel method by which the dearly departed was sent. So, with Imogene, I did what I always do when I'm at a loss for words. I said nothing.

Imogene must not have needed any encouragement from me to keep talking. Maybe she was a little like her sister in this respect. "I'm sure that if Phyllis really did tell Orval a story like that, she made it up. Just to hurt him."

From Imogene's tone, you might've thought she was recalling some cute thing her sister had done. Apparently Imogene didn't think there was a thing wrong with making up a story of infidelity and telling it to your husband.

Come to think of it, though, I myself would've preferred that to what my own ex did. The day Claudzilla left, she'd thoughtfully taken the time to tell me about every one of her infidelities. Only she hadn't been making them up.

"That's all it was," Imogene was saying. "Phyllis just told Orval that story to pay him back a little. For all the things that slimeball had done to her."

I immediately amended my first thought. Apparently Imogene didn't think there was anything wrong with telling your husband lies about being unfaithful—if the husband in question was, as she so quaintly put it, a slimeball.

I glanced back over at Vergil and the slimeball in question. Orval had apparently run out of sobs at last. He was tearfully reciting names and addresses to Vergil, who was busily scratching away in his notebook.

Imogene followed my eyes. "The man's a slimeball, all right," she said. "You know it, and I know it. I bet even Orval himself knows it."

I wasn't sure about that. It's been my experience that slimeballs don't generally see themselves as slimeballs. They're funny that way.

I didn't argue with Imogene, though. I just nodded as she moved a little closer to me and lowered her voice. "So. Are you going to tell the sheriff what you know?"

I didn't rightly know how to answer that one. Being as how I couldn't think of anything particular that I knew, it didn't seem likely that I was going to tell it. I decided to go with a real noncommittal answer.

"Huh?"

Imogene must not have been impressed by my snappy comeback, because she stepped back and just looked at me. Like maybe she was wondering if she were talking to someone whose IQ was every bit as lofty as the Gunterman twins'. "I *said,* are you going to tell the sheriff what you know? About Phyllis and all." This time Imogene spoke a lot slower and a lot more distinctly. Exactly the way you might, say, to Jeb or Fred.

I glanced over at the two of them, now standing about two feet on the other side of Vergil and Orval. In his zeal to get the names and addresses of Orval's customers, Vergil had overlooked telling the brothers to resume their positions in front of Phyllis's front door. So the two of them were, as they say in the military, at ease. Fred, at that moment, was picking his nose. Jeb, no doubt the more intellectual of the two, was squatting on the ground, his face twisted in intense concentration. He was retying the shoelaces of his right shoe. As Jeb concentrated, his tongue protruded about a half inch out of the left corner of his mouth. From where I stood, it looked like shoelace tying might be a project that could keep Jeb occupied for the better part of a day.

I can't say that these two had the sort of professional

image that I particularly wanted folks to confuse *me* with. I tried to answer Imogene real quick this time. No hesitation at all. "Frankly, I consider anything that Phyllis told me to be confidential, and I wouldn't divulge it unless I had to."

Imogene's eyes widened. I was pretty sure she didn't think I knew words with as many syllables as "confidential."

On a roll, I hurried on. "Or, to put it another way, I'd say that this entire matter falls under the auspices of client-detective relationship, and as such, should be considered strictly confidential." As I spoke, I was pretty sure Imogene's eyes now held new respect. Either that, or she was staring at me, wide-eyed like that, because she was afraid any minute now I would pull out a thesaurus. I nodded once again in her direction and added, "That is to say, of course, that I would have to divulge such information only under subpoena, which I tend to believe—"

Thank God Imogene jumped in at that point. I was getting tempted to use phrases like "vis-à-vis" and "party of the first part." In a second or two, even *I* wouldn't have known what I was talking about.

"I don't mean just what Phyllis *talked* to you about. I mean *everything.*" Imogene emphasized that last word and gave me a significant look.

The significance of which, of course, completely escaped me.

I stared back at Imogene. I was real afraid that the expression on my face probably mirrored the one on Jeb's. He was at that moment staring dully at his tangled shoelace, his eyes bewildered.

"Phyllis really wasn't like what you might think, Haskell," Imogene went on, leaning even closer and lowering her voice to a whisper. "She was just real confused these last few days. That's why she did what she did."

I had only one small question. Did what? Apparently Imogene was under the impression that she was talking about something with which I was already well acquainted. She must've concluded a lot more than she should have from my referring to Orval as "Loverbug."

"I see," I lied.

Imogene nodded, running her hand through her hair again. "Phyllis thought those tapes were her ticket out of the mess she was in."

I stared at Imogene, trying real hard not to look as surprised as I felt. Tapes? *Plural?* Had there been more than the one tape I listened to? This stood to reason, since there had been *three* tape recorders. Wouldn't it necessarily follow, then, that there had been at least three tapes? But had *Phyllis,* of all people, made them? I would sooner have believed that Mr. Ed himself had made the tapes, rather than think that Phyllis had recorded her own husband in bed with another woman.

It just didn't seem possible. And yet, if it were true, then Phyllis was clearly every bit as open-minded as Orval had said she was. And she had cleverly disguised her amazingly modern attitude by wearing an old-fashioned green gingham square dance dress.

I stood there, going over it in my mind. Could all that really be so?

Imogene reached out and touched my arm. "I know what you're thinking," she said.

I strongly doubted it.

"But you've got to understand, Haskell, Phyllis just wanted to get enough money to get away from Orval. She wasn't a bad person, she was just real desperate."

I tried to hold my face perfectly still so that it wouldn't reveal in the slightest how very badly my jaw wanted to drop open. Having heard this last bit, now I wondered if Phyllis wasn't making some kind of sex tapes starring Orval the Cowboy Repairman. And *selling* them. Now, this took open-mindedness to a whole new dimension. If this were true, old Phyllis had been blazing new frontiers in open-mindedness.

I gave Imogene a quick smile, something hard to do while the blood is draining from your face. "Look," I said, holding up my hands, "don't worry. I always try not to make judgments of people." I did not add that one good reason I wasn't judging Phyllis was that I didn't know what the hell Imogene was talking about, but I reckon I sounded reassuring.

Imogene actually looked relieved. "I knew you wouldn't tell Vergil about all this. I knew we could trust you, Phyllis and I."

I gave her what I hoped was a smile every bit as reassuring as I sounded. "You can trust me not to say a word."

I believe I can say at this point that I was telling Imogene the absolute truth. How can you say a word about something you know nothing about?

Imogene looked back over at Orval, who was, unbelievably, *still* giving Vergil names and addresses. Apparently the list had been slowed up some because Orval was having some trouble spelling some of the names. "All this was his fault, you know," Imogene said. *"He* drove her to it." If I didn't know better, I'd say there was something real close to hatred in Imogene's voice now. "If it hadn't been for that asshole and the way he ran around on her, Phyllis would never have made those tapes. She wouldn't even have thought of such a thing."

As if on cue, a guy from the crime lab walked out Phyllis's front door the exact second the words were out of Imogene's mouth. Imogene's face went pale again when she saw what the guy was carrying.

His hands in clear plastic gloves, he had all three tape recorders.

"We found these in the kitchen," the guy told Vergil. "Two of them are empty—" here Imogene's eyes flickered to mine; there seemed to be a question in her eyes, but before I could say anything, she looked away, back over at the crime lab guy "—but the third still has a tape in it," he was saying. "I think you'll want to listen to it, Sheriff."

Under other circumstances, that might've been true. In this case, though, the crime lab guy was wrong. Vergil clearly did not want to hear it. Not with Imogene standing less than three feet away.

After the crime lab guy pushed "play" on the recorder, it took Vergil at least a full minute, though, to realize what it was he was listening to. I think this was on account of Vergil's hearing not being quite what it used to be. Vergil moved a couple of steps closer to the crime lab guy and leaned forward, screwing up his eyes, of all things, as if that might help him hear better.

The tape was at a real good part, the part where the Unknown Giggler was saying, "Oh, yes, oh yes, oh-h-h YE-E-ES" over and over. And sounding as if her asthma had gotten real bad.

I'm pretty sure everybody but Vergil caught on right away to what was going on.

Even Jeb and Fred. Fred immediately stopped picking his nose and nearly tripped over Jeb, trying to get closer. Jeb gave up tying his shoelaces, and for a second he and his brother tried to shoulder each other out of the way, like two elementary school kids trying to cut ahead of each other in line. They settled for standing shoulder to shoulder, as close to the crime lab guy as they could get.

Listening to that tape, the twins started grinning so wide, you might've thought they were trying to land a part in one of them Doublemint commercials. Which was, let me tell you, a scary thought.

Orval, on the other hand, was not grinning. Far from it. Orval must've recognized those "oh-yeses" from the get-go. "Hey, where the hell did you get that?" Orval said. "What the hell do you think you're doing?"

For a man who insisted he was just exercising, Orval was suddenly awful irate. Can you believe it? Just because folks were listening to his aerobics tape. "Gimme that!" Orval yelled, making a wild grab for the tape recorder.

It was as if somebody had tried to shut off the twins' favorite program. Their Doublemint grins quickly vanished, and both deputies moved threateningly toward Orval, just as he was making his grab.

Orval immediately seemed to see the error of his ways, drawing his hand back so fast, you might've thought the tape was hot.

Which, in a way, I reckon it was.

Putting some distance again between himself and the twins, Orval looked as if he might cry again. *"I said* where did you get that? That's private, you know."

As if we needed this pointed out to us.

The crime lab guy answered Orval's question as if Vergil has asked it. Looking straight at the sheriff, he said, "We found this in the cabinet over the refrigerator."

At that moment the Unknown Giggler had switched from repeating oh-yeses to repeating, "Orval, Orval, Orval." Sort of like an out-of-breath cheerleader.

Vergil had evidently heard enough by now to realize what it was. Either that, or he'd just remembered that there was a lady present. The sheriff turned not just pink, but bright red, gave Imogene a quick look, and apparently decided that Orval's aerobics were not suitable for mixed company. "Turn that off!" he snapped. Both twins immediately looked crestfallen. "I'm real sorry, ma'am," Vergil said to Imogene. "Real sorry."

I believed him. Even Vergil's salt-and-pepper hair seemed to have a red sheen to it. Vergil turned and glowered at Orval. "Does this—this—this—" Here Vergil gave up trying to find a word for it. "Does this belong to you, Orval?"

Orval looked hurt that Vergil would even suggest such a thing. "It does not!" Orval was doing righteous indignation again. "I'll have you know that I would never, *ever* make a disgusting tape like that. *Never!* Why, that's nauseating. That's—that's *nasty!"*

Orval appeared to be forgetting here that it was *he* himself who was doing the disgusting, nauseating, and nasty things that we were listening to.

Vergil must've concluded that this was worth pointing out to him. "Isn't that *you* on the tape?"

Orval started twisting his cowboy hat again. "Well, yeah, that's me, all right. But I never saw that tape before in my life."

Vergil blinked. "Never?"

Orval's voice was earnest. "Now, Sheriff, would I make a disgusting tape like that and keep it right in my house? Where my wife might find it?"

Orval probably should've given that statement a little more thought. Vergil took a real deep breath, and sighed, his eyes infinitely sad. "Orval," he said quietly, "I thought you told me Phyllis didn't mind you *exercising.*"

Orval was stammering now. "Well, now, uh, sheriff, it's one thing to know about it, but, uh, it's an entirely different thing to *listen* to it."

Orval's credibility was once again right up there with Richard Nixon's. Vergil cleared his throat. "Who's the lady, Orval?"

Orval shuffled his feet uneasily, twisted his hat a couple more times, and finally blurted, "Flo."

That was all he had to say. Vergil, Jeb, Fred, I, and even the guy from the crime lab all nodded. I reckon there's not a male over sixteen in Pigeon Fork who doesn't know about Flo Pedigo. In her early forties, with hair the color of garnets and the figure of an awfully healthy twenty-year-old, Flo is what you call a real friendly sort. In fact, I reckon Flo has a lot in common with Will Rogers. She never met a man she didn't like. She particularly likes him if he has twenty-five dollars. More if the man wants her to like him for over an hour.

This is not to say, mind you, that I know this from personal experience. I've just heard Flo's price list around town. Really. Besides, if I ever end up actually having to *pay* some woman to go to bed with me, my ego will be in worse shape than it's already in.

I've also heard Flo's price list from Vergil. In real loud, outraged tones. Vergil used to arrest Flo on a regular basis. Only trouble was, she never seemed to have bail money, and while she was awaiting trial in his jail, she kept telling dirty stories to the other prisoners. And doing stripteases. After a while, it got to where a lot of the men around Pigeon Fork were *trying* to get themselves arrested when Flo was doing time.

The week the seventeen-year-old Toomey kid threw a brick through Vergil's office window—and then just stood there, out on the front porch, happily waiting for Vergil to haul him in—Vergil pretty much decided that he'd let Flo alone, if she'd let him alone.

You could tell Vergil wasn't any too happy to hear her name, though. He actually winced. Then he made Orval go through his whereabouts during the day all over again. Several times. It took forever. Vergil, however, did get Orval to finally admit that he'd had quite a bit of traveling time between jobs.

And, during that traveling time, he'd had no alibi.

"But, Sheriff," Orval wailed. "If I'da done this to my sweet wife, I woulda had to drive all the way back home, and then all the way back, in order to make my afternoon appointment!"

I wasn't sure what exactly was his point. Was it that it would've been too much trouble to murder his wife? Or that it would've put too much mileage on his truck?

Orval hurried on. "And—and Phyllis left that note! With the seven on it! What's a seven got to do with me?"

In my opinion, it might've been his IQ, but I didn't say anything.

Vergil seemed unmoved by either of Orval's arguments. You could almost see the sheriff mentally penning Orval's name on an arrest warrant.

Me, I wasn't so sure. Unless Orval had real talent as an actor, I'd say he was telling the truth when he said he'd never heard the tape before. I'd also guess he was seeing the tape recorders for the first time. Orval really did look like he'd just been poleaxed. So, if he didn't know Phyllis had even made these tapes, why would he have killed her? She sure didn't seem to be getting in the way of his exercise program.

I couldn't help but notice, however, that while Vergil was drilling him about his day, Orval was also looking quite a bit less sad that his wife had met an untimely end. Orval must've realized that if *he* didn't make that tape, it had to have been Phyllis who'd made it and hidden it in the kitchen.

Vergil may have been homing in on Orval as a suspect, but Imogene, surprisingly, was not. While Orval continued to protest his innocence, Imogene once again moved closer to my side. "I don't believe for a minute that Orval did this to Phyllis," she whispered. "He may be a slimeball, but he's not a killer. It's got to be one of those people on the tapes, don't you think?"

Actually, the answer to that was no, I don't think, I'm beyond thinking right this minute, I'm using up all the brain power I've got just trying to follow what in the world you've been talking about. I settled instead for just nodding, however, and saying in as nonchalant a voice as I could muster, "You know, we ought to get together and go over all we know." What I meant, of course, was that we needed to go over all *Imogene* knew, but I didn't think I really ought to spell that out for her.

Imogene blinked and then just stared at me for a long moment. Like maybe she was sizing me up. I wondered uneasily if she might actually suspect that *I* had something to do with her sister's death. Apparently, though, Imogene decided that somebody who looked like Howdy Doody probably wasn't murderer material. "You're right," she finally said. "We do need to talk. I'll come by your place later tonight, OK?"

I gave her directions, and when I was done, she took a deep breath. "I'm not going to let whoever did this to Phyllis get away with it, Haskell. You mark my words. I'm *not*." As she said this, Imogene gave her fist a determined shake.

"Maybe Phyllis shouldn't have made those tapes, but she sure didn't deserve this."

I nodded, wondering how in the world I was going to get Imogene to tell me all she knew without revealing one small, insignificant thing—that *I* didn't know anywhere near as much as she apparently thought I did.

It was sure going to make for an interesting evening.

9

It was getting dark before Vergil finally let us all go home. We would've gotten away a little sooner, except that Vergil had the guys from the crime lab fingerprint Orval and Imogene—and, oh yes, *me*. This, even though Vergil had said earlier that he thought Phyllis's house had been wiped clean.

Vergil was, oddly enough, even more thorough with me than he'd been with Orval and Imogene. With them, he'd just got their fingertips and thumbs. With me, Vergil insisted that the lab do my fingers, thumbs, full handprints, and both palm prints. For a while there, I thought Vergil might actually have them do my elbows and knees. Vergil told me he was doing all this just for elimination purposes, but I wasn't so sure. Before the crime lab guys started in on me, I tried pointing out to Vergil that my fingerprints were already on file back in Louisville, being as how that's one of the things they always do when you sign on to the police force. Vergil, however, evidently didn't want to bother sending away for my prints. Either that, or he was intent on punishing me a little for causing yet another homicide to pop up in Crayton County. This last was the one I tended to believe. I may have been getting a little sensitive here, but I thought Vergil actually seemed to enjoy watching the crime lab guy dirty up my fingers with black ink.

He also seemed to enjoy something else. While the crime lab guy was printing me, I said to Vergil, just like I was making conversation and nothing more, "You know, if I could have me a Xerox copy of that note Phyllis left, it would sure be a big help."

Vergil didn't even blink. "Yep," he said, "it would be a big help, wouldn't it?" That was all he said. He didn't say, *no. I couldn't have it,* and he didn't say, *yes, I could.* He just turned and walked away. If I didn't know better, though, I could've sworn old Vergil had come real close to actually smiling.

That man does love to torture me.

I watched him walk away, and contemplated my next move. Maybe I should show up at his office tomorrow morning early and beg.

My fingertips still looked a tad gray as I finally drove home. That black ink is right hard to wipe off. On the way home, I had almost a half hour to think. It didn't do much good, though. I watched the headlights of my Ford pickup bouncing along on the two-lane highway up ahead, and all I seemed to be able to come up with were questions. The biggest one, of course, was, What did Phyllis's dying clue mean? Why would she have written a seven, of all things? If, of course, it really was a seven. Could Phyllis have been in the act of writing a letter, like a T, for instance, and run out of strength before she could finish?

When I got through wondering about that, I wondered what in hell Imogene had been talking about. Had there really been more than just the one tape I'd listened to? If so, then had Phyllis gotten herself a hobby? Something on the order of making sex tapes for fun and profit? Where, then, were these other tapes? Had Phyllis's killer taken them after the murder? Was that why Phyllis had been killed? To get the tapes?

Oh yeah. I was real good at coming up with questions. It was the answers that I had a problem with.

When Imogene showed up at my house later, I sure hoped she brought some answers with her.

I must've been a lot more tired than I thought, because it didn't occur to me until I was heading up my driveway that there were two other folks in town who'd also had break-ins like Phyllis's. And if there was even the slightest chance that what had happened to Phyllis could in any way be connected to her earlier break-in, then these two other folks should be warned.

Even if you no longer worked for them.

Driving up my hill, I could hear Rip, as usual, up there on my deck, barking and howling and carrying on. It was real black outside by then, but I've got me two big porch lights on either side of my front door that switch themselves on once it gets real dark out. I would've liked to think that maybe old Rip just couldn't see that it was me, but being as how my entire front yard and a good part of my driveway were lit up like a Christmas tree, I knew Rip *had* to know who it was. If anything, he barked even louder once I pulled up right in front of the house, and that dumb dog could get a real good look at me.

It *had* been yet another long day. If anything, Rip sounded more desperate today than he had yesterday. Which was going some.

That, of course, meant I had a choice to make. The SPCA might've disagreed with me, but making that choice didn't take long. It seems pretty open and shut that if you can only do one thing at a time, and you have to choose between warning somebody about possibly being *murdered*—or carrying your insane dog downstairs to the yard to do his business—there's really only one way you can go.

Rip, however, did not see it my way.

He kept on barking and howling, like he always does, right up until I got out of my truck and started up the stairs to my deck. Then, again like always, Rip stopped with his bark-at-the-guy-who-lives-here routine, and went right into his thank-the-dear-Lord-he's-home ritual. This last was his usual hysterical combination of wriggling all over, and dancing back and forth, and jumping in the air with joy. I've always wondered how that dog could stand to do that with a full bladder.

When I was almost to the top of the stairs, Rip abruptly cut the hysterics and scooted over to the edge of the steps. And waited.

This, of course, was where his and my evening routine abruptly varied. "Just a minute, Rip," I said. "I've got a couple of calls to make, and then I'll be right back for you. OK, Rip?"

I don't know why I said this to him. I guess I just thought he deserved an explanation. Of course, I knew full well that all Rip really heard was, "Blah, blah, blah, *Rip,* blah, blah, blah, blah, blah, blah. Blah, *Rip?*"

I stepped past him and hurried across the redwood deck, toward my front door.

Rip was still sitting there at the edge of the steps, a horrified look dawning in his brown eyes as he watched me disappear through my front door.

Right up to then, I'd thought Rip was taking the delay real well. Like maybe Rin Tin Tin would've. With perserverance and courage and all.

That, of course, was before Rip started the howling.

And the whimpering.

And the shrieking in sheer agony.

Maybe jumping up and down like that had been harder on his bladder than I thought.

Looking up Ruta Lippton's number in the phone book seemed to take forever. Particularly with Rip carrying on like that outside. By the time I dialed her number, Rip had apparently decided that keeping his vigil at the edge of the stairs and merely howling his head off was not doing the trick. This appalling situation no doubt called for more direct action.

Like, for example, an assault on the storm door that opens into my living room.

I was already in the kitchen by then, with the receiver to my ear, listening to Ruta's phone ring, so I couldn't actually see what Rip was doing. If I had to guess, though, I'd say, from the way it sounded, Rip was throwing himself bodily against my front door. Apparently the impact was knocking him senseless, because there was always this short pause after the huge booming noise. Then, of course, after the short pause—during which, no doubt, Rip regained consciousness—there was this scritch-scratching noise. This, I decided, was the sound of Rip scrambling for traction on my redwood deck. After that, of course, came another door-rattling boom. It went on and on. BOOM, pause, scritch-scratch, BOOM, pause, scritch-scratch . . .

Ruta had not answered yet, so I put my hand over the receiver and yelled, "Rip, no! No, boy! Cut IT OUT! NO, RIP, NO!" I thought I sounded pretty fierce.

Outside on the deck, there was a short pause. Then, you guessed it, a scritch-scratch, followed by a BOOM, then another pause, another scritch-scratch . . .

This is a real distracting thing to have to listen to while you're trying to convince somebody they could be in danger.

Maybe that's why Ruta really didn't seem to take what I had to say seriously. I told her about what had happened to Phyllis, and about Phyllis's break-in, and all Ruta said was, "Yeah, I heard. Ain't that a crying shame?"

"Ruta," I said. "What I'm trying to tell you is that Phyllis Carver had her house broken into, and nothing taken, *just like yours.*"

"Whaddya know," Ruta said. She paused and then said, "Well, um, it's been nice talking to you, Haskell."

Obviously the woman was not getting it.

"Ruta," I said, "you could be in danger."

"Pish posh," Ruta said.

I gripped the phone a little tighter. The woman could be on somebody's list of Folks To Be Murdered, and Ruta's reaction was "Pish posh."

"Look, Haskell," Ruta went on, "Lenard's right here. You don't have to worry about me."

"Listen, Ruta—" I began, but she interrupted me.

"Haskell, I don't want to sound mean, but you might as well give up. I'm not going to hire you back again. I've made up my mind, and that's final."

Apparently Ruta thought my phone call was just a scare tactic to drum up more business.

"Ruta—"

That was all I got out before Ruta interrupted me again. "Is that thunder?"

I reckon you already know what it was. Rip had evidently decided that he wasn't making a big enough dent in my *front* door, so he'd run around on the deck to my back door. Which is just off my kitchen. So now I could hear the scritch-scratch of his toenails a lot clearer just before he threw himself against the door.

Explaining all this to Ruta, though, might be a tad embarrassing.

"That's thunder, all right," I said.

"Hm. It's not supposed to rain," Ruta said. With that final weather report, she hung up. If she said good-bye, Rip's crashing against my back door drowned it out.

Unfortunately, Rip's body-slamming my back door did *not* completely drown out what all June Reed had to tell me.

I said my piece, and June immediately responded with, "Haskell, Winslow and I are very sorry to hear about that Carver woman. We really are. It's just a tragedy. *But* I thought I made myself clear." June's lotion-voice had ice floating in it. "You are *not* working for me and Winslow anymore. Our house being broken into is no longer any of your business. Got it?"

I got it, all right. June was definitely crossed off my list of favorite high school cheerleaders. "Look, I just thought I ought to tell you," I said. It sounded lame even to my own ears.

"So you told me," June said, and hung up. Rip at that moment was not making contact with my back door, so I knew for sure this time that June had definitely *not* said good-bye.

Apparently I had tortured a mentally ill dog for nothing.

Rip, though, was surprisingly forgiving. At least, he was until after I'd picked him up and carried him downstairs. He even tried to lick my ears a couple of times before I put him down in the yard.

It was on the return trip that Rip started squirming and growling under his breath and finally erupted into full-blown barking. Even when I put him down on the deck so that he could follow me inside on his own steam, that fool dog kept right on barking. There wasn't anybody else around, and I didn't hear any deer or rabbits or anything moving around out in the woods. So I was pretty sure that this was Rip's way of giving me a tongue-lashing for being so tardy in performing my duties.

"Hey, I'm sorry, Rip," I said.

Rip kept right on barking even after he and I moved inside.

Rip knows he's not supposed to bark in the house for no good reason, so right after we went through the front door, he started doing his mumble-barking under his breath. This was almost as irritating to listen to as his assaults on my doors. It sounded as if he were trying to bark with his mouth full. I ignored him, and went into the kitchen to make myself the kind of gourmet meal we bachelors are famous for. Microwaved hot dogs topped off with microwaved pork and beans straight from the can.

Being as how I felt so guilty about what I'd done to him earlier, I gave Rip a hot dog, too. *With* the bun. Usually when I do this kind of thing, Rip looks at me with surprise, like he thinks this may be some kind of trick. Tonight he seemed to take it as his due, wolfing down that hot dog in two big gulps. He even sat there for a second afterwards, staring at me expectantly, like maybe he thought he deserved more than this, considering what he'd been through.

I ended up making him another hot dog. I know. I know. I'm a pushover.

A half hour or so later, I had cleaned up the kitchen, put my dishes into the dishwasher, and just turned it on, when

Rip started barking out loud again. Skipping the mumble-barking altogether and going straight for the real thing. For a second I thought maybe Rip had decided he hadn't given me enough of a tongue-lashing before, and he was trying to make up for it. Then I heard the car heading up my driveway.

Even over Rip's barking, it's generally pretty easy to hear when a car's coming. Because my hill is so steep, a car's motor is usually straining real good by the time a car gets to the top.

Imogene's red Mustang was no exception. It groaned to a stop in front of my A-frame, and Imogene headed toward my front door, shaking her head. When she saw me standing there, she said, "You ever think about getting a chair lift?"

I figured that was one of them rhetorical questions, and it didn't need an answer. Besides, even if I'd wanted to say anything, I wouldn't have been able to, on account of Rip's carrying on.

I think his bladder problems earlier had left him in a real bad mood. Rip not only barked at Imogene, he growled at her. I was pretty sure, though, that Rip was not making some kind of character judgment. He was just enjoying being rude.

I've got to hand it to Imogene. She didn't do anything stupid, like put her hand out and say, "Nice doggie." Nope, she just stood there at my open door, waiting for Rip to calm down. She was still wearing the navy blue suit she'd had on earlier, and I couldn't help but notice, her slip was still showing in the back.

I tried not to stare at it. Was this a standard look for her, or was she just too upset to notice? Lord knows, of course, she had good reason to be upset.

Rip, however, might've had Imogene beat in the upset department. "Rip," I said, "quiet." I also said, "Hush now, Rip. Quiet, boy! Hush! QUIET! Rip, will you SHUT UP!"

I think Rip is getting to be real obedient. He quieted down right after that, and contented himself with just giving

Imogene's shoes a quick sniff as she walked past him. Then he padded over to his favorite plaid chair, and lay down in front of it.

It was when she walked by me that I realized that Imogene had probably cried all the way here. The tip of her nose was real red, her eyes looked puffy, and her freckles almost blended into the general pink of her face. It made me feel a lot worse about Rip being so rude to her.

It also made me wonder what in the world to say to her. Like I said before, I'm real bad in situations like this.

Imogene stepped past me into my living room, and right away she did two things that made me start liking her. One, she walked right over to my blue wraparound couch, stepped around the wooden wire spool that I use as a coffee table, and sat down. This may not sound like much, but I've had women come in and immediately start cleaning up. Picking up magazines and newspapers and dog toys, and putting them away for me.

My house is not quite the Bermuda Rectangle my office is purported to be, but you can tell both places have the same decorator.

I've also had women come in and look wildly around, their eyes showing the whites all around. One woman I went out with only once, oddly enough, actually refused to sit on my couch until she'd taken a handkerchief out of her purse and put it between her and the couch cushion. She'd looked as if she were sitting on a place mat.

The Amazing Imogene did none of these things. She just sat down—without benefit of a handkerchief—and glanced around the room. "This is cozy," she said.

She actually sounded as if she meant it. What a woman.

I sat down on the other end of my wraparound couch, facing her, and for a second my mind went totally blank. How do you politely bring up all the things I wanted to discuss with her? Surely it was even more rude than Rip had just been to blurt out, "So, Imogene, why do you think your sister was murdered today?"

Imogene didn't look as if she knew how to get started either. She just sat there, looking ill at ease, fidgeting a little with the red bow at her collar.

It was at that moment that my water pump came on, and Imogene did the other thing that endeared her to me. She didn't even flinch. Or jump. Or say, "What the hell is THAT?"

Being as how I live too far from Pigeon Fork to have city water—and I've yet to go to the expense of digging a well—my house is on a cistern. Every time I run my dishwasher, or wash my clothes, or do anything that takes a quantity of water—my water pump kicks on. There are, no doubt, quieter pumps. This one puts out a real loud hum. I've had folks visiting from Louisville go into my bathroom, flush, and nearly have a heart attack.

After they start breathing regularly again, I always have to go into this lengthy, boring explanation of my water supply. Believe me, trying to explain what a cistern is to somebody from the city is not easy. They generally seem to think it's something pretty disgusting. I believe that's because folks from the city generally seem to confuse cisterns with *cesspools*.

I usually just tell them that a cistern is sort of like having a concrete basement under my side porch. Only this particular basement is filled with water. Not sewage. *Water.* My cistern fills up with water draining off my roof, and sometimes, when there hasn't been a rain for a while, I get water delivered, pumped off the truck directly into my cistern. Which, in turn, is pumped by my water pump all over the house. After which, I just turn on the tap like anybody else.

When my pump went off, Imogene—Lord love her—just cocked her dark head to one side and said, "Oh, you're on a cistern, too. So am I. It's a nuisance, isn't it?"

I never thought complaining about the inconveniences of living on a cistern could be such a icebreaker. By the time Imogene had said that paying twenty-five dollars for two-thousand gallons of water was highway robbery, and I'd said that if she thought that was bad, I had to pay *thirty* dollars on account of my hill being so steep, it seemed like we could've been old friends.

Imogene apparently thought we actually were. "You know, Haskell, I remember you from high school. You were two years behind me."

I stared at her, surprised. Surprised that she remembered *me*, and I didn't recall her at all. And also surprised that this woman sitting in front of me on the couch, looking cuter by the minute, had to be two years older than me. Imogene sure didn't look it. In fact, I would've taken her for being Phyllis's younger sister.

I didn't have time to feel flattered about Imogene remembering me, though, because right away she said, "I probably shouldn't tell you why I remember you, but I'm going to, anyway." She looked down at her lap for a second, and then said, "All the kids in high school used to call me Spatterface, too."

I just looked at her. So much for being flattered. "No kidding," I said. What a thing to have in common. It gave you a real warm feeling, all right.

I braced myself for Imogene to say something about Howdy Doody, but she didn't. Instead, she just nodded, and I saw that her eyes were filling up. To show you what an idiot I am, I was actually thinking, Lord, this woman is real sensitive if being called names almost twenty years ago still hurts her feelings this bad today, when Imogene said, "Phyllis used to get so mad at them when they called me Spatterface." Imogene was blinking hard now. "God, I can't believe she's gone."

While Imogene kept blinking back tears, I sat there like a bump on a pickle, not knowing what to say. Or what to do. I was pretty sure that I didn't have any more Kleenexes in my house than I'd had back at my office. If Imogene was going to need something to cry into, the best I could do was a paper towel from the kitchen.

Before I could get up to get her one, Imogene pulled a rumpled Kleenex of her own out of her suit pocket. It looked the worse for wear, but it was probably a distinct improvement over my paper towels. Imogene dabbed at her eyes a second, and then looked back up at me. Her face was not what you'd call gorgeous or anything, but her eyes really were pretty. Fringed in thick, curly lashes, they were mainly hazel, but they had a definite green cast. Sitting this close to her, I could make out several gold flecks glinting in them. It was as if Imogene's eyes, like her face, were sprinkled with tiny golden freckles. "I'm sorry, Haskell, I really am," Imogene said, "I—I just can't seem to stop crying."

I reached over and patted her hand. "There, there," I said. I believe I've mentioned before that I have no idea what this is supposed to mean, but it's what everybody seems to say in situations like this.

It must've been the right thing to do, because Imogene gave me a grateful look. She sniffled a little bit more, and then she cleared her throat. "You used to live in Louisville, too, didn't you?"

I think we were both relieved to be on safer ground. "Sure did," I said.

Imogene nodded. "I lived there myself for six years. Just moved back last October."

"No kidding." I know I'd said this before, but her crying had really rattled me. It was all I could do to come up with "no kidding."

Imogene swallowed. "Phyllis never left Pigeon Fork. Mama and Daddy moved us all here when we were both real little, and Phyllis never left."

From the way Imogene said it, I couldn't tell if she thought this was a bad thing or not.

"Phyllis married Orval right out of high school, and that slimeball started running around on her right away."

There was no doubt this time. *This* was a bad thing.

In fact, I think you could categorize every single thing that Imogene had to say about Orval as bad. According to Imogene, Phyllis had caught Orval running around on her about every other month.

"Every time Orval got caught," Imogene said tearfully,

"he would swear to Phyllis that he'd never, never do it again. Can you believe it?"

Actually, I was having trouble believing any of it. Mainly because I found it real hard to swallow that a bald-headed cowboy repairman could be all that attractive to the opposite sex. It sounded like Orval, *married,* had done a lot better than me, *single.* I think I was getting depressed again.

Imogene took a deep breath. "This last time was the final straw."

Imogene explained that Phyllis had suspected something was going on for some time. Then, two weeks ago, Phyllis had been cleaning her bedroom and found a cigarette butt with lipstick stains on it beside her bed.

Imogene took a deep breath. "Phyllis doesn't smoke."

I nodded. Maybe estimating Orval's IQ at seven was a tad optimistic.

"Do you know what Orval told her?"

I hated to guess.

"He actually told Phyllis with a straight face that the cigarette must've been caught on the bottom of his shoe, and he'd tracked it into the house himself."

I was, once again, at a loss for words. Orval had stepped in something, all right, but it hadn't been a cigarette.

Imogene was on a roll now, her voice getting angrier. "That's why Phyllis bugged their bed. To find out for sure if Orval was lying." Imogene wiped her nose, and then looked over at me. "But, of course, you already knew that, didn't you?"

I just looked at her. This was the part I'd been dreading. The part where I was supposed to act as if I knew a hell of a lot more than I did. "Of course," I said.

I think I said it with real conviction.

Imogene nodded again. "Phyllis thought she was being so smart. Sticking that voice-activated recorder under their bed. Then, of course, she recorded that awful tape we heard earlier." Imogene's voice was getting shaky. "I don't know. Listening to that tape did something to Phyllis. For a while there, I thought she might actually be having a breakdown.

Screaming and crying. Then, finally, she made up her mind. She was going to leave Orval once and for all. She came up with this whole scheme so she could move to another city and start a-a-a new life!"

Imogene went into full-fledged weeping here. I patted her hand some more and said, "There, there," quite a few times, but unlike earlier, it didn't seem to help. It was a full minute before she stopped.

"I know what you're thinking," Imogene said.

She'd said this earlier. I had a feeling she didn't know my thoughts any more this time than she had then.

"You're thinking I didn't try to stop her, but, Haskell, I did. I told her that the whole idea was stupid, that she wasn't thinking straight, but Phyllis wouldn't listen to me. She wanted to get away from Orval, and she didn't have any money of her own. Orval paid all the bills, and he only gave her just enough to buy groceries."

This could explain why Phyllis's closets held a lot more clothes belonging to Orval than to Phyllis. That poor woman. After living with Claudzilla, I never thought I'd ever feel sorry for a woman who wasn't allowed to shop, but I did.

Imogene sounded angry again. "Did you know that slimeball even took the money Phyllis made as a part-time secretary?"

This seemed safe to admit. "No, I didn't know that."

"Well, he did. That's why Phyllis needed to come up with a way to make some quick money. She was sure her plan would work like a charm. She'd learned a lot about electronics from Orval, and she was convinced it was going to be easy."

Her eyes were fixed on my face. I shook my head regretfully. "What a thing to do," I said. Whatever it was.

Imogene was shaking *her* head regretfully, too. "I would've given her some money myself if I'd had it. But with the real estate market the way it's been, I just didn't have it to give."

I shook my head regretfully some more. My thinking here was to keep Imogene talking until she finally spilled the beans. Unfortunately, it looked like there were quite a few beans to get through before she got to the ones I wanted to hear about.

"And both our parents are retired, living on Social Security," Imogene said. "So there was no use asking them."

I nodded. Right. Right. So Phyllis didn't have any money, so she decided to—what?

Imogene was nodding, too. "And, of course, it was bugging her own bed that gave Phyllis the idea."

I just looked at her. What idea? That's what I thought. What I said was, "My, my." I don't think you can get any more noncommittal than that. I also think I was showing real patience here, considering by this time what I wanted more than anything was to grab Imogene by the shoulders and scream, WHAT IN HELL ARE YOU TALKING ABOUT?

Imogene was back to shaking her head regretfully again. "Phyllis actually thought all she had to do was sneak into the houses of some folks she'd heard gossip about, bug their beds, and find out if the gossip was true. If it was, she thought she'd just play the tape for the folks involved, collect a couple thousand dollars worth of getaway money, and that would be that. Phyllis actually thought it would be a snap."

Uh-oh. I swallowed and just stared at Imogene. Because, of course, I realized right then what Imogene was talking about. And what Phyllis had thought would work like a charm.

Blackmail.

Phyllis Carver's new hobby for fun and profit had been blackmail. Also known as extortion. Also known as a jim-dandy motive for murder.

Lord.

"You know whoever did this to Phyllis is probably one of

the folks she taped." I said it real slow, hoping that Imogene would take my lead.

She did, but I think I knew, even before Imogene said their names, exactly whose beds Phyllis had decided to bug.

Imogene was nodding her head vigorously. "I know. It's got to be either Winslow Reed or Ruta Lippton, don't you think?"

I swallowed again. It made sense to me.

10

I don't know. I reckon I've always pictured blackmailers as sleazy little men with greasy hair, pointed Italian shoes, and wet-lipped grins. I never once pictured a blackmailer as a horse-faced woman in a green gingham square dance dress.

But, as a private detective, you don't ever want to give the impression that you're shocked. It's real bad for business. Clients aren't any too inclined to take you into their confidence if every other second you keep looking as if a bombshell has just gone off in your lap. Nope, the attitude you always want to project is one that says, "I've seen it all and I've heard it all and the best you can do is repeat it."

That's why I put on my best poker face as Imogene went on.

"Phyllis heard through the grapevine some rumors about Winslow and a waitress over at Frank's Bar and Grill by the name of Leesa Jo Lattimore," Imogene said.

My poker face felt as if an earthquake went through it. I didn't want to interrupt Imogene, but I knew Leesa Jo. In her late twenties, with a creamy complexion and long blond hair that she wore in a thick plait down her back, Leesa Jo wasn't exactly the sort of woman you'd forget in a hurry. I

147

didn't know her real well, mind you. In fact, our relationship up to now had been pretty much confined to my ordering from Frank's menu, and Leesa Jo going back to the kitchen and getting me what I'd ordered. We'd enjoyed this kind of intimate relationship once or twice a week for almost six months now—in fact, ever since I'd caught sight of Leesa Jo sashaying around Frank's in a real tight, short, black skirt.

A couple of times I'd even tried to change our relationship to something even more personal, but every time I got up enough nerve to say anything to Leesa Jo that didn't involve what I wanted on my salad or how I'd like my burger cooked, Leesa Jo always seemed to come up with a real pressing problem back in the kitchen. In order to ask her out, I would've had to trot alongside her, dodging around tables. Perhaps impaling myself on the corner of one. With an obstacle course like that ahead of me, it wasn't long before I decided that Leesa Jo was telling me loud and clear that she just wasn't interested in being on my menu.

And now, come to find out, Leesa Jo Lattimore was Winslow Reed's dish on the side. Winslow, you remember, the only guy I knew who'd dated *less* than I did in high school.

It appeared, then, that there were women in the world who would rather go out with married ex-nurds instead of me. I know I've said this before. But a thing like this could really hurt a guy's feelings.

Imogene was hurrying on. It was as if the words she had to say tasted real bad, so she was trying to spit them out as fast as she could. "Phyllis also heard some gossip about Ruta Lippton playing fast and loose on her husband when he was out of town. Word was that both Winslow and Ruta entertained their 'guests' right in their own houses, right under their spouses' noses, and that they both did their entertaining as often as twice a week." Imogene would never have made a good private detective. She definitely sounded shocked.

My poker face, on the other hand, was still intact. I'd even added a sort of jaded smirk.

Imogene stared at me. "You're looking kind of sick to your stomach. Are you feeling OK?"

Maybe the smirk was a bit much. I dropped it and nodded. "I'm fine. Go on."

"Anyway," Imogene went on, her eyes still resting uneasily on my face, "Winslow and Ruta both appeared to be very well off, so Phyllis thought they ought to be able to afford to send her on her way without it being too much of a pain in the pocketbook."

Imogene's point here seemed to be how considerate Phyllis had been.

I gave her a weak smile. I had a pretty good guess that neither Winslow nor Ruta looked at it that way. As a matter of fact, it definitely looked as if one of them had decided to take a much more economical approach to the problem Phyllis presented. Instead of getting rid of any actual money, they'd decided to get rid of Phyllis.

According to Imogene, a few days ago, Phyllis had phoned her, actually laughing about how she'd broken into both Winslow's and Ruta's homes, and they hadn't even known it. "It had been even simpler than she expected it to be," Imogene said, "since folks around Pigeon Fork don't generally lock their doors." Phyllis had just waltzed right in, put the voice-activated recorders under Winslow's and Ruta's beds, and then left without tipping either one of them off. Since she wasn't sure when the lovers were supposed to meet, Phyllis's plan had been to check on the tape every few days or so to see if she'd recorded anything incriminating.

It hadn't taken all that many days, though. Phyllis had hit pay dirt on both Winslow *and* Ruta right away. "Phyllis called me up yesterday, giggling like she thought it was the funniest thing in the world." Imogene was blinking back tears again. "It was awful, Haskell, just awful."

When Phyllis had returned to retrieve the tape recorders, she'd made it obvious that she'd been in the Reed and

Lippton homes. So that, when she called Winslow and Ruta and asked for payment to keep quiet, they'd already be rattled. "In fact, I'm pretty sure that was the surprise Phyllis was planning on showing me today," Imogene said. "After my going on and on about how her scheme would never work, Phyllis was going to show me to my face all the money she'd collected."

I took a deep breath. So Phyllis had probably been meeting either Ruta or Winslow, or *both,* earlier today. For payment. It looked like she'd sure gotten herself paid, all right.

"After going and getting the tape recorders," Imogene said, "Phyllis started thinking that she shouldn't have made it so obvious that she'd broken in. She started worrying that Ruta or Winslow would go to the police. Or that they'd go to the only private detective here in town." Here Imogene gave me a significant look.

Imogene didn't have to say any more. It was instantly all too clear why Phyllis had come to me, acting as if her own house had been broken into. She'd wanted to find out from me if Winslow and Ruta had reported their break-ins. And she'd wanted to throw suspicion off herself. Surely no one would suspect that *Phyllis* was the one doing the breaking in, if she herself had been a victim.

This also explained why Phyllis had been so nervous when I was going through her house. Phyllis had no doubt been worried that I might figure out that she'd faked the whole thing. Maybe she'd even been afraid that I'd find the three tapes.

I moved on the couch uneasily. Obviously Phyllis had grossly overestimated my brilliance. I had, in fact, been completely taken in. I'd even told her exactly what she'd wanted to know. That Ruta and Winslow had indeed come to me about their pseudoburglaries.

I had to admit it, I was impressed. Phyllis had been right. She certainly wasn't dumb. Unless, of course, you happened to think it was dumb to get yourself into the kind of spot where a number of folks would want to murder you. That might've been poor planning.

Phyllis must've called Winslow and Ruta right after I'd left her house yesterday. To play the tapes for them and make her demand for getaway money. No wonder both Ruta and Winslow had wasted no time calling me to get me off the case. They hadn't wanted me to find out that they were being blackmailed.

And they, for sure, hadn't wanted me to find out why.

That is, one of them had fired me for that reason. The other had fired me simply because I was no longer needed. Because Phyllis herself was not going to be a threat much longer.

I suddenly felt real tired. "Imogene, why didn't you tell all this to the sheriff earlier tonight?"

Imogene stared at me as if I'd asked her why she didn't drink and drive. "Haskell," she said, and from her tone, you might've thought she was talking to a preschooler. "If I did that, Vergil would think that Phyllis was a blackmailer!"

I just looked at her. There was, no doubt about it, every chance that he would reach that conclusion.

Imogene started twisting the Kleenex she held in her hand. "Haskell, I'm not about to dirty my baby sister's reputation. I—I won't have Phyllis remembered that way!" Her tone was outraged.

I had to admire Imogene's loyalty, but the truth was, there were at least a couple of folks here in town who were going to remember Phyllis in *precisely* that way.

Being as how Imogene seemed to be getting real upset, I put my next question as gently as I knew how. "Why didn't you tell the police what Phyllis was planning to do? *Before* she did it."

I probably shouldn't have brought it up, because Imogene looked as if she suddenly tasted something sour. She looked across the room, directly, in fact, at Rip. He was curled up in front of the plaid chair he considers his, and was snoring real loud. You could tell, though, that Imogene didn't really see him. She didn't even seem to *hear* him, which was going some. "I should've told the police," she said. "I know that now, but I—I didn't want to get Phyllis in trouble. Haskell, I didn't want her to get *arrested.*"

I didn't say what I was thinking, of course. But *arrested* did seem to be preferable to *murdered.* Imogene looked back over at me with those gold-freckled eyes. "I wish now I had gone to the police. I really do. I really, really do."

I believed her. I was now feeling mean for even mentioning it. Imogene's eyes were brimming with tears. "I should've, I know that now, I should've," Imogene repeated, her voice distracted, "but, you know, I didn't really think that she'd actually go through with all this. It was such a preposterous scheme. I didn't really think Phyllis was serious."

What could I say? Phyllis *had* been serious, all right. Dead serious.

Imogene was now looking as if she might break into outright sobs. And me still without any Kleenexes. And the Kleenex in Imogene's hand looking as if it was real close to disintegrating. I made up my mind then and there not to ask her any more questions that sounded even faintly accusing. The way it looked, Imogene was doing enough of that all by herself.

"You know, Haskell," Imogene said, and her voice held horror now, "I think Phyllis was actually enjoying herself these last couple of days, causing Winslow and Ruta all this grief. She told me she thought they deserved it! She said that she and the Reeds and the Lipptons all went to the same church, and that religious folk like them shouldn't be running around on their spouses, anyway."

But it was OK for religious folk to dabble in a little blackmail? I didn't say a word, though. I just let Imogene keep talking.

Imogene was drawing a ragged breath. "It was like Phyllis was acting out all her anger at Orval on Winslow and Ruta. She—she even seemed to enjoy playing a little bit of each tape for me on the phone." Imogene paused here, and then said something that made me almost drop my poker face. "But then, you've already listened to those tapes yourself, haven't you?"

I just stared at her. What in the world had given her that idea? "No, no, I haven't heard them."

It was now Imogene's turn to stare at me. "Sure you have."

I was fairly certain I wouldn't have forgotten a little thing like that. In fact, I'd say, a significant portion of Orval's tape had been pretty much scorched into my brain. "Imogene, I haven't heard them," I repeated.

Imogene made a noise that sounded downright disbelieving. "You *had* to have listened to the tapes before the sheriff got there. That's how you knew about that Flo woman calling Orval 'Loverbug.'" Imogene said that last word with obvious distaste, but there was a trace of pride in her manner. As if she were almost gloating about the way she'd reasoned all this out. "I figure you must've been interrupted when you were removing the tapes, and you had to leave Orval's tape behind. But you've got the other ones. Sure you do." Her tone was that of a kindergarten teacher trying to coax a naughty boy into confessing.

I hated to tell her that her logic was a tad faulty. "Imogene," I said, "I'll admit that I did find the recorder with Orval's tape in it, and I did listen to it before the sheriff got there, but there was only that one tape. The other recorders were empty."

Imogene just stared at me for a long moment. I couldn't make up my mind if she just didn't believe me, or if she wasn't sure she'd heard me right.

"You mean, you really didn't take the other tapes? You don't have them?"

I shook my head.

Imogene's freckled eyes were getting real big. "You really *don't* have the tapes?"

I shook my head even more emphatically. What was it going to take to get her to believe me—something notarized?

"But there were *three* tapes," Imogene said. "And if you didn't take them, then—then, it must've been the—the—the—"

I decided not to complete her sentence for her, but it looked like Imogene's logic was right on target this time. I nodded my head yet again.

Imogene abruptly got up and walked over to stand in front of my wood stove. She just stood there, her back to the stove, shifting her weight from one foot to another, as she digested this last bit of news. You might've thought that the stove was actually putting out some heat, and that Imogene was warming herself in front of it. If, of course, you didn't know that we were in the middle of one of the hottest Mays on record, and that even though it was dark outside, it hadn't cooled off much. My central air was still running full-blast, and my guess was, that black metal stove was the coldest thing in the room.

With Imogene standing up like that, it was real easy to notice that her slip was still showing. In fact, it looked as if it had slipped some more. A good inch of white lace was now showing beneath her navy blue skirt.

I averted my eyes.

"Imogene, do you remember anything about the tapes you heard?" I asked the question as gently as I could.

Imogene gave me a look. "Actually, the only tape I remember well was the one of Orval. I really didn't listen any too close to the others." She shuddered a little and wrinkled her nose. I think I could assume from that assortment of gestures that the tapes were not the sort of easy listening she enjoyed.

"Don't you remember anything?"

Imogene gave me another look. *"I said* I didn't much listen to the others. *I* wasn't all that interested."

Her tone seemed right snippy all of a sudden. I couldn't tell if Imogene was mad because I hadn't walked off with her sister's tapes. Or if she was suggesting that *my* interest in those tapes, unlike hers, was something more than strictly professional.

"Look," I said, "I just wanted to know if you remembered anything that might help in—"

I was clearly wasting my breath. Imogene obviously was not listening. Instead, she just stared at me. "If you didn't take those tapes," she said slowly, interrupting me, "then you didn't know any of this before I told you. No wonder you've been sitting there looking so flabbergasted."

I swallowed. No doubt about it. I needed to do some work on my poker face. "Well, now, I wouldn't say I was *flabbergasted* exactly—"

That apparently was not the subject Imogene wanted to discuss. "Haskell, you're not going to tell the police what I just told you, are you?"

I had to tell her the truth. "I don't know if I can keep it a secret—"

"You've got to!" Imogene burst out. "Phyllis wasn't a bad person. She just made a little mistake!"

Phyllis's little mistake was a beaut. "Look, I'll do what I can, but I can't promise anything," I said.

Imogene came over and sat down beside me on the couch. In the movies, I do believe this is generally the part where the cute sister of the victim starts using her feminine wiles on the jaded detective, convincing him to do God knows what all. If that turned out to be the direction we were headed, I can't say I minded.

Imogene, however, just sat herself down, and didn't make a move to get any closer. With at least two feet between us, she stared at me with those pretty, hazel-green, gold-freckled eyes of hers. "Haskell," she said, and her voice shook just a little. "I'm begging you, please don't tell Vergil, please? Can't you please help me find out who did this to Phyllis without dragging her name through the mud? I'll pay your regular fees and everything, but I don't want her reputation destroyed!"

The pretty eyes gambit was probably a better ploy than the feminine wiles bit. "Imogene," I said without hesitating a bit. "I'll do my best." Actually, I wasn't telling her anything new. I was intending to work on this case whether I was being paid or not. I owed Phyllis that much. Even if she did go in for real strange hobbies.

Imogene beamed at me. "If you're working for me, then won't that thing you said earlier apply here?"

I wasn't following her.

"What you said back at Phyllis's house. About everything between client and detective being confidential. If I've just hired you, you *have* to keep everything I've told you quiet, don't you?"

I swallowed. Apparently Phyllis had not been the only Mayhew sister who was smart. The only trouble was, I'd just been talking off the top of my head earlier. I was pretty sure that the client confidentiality thing only applied to lawyers. And if I got caught withholding valuable information in a murder case, I could be hip-deep in what my daddy used to call deep, dark doo-doo.

I decided to tell Imogene the truth. "Like I said before," I said, "I'll do the best I can to keep all this between you and me. But I'm not sure I can."

Imogene's face fell.

"I can promise you this," I added. "If I end up having to tell, I'll tell you first."

Imogene brightened, got up, and walked over to the stove again.

Once again, of course, giving me a good view of her slip. It looked like it was falling fast. A good inch and a half was hanging out in the back now.

Imogene sighed. "Well, I guess I'd better be on my way. The whole family's congregating at my parents' house tonight. Aunts and uncles and cousins. Folks I haven't seen in years." Her eyes were tearing up again. "I guess that's a nice thing about my family. The way we all pull together when something awful happens." She swallowed, blinking fast. "But, God, it's going to be so strange for everybody to be there. And not Phyllis."

I couldn't help feeling real sorry for her. I also couldn't help picturing Imogene walking into her mother's house.

156

With her whole family there. And every one of them turning to look at her.

And seeing her slip.

It seemed real mean not to tell her. And yet, how did you go about it? What would be a nice, tactful way to put it? My own mother, God rest her soul, always used to say a real quaint thing in situations like this. She'd tell the slipper in a loud stage whisper, *It's snowing down south*. Leave it to my mom. I think she had a euphemism for everything.

Imogene was now dabbing at her eyes with her crumpled Kleenex. I was pretty sure if I up and said, real casual-like, "By the way, Imogene, it's snowing down south," she'd look at me as if I were out of my mind.

Maybe, then, I should say something a little more direct. Something like *Pardon my slip*. Would she get what I meant?

I'd already opened my mouth to try this one out when Imogene finished wiping her eyes and said, "Can you point me toward your bathroom, Haskell? I guess I'd better fix my slip before I leave. If I walk in looking like this, Mama might die of embarrassment. She's fussy that way."

I actually had to pretend my jaw was wired shut to keep it from dropping open. Then I pointed the way upstairs to my bathroom and, wordlessly, watched Imogene head out of the room.

Imogene already knew. She might actually have known all along. Apparently Imogene—unlike her mother—was not at all fussy about her appearance.

After living four years with Claudzilla, who had been known to spend hours in front of a mirror, making sure not a hair was out of place, I couldn't help but be amazed. And kind of impressed. Imogene may be a tad on the relaxed side, but she sure was a refreshing change.

When Imogene returned, her slip was no longer on view and her hair had obviously just been brushed. She'd even put something shiny on her lips, but that appeared to be about all. She wasn't wearing any blush or eye stuff or anything else women always seem to be putting on their faces. Imogene looked right nice, though. In a real healthy, back-to-nature sort of way.

"So what's our next move?" she said as she walked into the living room.

I didn't like the use of that word, "our." Getting to my feet, I said, "*My* next move is to talk to Winslow and Ruta again."

If Imogene noticed the way I emphasized the first word in that sentence, she didn't act like it. She just nodded, moving toward my front door. She had to walk right past Rip, but either he'd made up his mind that she was no threat, or else his earlier temper tantrums had left him exhausted. That dumb dog kept right on snoring as Imogene and I walked out on my deck. Just before she left, Imogene wrote her home and work numbers down on a piece of paper, handed it to me, and said, "Call me and let me know what you find out."

I stood out there on my deck, watching Imogene's red Mustang disappear down my driveway, and considered finding out quite a few things. Maybe finding out if Imogene had herself a boyfriend. Maybe finding out if she'd like to go out with me after all this was over.

I folded up the paper Imogene had given me and stuffed it in the back pocket of my jeans. Then again, maybe not. The last I'd heard, women preferred *married* guys over me.

Imogene's headlights had no sooner disappeared down my driveway when another set of headlights appeared, heading up. For a second I thought maybe Imogene had forgotten something. Then, of course, I recognized the car.

There aren't too many folks around these parts driving a car with the word "Sheriff" stenciled on the side.

Rip may have decided that Imogene was OK, but he apparently had serious reservations with regard to Vergil. When Vergil's car pulled up out front, Rip woke up and began doing his scene from *Cujo* again. Snarling and baring his teeth. Jumping up and down, and clawing at the screen door in back of me.

Unfortunately, I'd left that screen door slightly ajar.

Which meant I got my exercise for the day chasing Rip all

around the deck, trying to grab his collar and haul his silly body back indoors. It also meant that Vergil sat out in his car for a while. Watching me, with eyes as sad as I'd ever seen them.

After I'd dragged Rip, whining like a baby, back inside and firmly shut the door, Vergil finally headed up my stairs. I could see right away that Vergil had been going at his hair again. It looked like his head had sprouted gray wings. His tan uniform was looking a little worse for wear, too. Vergil climbed up my stairs at a pretty good clip, being as how he'd wasted a lot of time watching Rip's Cujo impression. When he got to my deck, Vergil cut things even shorter by skipping the part where he says my name by way of greeting. Instead, he just blurted out, "OK, I've come all the way out here, and I've driven up the side of your mountain—"

Vergil always acts as if I live on one of the Alps. And that he has to drive to Switzerland to see me.

"—and I've sat out there waiting for you to get your dog under control." At this point both of us could hear Rip whining behind the door in back of us. I chose to ignore it. "I've gone to a heck of a lot of trouble to talk to you," Vergil went on, "so's you better tell me the truth."

I wasn't sure what Vergil's inconvenience and my truth telling had to do with each other, but I didn't have any intention of lying. I nodded my head. "What do you want to know?"

Evidently it wasn't going to be as easy as that. Vergil has always believed in the big buildup. "I didn't want to ask you this in front of everybody at Phyllis's house," he said, "being as how I didn't want to make it look like I was accusing you of anything—"

I nodded again. Let me see now. Vergil didn't mind comparing me to the Black Plague in front of Jeb Gunterman, but according to Vergil, there *was* something he minded talking to me about in public. This ought to be good.

"I sure don't want you taking this the wrong way—"

OK. OK. "Vergil," I said, "what is it?"

Vergil answered me with one of his prize-winning sighs. Finally, the sigh done, he said, "You didn't happen to take a couple of tapes out of them two tape recorders, did you?"

"No, I didn't." Maybe I answered too quick, or maybe Vergil was already real suspicious. Whatever the reason, Vergil just looked at me level-like for a long moment. Like maybe he was trying hard to make up his mind whether I was lying or not.

I stared right back at him, without blinking, just like I used to back on the playground, when some kid accused me of something. The only trouble was, even back then, I always looked guilty, even when I wasn't. Just knowing somebody thought I'd done something was all I ever needed to make me feel like I'd done it.

Once again I must've looked guilty as hell, because after Vergil got finished staring at me, his eyes now infinitely sad, he cleared his throat and said, "You *do* know that you can get yourself arrested for taking something from a crime scene?"

Vergil is always doing this. *Instructing* me. As if I really was still out on that playground. I nodded for the third time. "Vergil, I'm telling you I didn't take anything out of Phyllis's house. *Not a thing.*"

Vergil stared at me some more, and then sighed again. This sigh wasn't as long as the one before, but what it lacked in length, it made up for in intensity. He cleared his throat again. "You working for Phyllis's sister now?" he asked.

Vergil had to have passed right by Imogene's car as she left. I nodded yet again—nod number four. I was starting to feel like one of those ceramic dogs folks used to keep in the back window of their cars. "Imogene wants me to look into all this for her," I said.

I didn't have to spell out what I meant by "all this." It was Vergil's turn to nod this time. "I figured as much," he said. "I reckon you'll be needing this, then."

He handed me a small, folded piece of paper and shrugged his shoulders. "I gave one to every police officer in town," he said, indicating the paper, "and I'm going to be showing it all around town personally. I reckon it wouldn't hurt a bit to have you showing it around, too." He stopped then and gave me another level stare. "Of course, I expect you'll be telling me *everything* you find out." Vergil put a little extra emphasis on the word "everything."

Once again I did a doglike nod, but of course, I was remembering the promise I'd just made Imogene. About not telling anybody how Phyllis had decided to blackmail a few of her neighbors for fun and profit. Now I was sure I looked guilty.

Vergil must've thought so, too. He kept right on staring at me, his eyes sort of squinching up. Like maybe he was trying to read my mind. "I'll be hearing from you, Haskell," he said. He didn't sound convinced, though. Turning abruptly, Vergil headed on back down the steps toward his car.

I watched him go, wondering if he believed what I'd told him about not taking the tapes. When Vergil had gotten in his car and was headed down my driveway, I opened the paper he'd given me.

It was a Xerox of the note Phyllis had left, with the mark that looked like a seven.

Either Vergil trusted me more than I thought, or he was giving me just enough rope to hang myself with.

11

Since the next morning was Friday, and I knew Winslow wouldn't be available until after two-thirty, when school let out, I decided to go talk to Ruta Lippton first.

I was particularly anxious to have myself a little chat with Ruta, anyway, being as how it had been *her* name on page seven of Phyllis's address book.

If, of course, that meant anything at all.

I got started real early. I got up, showered, pulled on a pair of jeans and a denim shirt, and made me and Rip some breakfast in record time. Then, of course, I carried Rip downstairs to the yard and then back up on the deck, made sure his food and water bowls were full, and I headed for Phyllis's house. The sun hadn't been up long enough to burn off the mist in the distance, so it looked as if the wooded hills around me were being steam-cleaned. The sun was slanting through the trees, like one of those scenes you see in fairy-tale books, and the morning air smelled fresh and clean. I rolled down the window on the driver's side of my truck, and drove down the gravel road leading away from my house, taking deep, satisfying breaths. It's mornings like this that remind me why I moved back here.

And, after what I'd seen yesterday, it made me especially grateful to be alive.

On such a morning, things that usually irritate the hell out of me don't bother me a bit. In fact, they seem kind of quaint. Like the way one of my neighbor's milking cows is always getting out of its electric fence during the night, and then—given any number of places it could go—it always seems to choose smack dab in the middle of the road. On this beautiful morning, it had done it again. About a half mile down the road, that dumb brown cow was standing motionless, facing me, totally blocking my way.

I reckon that cow stared at me and my truck for a good five minutes. With its huge, sad, brown eyes. More or less making the point that cow-pedestrians always have the right of way.

There are not a whole lot of ways you can argue with a cow. They're too big to push out of the way, and they pretty much won't listen to reason. It wasn't as if I could back up and go another way, either. The only way out to the blacktopped state road was through the cow. And since my gravel road is bordered on both sides by electric fences, there's no way you can pull around.

Today, though, all I did was honk my horn a couple of times. I didn't even yell at the animal. Or curse its owner, like I usually do. The cow must've been in a real good mood, too, because eventually it flicked its velvety ears a couple of times, turned, and ambled over into the long gravel drive-way leading to my neighbor's house, letting me pass. That cow might've been giving me a dirty look as I went by, but being as how I wasn't up on cow body language, I didn't know it.

I reckon I could've stayed in bed and slept another hour or so, maybe avoiding the cow altogether, if I'd wanted to go by the Curl Crazee to see Ruta. I could've just dropped by after nine, when the shop opened. It was worth it to me to lose the extra sleep, though, *not* to have to go in there. I don't know why, but somehow, standing around inside a beauty shop makes me feel about as welcome as a weasel in a chicken house.

I got to Ruta's house right at eight o'clock. Oddly enough, there were no cows blocking the road into the Twelve Oaks subdivision. I expect they wouldn't dare.

Ruta herself answered the door. If anything, she looked even more curl-crazy than she had two days ago at my office. Her brown hair was still a mass of tight three-inch cork-screws, but it looked as if maybe some of her spit curls had had babies since I'd seen her last. Now tiny spit curls nestled between the larger spit curls, framing Ruta's face in various-sized circles all the way around.

Ruta had obviously been up awhile, because she was already dressed for work in her pink uniform with matching pink socks and pink Reeboks. Evidently, though, she hadn't been up anywhere near long enough, because she hadn't yet closed the large gaps in the front of her uniform with the safety pins she'd been using at my office earlier. A couple of the buttons on Ruta's massive front looked to be under tremendous strain. It took real concentration on my part not to look in that direction.

Ruta also had not quite finished making up her face. She'd gotten to some of it, however. The skin on her face was already several shades darker than her throat, and she'd already done her Spuds eyes. It was her mouth, though, that I couldn't help staring at. Without any lipstick, Ruta looked as if she'd recently undergone a mouthectomy. In fact, until she opened her mouth to speak, I would've sworn that Ruta's entire face below her nose was solid chin.

First impressions are a little iffy to go by, but in my opinion, when Ruta opened her front door, she didn't look in as good a mood as that cow in my road. Maybe Ruta didn't appreciate being interrupted while she was troweling on her makeup. Her mood didn't seem to improve any after she saw that it was me standing there on her front porch. "Haskell Blevins," she said, "what in blue blazes are you doing here at this hour of the morning? I thought I told you that you're off the case. Don't you understand good English?"

Apparently Ruta was not a morning person. "I'm not working on *your* case, Ruta," I said, real easy-like. "I'm working on the Phyllis Carver case, and I need to ask you a few questions."

Ruta swallowed once before she answered, and her eyes looked as if something bright flickered in them for about a half second. "Questions? About Phyllis Carver? You mean, that woman who was murdered?"

I nodded. "That's the one," I said. On my way here, I'd already come to the conclusion that the best approach in this situation was probably the blunt approach. "You might also refer to Phyllis as that woman who was blackmailing you."

I could've sworn the second I said that, some of the curl went right out of Ruta's hair. Her heavily mascaraed eyes bobbled up and down a couple of times, and for a long moment she didn't say a word. She just stared at me, her invisible mouth making a perfect round O. Ruta's eyes now might've been a little bigger than that cow's. She swallowed again and said, her voice sounding as if she'd just taken a big gulp of sand, "I—I don't know what you're talking about."

If she didn't, the blood was draining out of her face for no reason. I gave her an easy smile. "Sure you do. I'm talking about that tape Phyllis made of you and your boyfriend."

Ruta's mascaraed lashes bobbled some more, and she darted a quick, furtive look over her shoulder. No doubt checking to see if Lenard was within hearing distance. Giving her corkscrews a vigorous shake, Ruta hissed, "I don't know nothing about no tape."

This was the woman who was talking to *me* about good English? "Sure you do," I said again.

"I don't neither," Ruta insisted. "And you can't prove I do, you can't—"

It looked like I wasn't getting anywhere. So I decided I'd best take a chance. "I can prove it, Ruta," I said, interrupting her. "Maybe you need your memory refreshed a little. I could go and get that tape and play it for you, if you like—"

"No-o-o!" The word seemed to erupt out of Ruta's mouth of its own accord. "I—I don't never want to hear that disgusting thing again," she said. She threw another quick look behind her, and then came outside to stand beside me on the porch. "Look, Haskell, don't you know Lenard's right inside?" Ruta was whispering now. "He's got a real bad temper, too, and I don't think you ought to make him mad."

To my way of thinking, I wasn't exactly the one who ought to be worrying about this.

Ruta hurried on. "You're not thinking about telling Lenard all this, are you?" She put a hand on my arm, and I could see right off how bad Ruta's hand was shaking. "Please, Haskell, don't tell him. I'm going to tell him myself one of these days. When the time is right."

I would bet that the time would be right just about when my dog Rip learned to do calculus. What I was thinking must've shown some on my face, because Ruta drew herself up and gave me a look. "It's not what you think, Haskell. I am, too, going to tell Lenard. Because Boyd and I are really, really, *really* in love."

I believed her. Three "reallys" sounded plenty serious to me.

"It's not just a fling with us," Ruta said. "In fact, it's only a matter of time until Boyd has enough money for us to run away together. Why, we'd be gone now, but Boyd is real proud. He doesn't believe in taking money from a woman—"

Boyd? There was only one Boyd that I knew of in Pigeon Fork. Boyd Arndell, brother to Zeke Arndell, who owned Arndell's New and Hardly Used Furniture. Boyd, as best as I could recall, had worked for his brother ever since he'd graduated from high school the year before me.

If the Boyd Ruta was talking about was Boyd Arndell, then I was confused. Because this Boyd would not only take money from a woman, he'd take it from a baby. If, of course, the baby let go first. If taking money from a baby required any actual effort on his part, Boyd would probably skip it. What I'm saying here is that *lazy* and *shiftless* were words that, if used in connection with Boyd Arndell, would probably be compliments. Word around Pigeon Fork was that Boyd had worked for Zeke since high school mainly because nobody else within a hundred-mile radius would hire him.

"Boyd and I belong together," Ruta was saying. "It's just a matter of time, is all."

She made them sound like Romeo and Juliet. Star-crossed lovers kept apart by a tiny little thing like a husband.

Lenard, however, was not a tiny little thing. Far from it. "Honey, who's that at the door?" a deep voice boomed from inside the house. At the sound, Ruta actually jumped.

"It's that detective in town, sweetheart. You know— Haskell Blevins?" Ruta said. Her tone had completely changed. It was now lilting, musical. Ruta could've been playing the adoring wife on a sitcom. "He's, um, asking questions about Phyllis Carver. You know, that woman who was, um—"

"Blown away yesterday?" Lenard finished for her, appearing in the doorway in back of Ruta. Lenard evidently believed in euphemisms every bit as much as my mom had. "Yeah, we heard somebody filled that broad full of lead."

What a nice way to put it. I was beginning to see what Ruta might not find all that attractive about her husband.

You could start with his looks. Lenard Lippton was about my height, but he would make at least one and a half of me. If you measured from side to side. It looked like the extra weight Lenard was lugging around was solid muscle, though, not fat. His hair was cut in that ever popular style from the sixties, the flattop, and his neck had a lot in common with Ruta's mouth. It was missing.

With a missing neck, a square jaw, and that flattop, Lenard gave new meaning to the word *blockhead*. Wearing jeans and a short-sleeved, pink-flowered shirt that revealed upper arms just about the size of my thighs, Lenard didn't look as if he were going to be featured on the cover of *GQ* any time soon.

I stared at the flowers on Lenard's shirt. They were pink petunias. There's a lot of men in Pigeon Fork who wouldn't be caught dead in a shirt with pink petunias on it, but Lenard was clearly a man who didn't have to worry about the local dress code. Hell, Lenard could probably wear a *dress,* and folks would compliment him on his good taste.

With Lenard standing there in the door, assuming almost the exact pose I've seen the Incredible Hulk do on comic book covers, I myself was tempted to say, "Nice shirt." Before I had a chance to, though, Ruta jumped in with, "Sweetheart, Haskell here is talking to everybody who knew Phyllis. That's, um, why he's here. Because we, um, knew her."

That pretty much explained the entire situation. Lenard, however, didn't look like he was completely buying it. "Oh yeah?" he said. His brown eyes definitely looked suspicious. "Well, we didn't know her. She just went to our church, that's all. We didn't know her from Adam."

I was pretty sure that Lenard really meant *Eve* here.

Debating whether or not they knew Phyllis, however, seemed pretty pointless to me, so I changed the subject. "Before she passed away, Phyllis left a note—"

Here I noticed Ruta's eyes did that flickering thing again. Lenard's eyes, on the other hand, didn't do anything. They just kept on staring at me, sullenly.

"—and I've been showing what she wrote to everybody who knew her. Just to see if they could figure out what she meant by it." I reached into my pocket, got me the copy Vergil gave me last night, and extended it toward them.

Both Lenard and Ruta stared at the paper for what seemed like an awful long time. "She made a seven?" Ruta finally said. If anything, her eyes looked a little relieved. Maybe Ruta had been afraid that Phyllis might have had the time to write out a complete account of everything Phyllis had found out about Ruta and Boyd.

Lenard didn't even blink. "That dumb broad just wrote a seven? That was it? Was she kidding, or what?"

Lenard was truly a sensitive soul. It looked as if he could stand a few more visits to church.

"Ruta," I said quietly, "your name appeared on page seven of Phyllis's address book."

Ruta didn't say a word. She just stared back at me. Lenard, however, had a real quick reply. "So what? So Ruta's name is in a dead lady's book. So sue us. That don't mean nothing." Apparently Lenard needed help in the English department as much as Ruta.

"I just thought I'd mention it, that's—" I started to say.

Lenard interrupted me. "Yeah, well, mention it somewhere else! If you think you can waltz in here and start making accusations about some broad we didn't even know, well, you'd better think again, you sawed-off, redheaded little runt!"

I stared back at him. I couldn't argue with being called redheaded, but sawed-off? And *little runt?* Lenard wasn't any taller than I was. I opened my mouth to point this out to him, but a sudden attack of sanity changed my mind. Let's face it. It probably wasn't the best idea to discuss it with him. Old Lenard here appeared to have a real short fuse. In fact, it could be that he had no fuse at all. He started at meltdown. "Now, Lenard," I said, trying to sound a whole lot more easygoing than I felt, being as how Lenard was now doubling up his fists, "I'm not making accusations. I was just giving you two some information, that's all."

I was not going to be real happy if I got myself punched in the stomach twice in as many days. It wasn't the sort of record I wanted to try for.

"If you ain't saying nothing, then what are you saying?"

This was Lenard, an obvious member of Pigeon Fork's intelligentsia, talking. It appeared likely that Lenard might be a blockhead in more ways than one.

I gave him an insincere smile. "All I'm doing is asking some questions. That's all."

Lenard was practically in my face by then, and I was giving some serious consideration to taking a couple of steps backward when Ruta squeezed in between us. "Haskell, I barely knew Phyllis. Really. I only saw her every Sunday in church. And that was it. Now I think you'd best be on your way, OK?"

Her suggestion made good sense to me. Ruta took my arm and began to lead me toward my truck. Like maybe I might've forgotten the way in the few minutes I'd been talking to her and her beloved husband.

Lenard stood his ground on his porch, watching us go. On the way, Ruta said real loud, so that Lenard couldn't miss it if he tried, "I only wish we could've been more help."

We were almost to my truck when Ruta gave Lenard a quick backward look. Lenard was still staring at us from the porch, but it was real likely he couldn't hear us from there. "Look," Ruta hissed, "I was at the Curl Crazee all day yesterday. I had one appointment after another, and I never left. You can check!"

I had my keys out and was opening my truck door. "What about Boyd Arndell?" I said. "Where was he all day?"

Ruta went as white as if I'd slapped her, turned on her heel, and headed back toward the house. Back on the porch, Lenard gave me one more sour look before he disappeared with his wife back inside.

I started my truck and pulled away. If Lenard ever found out about Boyd and Ruta, I would not only hate to be Boyd, I'd hate to be anybody within a five-mile radius of Boyd.

There was really only one place to head after that. Arndell's New and Hardly Used Furniture. It was a little early for it to be open yet, so I killed a little time going by my office. Seeing if love had perhaps changed Melba for the better, and out of the goodness of her heart, she'd actually taken some messages for me.

It was after eight-thirty, which was when Melba was

supposed to start work, but she was nowhere to be found. Maybe love doesn't conquer all, after all.

I looked for Melba all over Elmo's, in every one of her hiding places. Between the aisles, back in the pharmacy, hunkered down behind the soda fountain counter. Melba is a creative hider. I even knocked on the girls' rest room, but either Melba wasn't in there or she was playing possum. All I found for my efforts was Elmo himself. Who glowered at me. I think he thought I might ask him to take messages for me again. I gave him a cheery wave and headed upstairs to my office.

Where I pretty much sat and did nothing until nine, when Arndell's opened. Even after it got to be nine, come to think of it, I didn't exactly rush down there. It was still too nice a morning for rushing. I noticed as I walked out my door that across the street a couple of old gents had already settled themselves on the neat white benches in front of the courthouse. Both of these old guys gave me a nod and a wave as I came down my stairs. I didn't know either one of them personally, but I nodded and waved back.

This is one of the things I missed when I was living in Louisville. If you waved at strangers on the street there, a lot of times they thought you were trying to warn them about something. Or that maybe you were flagging them down for some kind of emergency. Here in Pigeon Fork you can wave at strangers all you want, and nobody thinks a thing of it.

When I got to the street, I turned to my right. I didn't have far to walk. Arndell's is on the same side of the street and in the same block as Elmo's Drugstore. In fact, the only thing between us is the Pigeon Fork Dry Goods Store.

Leroy Putnam, who owns the dry goods store, apparently had decided—like me—that even though it was only May, it was undeniably summer. His store already had swimsuits in one of its two narrow display windows. Leroy had gotten real arty with the swimsuits, too, laying out men's, women's and children's suits on a big pile of sand with a toy shovel stuck in it. Evidently he hadn't been able to come up with real seashells, so he'd made do with a bunch of starfish and seahorses that he'd cut out of brightly colored construction paper. These Leroy had scattered here and there on the sand. I figure what the display lacked in authenticity, it made up for in originality.

The other window was even more original. It still had an Easter theme, even though Easter had come and gone. I suspected Leroy was so proud of this window, he hated to take it down. It was obvious he'd really gone to town on this one, cramming into that narrow window just about everything you could think of that had to do with this particular holiday. There were Easter bunnies in assorted sizes and colors, Easter eggs, a big bouquet of plastic Easter lilies, and at least a dozen Easter baskets. Leroy apparently also wanted folks to know that he knew very well that Easter was not just a secular holiday, because he'd even put a three-foot plastic Christ on the cross in the left-hand corner. It was a little disconcerting to see Jesus looking down on a bunch of Easter bunnies, but I reckon it was the thought that counted.

I was still looking back at Leroy's Jesus-and-the-bunnies window when I got to Arndell's. Not watching where you're going is not a real smart thing to do in front of Arndell's. Especially on warm-weather days. You're safe enough during the winter, or on days it rains, because the sidewalk is clear then. Zeke Arndell, however, believes in luring his customers inside, so on nice days the sidewalk outside his store is crammed with the stuff Zeke considers his latest prize merchandise. On this particular morning he'd put out an old humpbacked trunk, a couple of green crushed velvet wing-back chairs, a tarnished brass headboard, and an ancient ringer washing machine. This last item I noticed in particular. Being as how I ran smack into it, cracking my ankle pretty bad on one of its legs.

I was tempted to let go with a string of curses, but there were folks going into the Crayton County Bank across the street. I wasn't about to draw attention to the fact that I hadn't been watching where I was going. In front of

Arndell's. On a *nice* day. It would've been like admitting in public that I was still an out-of-towner.

Instead, I just rubbed my ankle some, trying to look as if I always limped like this, and finished picking my way around all the stuff on the sidewalk, slowly making my way toward the front entrance. I stepped around a chifforobe with a slightly buckled finish, an oak end table on top of which Zeke had put a hand-lettered sign that said "BRAND NEW!" and a girl's faded red Schwinn bike. Zeke, I do believe, defines the word *furniture* real loosely.

Zeke was nowhere to be seen when I walked in, but I spotted Boyd right away. This was amazing luck, because it's not real easy to locate anything inside Arndell's. This is because Arndell's is as big as a warehouse inside, and it doesn't do what a lot of other furniture stores do. You know how furniture stores often arrange chairs and sofas and whatnot into room displays, so that you can pretty much see how the stuff is going to look in your own home? Zeke apparently thinks this is a waste of valuable space. Instead, he just sets everything out in long, straight rows, from the back of the store to the front of the store, in no particular order. A sofa could be next to a refrigerator, a dining room set right next to a bed. Arndell's, in fact, looks a lot like a furniture library, with rows and rows of furniture waiting to be checked out. Only there's no Dewey decimal system to help you find anything.

That's why finding Boyd so soon was such a lucky break. I'd pictured myself going up and down Arndell's narrow aisles searching for Boyd with about as much luck as I'd had earlier when I'd looked for Melba. But no, there Boyd was over in the first row, two dressers and a lawn mower from the front. Boyd appeared to be doing some checking out of his own. He was in the act of personally testing a black Naugahyde La-Z-Boy—a piece of furniture no doubt named after Boyd. Dressed in brown twill slacks and a plaid shirt, Lazy Boyd was completely stretched out in the lounger, eyes closed, hands behind his head.

This was Boyd at work.

"Boyd?" I said. "Can I talk to you a minute?"

Boyd gave a sudden jerk, but only opened his right eye. "Whuff?" I believe that's an exact quote.

"Boyd?" I repeated. "Can I talk to you?"

Long-limbed and wiry, Boyd Arndell has a long, angular face, with a long, straight nose and real full lips. His lips are so full, he almost looks as if he's wearing a set of those fake wax lips that kids wear on Halloween. Boyd also has thick black hair that he combs straight back from his face. When, of course, he combs it. Right now his hair was hanging in his eyes. He made no move, however, to brush it out of the way. Instead, he just yawned and stretched for a while before he got around to answering me. "OK, sure, Haskell." Boyd always talks real slow, as if actually forming entire words is too much of an effort. "Uh, you wanna look at some furniture?"

What a sales pitch.

"Nope," I said, giving him the insincere smile that I think I perfected with Lenard earlier, "I want to ask you a few questions about you and Ruta Lippton."

Boyd didn't even blink. He yawned and stretched once again as he got to his feet. I noticed he did not brush the hair out of his eyes this time, either. He just kept staring at me through it, as if he were peeking through a black curtain. "Me and Mrs. Lippton? I don't know what you're talking about."

"Come off it, Boyd. I know all about you two. Ruta told me herself."

This seemed to refresh Boyd's memory some. He blinked slowly, and looked only slightly more alert. Finally he gave a slow shrug and drawled, "Hey, what can I say? I was just trying to be a gentleman, you know, trying to protect the lady's reputation." He gave me a slow grin. "Generally I like my women to still be in their twenties, you know, and old Ruta is getting on up there, but hey, what man would pass up the chance to play with those knockers of hers?" At this point Boyd managed to wink and smirk at me all at the same time, a feat which, no doubt, should earn him extra points for degree of difficulty. "Haskell, I tell you, you ought to see that old broad in bed. I swear, she could be one of the Flying Wallendas."

I just looked at him. Boyd was quite the gentleman, all right.

Boyd was now shaking his dark head, giving a low whistle. "Lordy, Lordy, a couple of times, while we were doing it, I was sure old Ruta was going to work herself up into a heart attack!"

I swallowed, still staring at Boyd. Unless I missed my guess, I'd say Boyd here, unlike Ruta, was not really, really, really in love.

Poor Ruta. It looked like both the gentlemen in her life were no gentlemen.

I probably shouldn't have said what I said next, but the fact was, after listening to Boyd here, I kind of wanted to wipe that smirk off his face. And I'd already more or less told Ruta what I was about to tell Boyd. "You don't have to tell *me,* Boyd," I said. "I've heard you two on tape."

That was a smirk-wiper, all right. Boyd looked real alert after that. "What—what do you mean? *Tape?*"

I gave him a look. "Didn't Ruta tell you about that? You two were recorded."

Boyd now looked downright startled. "Wha-a-at?" As he said this, Boyd sank back down on the La-Z-Boy, staring straight ahead. It looked like maybe his knees had given out under him.

"I thought you knew," I said, shrugging my shoulders real casual-like. I was telling the truth. I'd fully expected Ruta would've mentioned it to him. Of course, maybe she knew Boyd wouldn't take the news real well. "There was a tape recorder under your bed."

Boyd actually brushed the hair out of his face after that one. "No, I didn't know." Anger was creeping into his eyes now. "That dumb broad never told me a thing about it."

I believed him. For no other reason than I was pretty sure Boyd was too lazy to go to all the trouble of faking surprise. Not to mention anger on top of it.

While Boyd was sitting there, looking stunned, I had another question for him. "Did you hear that Phyllis Carver was murdered?"

Boyd now looked genuinely confused. "Sure, I heard, but what's that got to do with—"

I interrupted him. "She left this note when she died." I had the copy of Phyllis's note out of my pocket by then, and I showed it to him.

Boyd stared at the piece of paper. If anything, now he looked even more confused. "A seven?" He stared back up at me. "I don't get it. What's all this got to do with me and Ruta? And who bugged our bed? And how did you happen to get ahold of the tape?"

I didn't answer him. "Where were you between quarter to eleven and three-fifteen yesterday?"

Boyd suddenly didn't look confused anymore. Apparently it didn't take even a lazy brain very long to figure out why I was asking. "Look, I don't know what you think you're getting at, but I was right *here!* I didn't even take a lunch hour yesterday. I worked here at Arndell's *all day long.*"

Frankly, I found it hard to believe that Boyd ever worked all day long in his life, but he was real specific. According to Boyd, yesterday he'd spent every waking hour from nine to six at Arndell's. No doubt testing La-Z-Boys.

"I hardly even knew that Carver woman," Boyd insisted. "Why you would think that *I* could have anything to do with her—"

I interrupted him, holding up my hand. "Hey, I'm not thinking anything. All I'm doing is asking questions."

Boyd stared up at me. "Well, I got some questions for you. *Who* bugged me and Ruta? And where the hell is that tape?"

I thought what I had to say to that should've sounded real comforting. "Don't worry, Boyd, the tape is in a safe place. And I'm not going to show it to Lenard, if that's what you're worried about."

Boyd, amazingly enough, didn't look the least bit comforted. If anything, at the mere mention of Lenard's name, Boyd's big lips seemed to twitch a little.

I decided that this was probably a real good time to take my leave. I turned on my heel and walked real quick out Arndell's front door.

I would've bet money that Boyd was on the phone to Ruta before I even passed Jesus and the bunnies.

12

After talking to Boyd, I was feeling downright antsy. Now there were two folks in town who thought I had tapes that I didn't. One of these two folks could easily mention this to Vergil, and then I would have some heavy explaining to do. Of course, since telling on me would also involve telling on themselves, it wasn't real likely that either Ruta or Boyd would be any too eager to do this, but you never knew. I was getting in deeper and deeper, and so far I hadn't even found one person who so much as lifted an eyebrow when they saw Phyllis's note.

What on earth could Phyllis have meant when she wrote that seven? If indeed it *was* a seven. And yet, what else could it be?

I decided maybe it would be best if I didn't wait until after school was out before I had myself a talk with Winslow. Surely a murder investigation was a good enough reason to interrupt a class for a few minutes. Besides, with a little luck, I might catch Winslow between classes, or during lunch.

I got in my truck, and headed on over to Pigeon Fork High. It's about six miles off Main Street, if you turn left at the only stoplight in town. You can't miss the school, with its stark two-story stone facade and its long, narrow windows grouped in five sets of five across the front of the building. The school sits back from the road on the left, right across the way from Metcalf's Flicks-To-Go, the video rental store. Back when I was going to Pigeon Fork High, all us kids agreed among ourselves that the school looked exactly like a prison.

I can't say I've changed my mind over the years.

During the day you can park right out in front of the school in the space usually reserved for school buses. I parked and headed inside. There I discovered things hadn't changed any more inside than they had outside. The gray linoleum floors were still yellowed from too many waxings, and the walls were still painted the same color they'd been painted the year I graduated. It's a color that's not exactly cheery. Gray. It's as if years ago whoever was in charge of the school's color scheme couldn't make up their minds, so they'd decided to go with something real noncommittal. Ever since then, I reckon nobody has had the courage to change it.

I didn't even have to *try* to remember where the principal's office was located. I headed right for it with the confidence of someone who'd been sent there quite a few times during my illustrious academic career. It wasn't, of course, that I was a rowdy kid or anything. High-spirited is the way I like to think of myself. The way my teachers thought of me is, no doubt, something else again. I actually had one of my old English teachers tell me at my ten-year reunion that he was real surprised I'd turned out to be a cop. On account of he couldn't believe anybody would ever give me a loaded gun.

I didn't particularly like him, either.

The tiny woman with the huge red beehive who was evidently now the school secretary looked at me with real regret when I asked for Winslow. "Oh, I'm sorry," she said, peering at me over her wire rims. "Mr. Reed called in sick today."

179

I was so surprised, it took me a moment to react. Then, of course, I turned on my heel and hightailed it back to my truck. As I pulled out of the Pigeon Fork High parking lot, I had an almost overpowering temptation to burn rubber. That would definitely have been like old times.

On my way *back* to Twelve Oaks, I couldn't help but think that, had I known Winslow was still home, I could've just headed straight over there from Ruta's. And saved myself some time and trouble.

No cars were in Winslow's driveway when I got there, but that didn't mean anything. The doors to the Spanish stucco garage were closed, so there was no way of knowing whether Winslow was really home or not. His calling in sick, though, sounded pretty feeble to me.

It sounded even more feeble to me when June answered the door. Apparently she, too, had taken the day off. Had she stayed home to nurse her ailing husband? Or could it be that *both* Winslow and June had suddenly come down with something? It was downright amazing how these flu bugs could sweep through a household. Or, at least, some kind of bug.

June, however, didn't look at all sick. Her glossy brown hair was pulled back from her face with a wide black ribbon, and she was wearing a lacy, white short-sleeved sweater over a pair of those clingy black stretch pants that have the stirrups over the feet. I've never particularly liked these pants on a woman. To me, they either look like a big black bandage, stretched to all get out, or worse, they look as if the wearer has caught her feet in something she couldn't shake loose. June here could possibly change my mind, however. Those pants made June's legs look real long and real lean.

I was not looking in the direction of June's legs, though, when she opened the massive oak front door. I was looking up. I hadn't forgotten about the wrought-iron bird balconies over the Reeds' door, and I was at that moment simply checking things out. It appeared that no birds were roosting up there right then, but I didn't think that was a situation I could count on lasting forever.

June gave me a flat stare for about a half second, glanced upward herself with a slightly quizzical expression, and then said, "Haskell. How nice to see you."

Her tone was downright cheery, and she followed this up with one of her patented cheerleader smiles, complete with dimples, but somehow I got the feeling June wasn't all that tickled to see me.

Maybe she was worried she and Winslow might give me the flu.

I gave her one of my own cheery smiles. "Is Winslow here? I went by the school, and they'd told me he was—"

June interrupted me. "Winslow isn't here right now," she said. A little too quickly, in my opinion. "I'm so sorry you missed him."

June didn't sound sorry. She also didn't seem to think there was any reason to explain why a man who was supposed to be home, sick, was not home at all. June just stood there in her huge doorway, staring at me with those huge brown eyes of hers.

No doubt Winslow was at the doctor's. Getting enough medicine for the both of them.

"Well, then, how about if I come in and wait until he gets back?"

June's eyes managed to get even bigger. "I wouldn't want to inconvenience you. It might be a while before—"

I interrupted her with another smile. "Don't mind waiting a bit."

This, of course, was not exactly the truth. I *did* mind waiting where I was. Being as how, at that moment, a couple of plump, gray birds had landed on the wrought-iron balcony directly above my head.

If June didn't let me in soon, I was going to have to shove my way past her.

For an interminable moment, June just looked at me. Then, thank God, she moved away from the door. I went through so fast, the breeze stirred the clothing of the conquistador in the hallway. June followed me, moving silently on the carpeted floor, as I headed into her perfectly kept living room. She took a seat on the Mexican-blanketed sofa, right next to one of the bullfighter lamps. I made myself comfortable on a bright red chair opposite her, right next to a huge cactus in a red, green, and yellow pottery container.

Or at least I tried to make myself comfortable. It was real hard to relax with that cactus within inches of my bare arms. That thing looked like it could leave some permanent scars.

It was June who spoke first.

"Look, Haskell, if this is about the death of that Carver woman, you might as well know that Winslow cannot possibly be a suspect. He had no motive. There was no reason to try to shut Phyllis up, because what she had to tell, I already knew."

For a second, I just stared at her. Up to that minute I'd had a pretty good idea the way this conversation was going to go, and this was definitely not it. In fact, I'd say the *last* thing I expected was June to practically admit that she knew all about Phyllis's blackmail scheme. Not to mention all about Winslow and Leesa Jo.

June apparently knew everything, though. She went right on, talking with as much ease as if she were recounting the plot to a soap opera, "Winslow and I have an arrangement, you see. I guess it's what was once called an 'open marriage.' He and I simply don't mind if the other one has relationships on the side. We both think that possessiveness and petty jealousy have no place in a relationship between mature, thinking people."

I think my mouth was hanging open now. This was definitely a different way to look at things. For my part, when I found out that Claudzilla had had herself what June referred to as "a relationship on the side," I reckon you could say I definitely minded. Call me immature. Call me unthinking. I closed my mouth, and then immediately opened it to say the only thing that came to mind. "No kidding."

June's dimpled smile got a little more crisp. "No kidding," she said. She reached over and straightened the shade of the bullfighter lamp on her right. It didn't look crooked to me. "I've known all about Winslow and his little liaison with that blond waitress for some time now," June went on. "Believe me, Haskell, I couldn't care less." She turned then and looked straight at me, her brown eyes appearing totally untroubled. "Winslow's little dalliances don't have anything to do with me. All I ask is that he continue to keep me in the style to which I'm accustomed, and that he practice safe sex."

I tried to match her smile with a crisp one of my own. I may be wrong here, but in my limited marital experience, safe sex never involved anyone other than your own spouse. In fact, as I recalled, Claudzilla had made it very clear from day one that—even though, apparently, *she'd* felt free to do otherwise—*my* having sex with anyone other than my spouse would definitely be unsafe. It might actually be fatal.

June was now shrugging her pretty shoulders, a gesture that seemed to indicate she was discussing something of no real consequence. "So many people actually get *divorced* over something like this. Can you imagine?"

I nodded. "I've heard it's happened," I said quietly.

June gave me an indulgent smile. "Winslow and I believe that marriage is a sacred bond. A bond you don't break just because of an inconsequential affair."

I blinked. A sacred bond that didn't involve fidelity?

June smiled again. "Of course, I've always insisted that Winslow be discreet." Here June leaned toward me and lowered her voice. You might've thought there was someone else in the room who might hear. I sure didn't see anybody. Unless you counted the conquistador. "There are so many narrow-minded people in this town," June said. "But my Winslow has never strayed from our agreement. He's never, *ever* stayed out all night." She gave me another cheerleader smile. "He always comes straight home to me. He's really a wonderful husband."

I returned her smile. Wasn't Winslow the thoughtful one. What a guy.

"So you see," June continued, "if you think Winslow had

any reason whatsoever to harm poor Phyllis, why, you're mistaken, that's all."

That did seem to sum it all up nicely. If, of course, you actually believed what June was saying. And I wasn't sure I did. Somehow, June just didn't seem like the type to overlook a little thing like infidelity. Could a woman who'd made her home into one giant souvenir of her honeymoon really be all that blasé about her husband's running around?

The fact was, up to now, I'd pretty much tended to agree with what Vergil had told Orval earlier at Phyllis's. I'd never known of a woman who *really* didn't mind if her husband wandered. And yet, here was June, telling me with her own mouth that I was wrong.

Lord. It made you wonder how on earth Winslow had pulled this one off. The man had apparently not only gotten over being the nerd he'd been in high school, but he'd actually managed to get his wife to agree to look the other way while he ran around on her.

Maybe he'd been slipping something into June's food. Or hypnotizing her while she slept.

Or maybe, just maybe, I'd been listening to what had to be the best performance this side of the Academy Awards.

If this was a performance, though, Winslow was equally good in a supporting role. He walked into the living room right then, coming in from the direction of the family room, and stopped dead when he saw me sitting there.

Winslow was not dressed in the sort of thing you'd expect to see on a sick man. He was wearing a short-sleeved, brown checked shirt with a button-down collar, tan slacks, argyle socks, and those hard-soled moccasins he'd been wearing earlier. He might've looked like a genuine dyed-in-the-wool yuppie had he not been wearing the peace symbol necklace he'd also had on earlier, and had he not pulled his shaggy blond hair back with a rubber band. Winslow's hair wasn't long enough to make a real ponytail, so he more or less looked like he had a small blond tumor on the back of his head.

I hadn't heard his car pull up, but the walls of this house

were thick enough, you might not hear much outside. Winslow could very well have just driven up in his car, and entered through the sliding glass doors. Then again, he might've been in the house all along.

Wherever he was, he was surprised to see me. Winslow almost did a double take, but June immediately covered for him. "Darling," she said, getting up and going over to link her arm through his, "I've just been telling Haskell here about our little arrangement."

Winslow scratched his beard uneasily, and generally gave the impression he wasn't all that eager to talk about it, but he backed up every single word June had said. I just sat there, taking it all in. Either these two were the best acting team since Richard Burton and Elizabeth Taylor, or they were actually telling me the truth.

After the two of them had cheerfully explained how unfaithful they were to each other—and how neither one of them cared in the least—I decided it was as good a time as any to show them Phyllis's note. I pulled Vergil's Xerox out of my pocket, got up, and walked over to where they were standing, extending it toward them. For some reason, I happened to be looking in June's direction when I showed the note to them. Maybe because she was standing directly in front of me. Maybe because she was a lot more fun to look at than Winslow.

June glanced at the mark on that copy, and immediately looked scared.

I swallowed, staring at her. The look of alarm was suddenly there—and then gone, just as quickly—but I was sure I'd seen it.

Winslow, on the other hand, kept right on looking at the paper, not even blinking. "A seven?" He looked back up at me. "She wrote a seven?"

I was still staring at June. "Well, we're not sure this is a seven. We think maybe it's something else—"

This was a leading question if ever I'd heard one, but June didn't pick up on it. I was half hoping that the look of fear might return to June's face, but the eyes she lifted to mine were now totally calm. "You know, you're right," she said slowly. "It really might be something else. It looks to me like Phyllis might've been trying to write a capital *I*, and then her strength gave out. That's why it ended up looking like a seven."

I swallowed again. It wasn't exactly difficult to think up somebody connected with this case whose name began with *I*. Imogene. What exactly was June saying?

June was peering at the paper again. "I knew both sisters back in high school," she said. Her tone was regretful. "Goodness, those two fought all the time. Just like two cats. Of course, it didn't help any when Phyllis took Orval away from Imogene."

I was hoping I'd heard wrong. "What?" I said.

June's eyes darted to mine. "Oh, didn't you know? Orval dated Imogene before he finally settled down with Phyllis."

After that little bombshell dropped in front of me, I was pretty flustered. I managed to wrap things up pretty quick, telling Winslow and June that if they thought of anything else, for them to get in touch with me, that sort of thing. It seemed to take forever to finally get out of there, though, on account of my mind going about a million miles an hour the whole time I was saying my good-byes.

Imogene and *Orval?* Lord. Talk about your Beauty and your Beast. All right, come to think of it, I reckon Imogene was not exactly your classic beauty, but she *was* right cute. It was Cutie and the Beast, then, because Orval, no doubt about it, was clearly a Beast. To my way of thinking, anyway.

It wasn't just the idea of the two of them together that bothered me, either. It was the idea that Imogene hadn't been totally honest with me. I had to admit it, I had started to really like the woman, and now I couldn't help but wonder if she had withheld information from me intentionally.

Could Imogene actually be involved in her own sister's death? Had all those tears yesterday been just a smoke screen? Was I really as colossally stupid about women as

Claudzilla always said I was? Maybe Claudzilla had been right, after all. Maybe the reason Imogene had looked so disgusted yesterday listening to that tape of Orval and Flo Pedigo was that Imogene herself was still in love with Orval. Was it possible that Orval could've been playing around with more than one woman at a time?

If so, the man was an inspiration to us all.

Of course, this brought up yet another reason for me to be feeling real flustered. Not to mention, depressed. I was beginning to suspect that even *married* folks in Pigeon Fork date a lot more often than I did. It was a good thing I didn't actually have in my possession all those tapes Phyllis had made, or else they'd probably depress me more. The sounds of other folks having fun in bed might be enough to drive me over the edge.

My mood didn't improve any when I got to my office. As I pulled my truck in back of Elmo's and walked toward the front, Melba actually came out and met me. "Haskell," she said in that lilting voice that I hadn't gotten used to yet. "I've been looking all over for you!"

Melba looking for me, instead of me hunting all over for *her*? Usually this sort of thing would be cause for celebration, but this morning Melba was not what you'd call a sight for sore eyes. She was wearing a filmy, black long-sleeved shirt, through which you could plainly see her black lace bra. This last garment looked filled to overflowing, and that was an estimation taken after only the *briefest* of glances. For want of any other place to look, I stared at the rest of Melba's getup. Besides the see-through blouse, she was also wearing a black skintight leather miniskirt, black fishnet hose, high-heeled black patent leather boots, and she'd stuck a black fishnet bow in the top of her beehive.

At 250 pounds, Melba had gone in for the Madonna look.

I couldn't help it. I stopped dead in my tracks and stared at her. If Melba opened her mouth and started singing, "Like a Virgin," I was going to take off running.

Melba did open her mouth, but thank God, she didn't

sing. Instead, she cooed, "I've got a message for you, sweetie, and I've even got the *name* of the person who called and left it."

Her tone implied that she expected praise for this.

"It was *Emma Jane*," Melba said. "She said she wanted you to call her at home."

I swallowed. I think I was showing real patience here. "Could the name have been Imogene?" I asked, real polite-like.

Melba waved a plump hand airily. "Imogene, Emma Jane, what's the difference? That's the only message I've got for you. Your phone hasn't rung for hours." Then, moving closer to me so that I caught a whiff of a perfume so strong, I actually gasped for air, Melba added, "Haskell, I also came out here to tell you something else! Dalton's done the most wonderful thing!"

I hated to ask, but as it turned out, I didn't have to. Melba hurried right on. "He's asked *me* to invest in his shopping center! Isn't that great?"

Uh-oh. I took a deep breath. "Melba," I said, "I didn't know you had any money to—"

She interrupted me, looking terribly pleased with herself. "Why, you silly, don't you know, I've got all that Social Security money that me and the kids have been collecting from the government since Otis died. I've been putting it all into CDs and a passbook account, saving for college for them and all, but I think Otis would be real proud if he knew he'd helped us buy into a great investment like this!"

On the other hand, Otis might be spinning in his grave just hearing her say the words. "Melba," I said gently, "you know, investing money takes a lot of know-how, and—"

"—and Dalton has the know-how!" Melba finished for me. She was beaming at me by then. "That's what's so wonderful about all this. He says I don't have to worry about a thing! Oh, Haskell, can you imagine? *Me*, the owner of a shopping center. Dalton says he can just see the two of us, walking through the mall, past the fountain in the center, having dinner in one of the restaurants. Oh, it's just so exciting!"

I tried to smile at her. "Then you've already given him the money?"

Melba waved her hand again. "No, no, not quite. My next Social Security check arrives and my CDs all come due the first of the month, so I told Dalton I'd give it *all* to him then!"

I didn't know what to say. Keeping the smile on my face was taking every bit of my concentration.

Melba, however, seemed to know exactly what to say. "Oh, Haskell, it's going to be a dream come true!" She tottered off back inside on her shiny high heels, giggling a little to herself.

I stared after her, feeling even worse than I had before. *Dream* was probably the word for it, all right. I gave a shopping center in Pigeon Fork as much chance of flying as, say, *my* sprouting wings and flying myself. I hated to think it, but either Dalton was one dumb son of a gun, or he was pulling a real ugly scam on poor Melba.

I was mulling over all this in my mind, and I reckon I was pretty distracted as I headed up my stairs. That's why I think everything took so long to register. For an interminable moment, right after I opened my door, I just stood there, motionless, on the landing just outside my office, and stared. It actually took that long for what had happened to sink in. And then, of course, it hit me.

My office had been broken into.

It was pretty easy to see how they'd done it. The wood right next to the lock on my office door was splintered all to pieces. Somebody had apparently just pried my front door open with a screwdriver.

It wouldn't have been hard to do. Out here in the country I've never bothered putting a dead bolt on my office door. On account of there not being all that many robberies.

Up to now, of course.

Inside, every one of the drawers of my desk was standing

open. The drawers of my filing cabinets had been dumped on the floor. All my books had been pulled out of the bookcases, and they lay scattered all over the office. My lamp was lying on its side, and the cushion to my desk chair had been sliced open. Handfuls of stuffing, like piles of soap suds, were scattered all over the room.

Even the small bathroom off my office had not escaped. The top of the toilet now leaned against the back wall, and the contents of the small cabinet in there looked as if they had exploded across the room. Nothing, however, appeared to have been stolen.

Obviously this was not a robbery. In fact, it looked as if someone had been searching frantically for something. It sure wasn't hard to figure out what that something could be.

Phyllis's tapes.

13

When I called up Vergil to report that my office had been ransacked, his reaction was the sort of sympathetic response you might expect from near-family. "How can you tell?" Vergil's tone was real sarcastic.

"Vergil," I said, and yes, my own tone might've been a tad testy. "I admit I may be a little on the sloppy side, but I do draw the line at throwing *all* my books on the floor."

For an answer, Vergil grunted. He did, however, agree to mosey on over and dust the place for fingerprints.

Mosey, he did. Vergil arrived a little over an hour later with the same guy from the crime lab that had been over at Phyllis's.

I made sure I didn't touch anything until Vergil arrived. So that he could fully appreciate the extent of the devastation in my office. That meant, of course, that I spent a good bit of the next hour staring at the mess.

When I got tired of doing that—and it became pretty clear that Vergil was not exactly *rushing* over—I spent the rest of the time going downstairs into Elmo's and asking folks down there if anybody had seen somebody going up my stairs while I was gone.

Nobody had seen or heard anything. Except, of course, for Melba. When I asked her, she immediately cocked her brown beehive to one side, gave the fishnet bow in her hair a little tweak, and said, "You know, Haskell, I *thought* I heard somebody climbing your stairs."

Melba looked downright pleased to have been proved right.

It had apparently not occurred to her at the time, however, to actually look and see who it was. "Now that I think of it," Melba said, "it didn't sound like you on the stairs. This guy's step was a lot slower than yours." She fluffed the filmy sleeve of her see-through blouse. "Who woulda guessed it was somebody sneaking up to trash your office!"

I just looked at her. Thanks so much, Melba, for your help.

Elmo, like Melba, had also seen nothing. My brother, of course, took this opportunity to once again remind me what a real dangerous profession I'd chosen for myself. "Mark my words," he said, rubbing his bald head worriedly. "You're a-going to get yourself kilt."

Elmo also had a few words to say once again about the thrill-packed world of drugstore management. I nodded, just like I was listening, because I didn't want to hurt his feelings. Elmo obviously loves his work, but to tell you the truth, if I myself have to go into the drugstore business, I'd rather be, as Elmo put it, *kilt*.

After Elmo got finished with his sales pitch, I went across the street to talk to the two old guys still sitting out in front of the courthouse—the same ones I'd waved at earlier in the morning. One thing I have to say for these two old guys. Unlike the folks in Elmo's, both these guys clearly remembered somebody going up my stairs.

One of the old gents—a guy eighty if he was a day, who was wearing a green coverall and had more lines on his face than a road map—was sure my intruder had been a girl. "A young chick," I believe were his exact words. I noticed when Road Map said these particular words that he appeared to have only three teeth left in his mouth. Two on the top, one on the bottom. It didn't make for real articulate speech.

The other old guy—this one in faded overalls and a yellowed V-neck undershirt—had Road Map beat bad in the teeth department. Overalls was the proud possessor of eight entire teeth, three on the top and five on the bottom. I noticed this impressive array while Overalls was cackling right after Road Map spoke. "Pshaw!" Overalls said. "It was *not* a girl neither." He pronounced the word *it* as if it were spelled with an *h*. Hit. "Sure as I'm sitting here, hit was a blond feller."

I nodded. That sounded like Winslow. Maybe this was why Winslow had called in sick today. He'd had a pressing appointment in my office.

Overalls was now scratching his grizzled chin and squinting his watery eyes in the direction of my office. "Or maybe the guy was black-headed," he drawled.

I just looked at him. Black-headed sounded pretty disgusting, but I was pretty sure Overalls here was talking about the guy's *hair*. If so, Overalls could've been describing Boyd now. The only thing was, how could you possibly confuse blond hair with black? Or, for that matter, a woman with a man?

Both Road Map and Overalls evidently had managed it. Overalls scratched his chin some more and nodded at me, his watery eyes now looking a tad clearer maybe. "It was one or t'other. I'm sure of that." He took a deep breath, looked over at Road Map, and said, "Or was he redheaded?"

I had the sinking feeling that Overalls was now getting the intruder confused with *me*.

After that, neither Road Map nor Overalls could make up his mind what the man/woman he'd seen had looked like. The two of them, however, did finally agree on the reason why. "Too much shade over there," they both told me. "You cain't see a thing."

There's only one tree in front of Elmo's, and it does not cast a bit of shade on my stairs. I nodded and thanked them both for their help. I almost wished I hadn't, though. They rewarded me with huge grins. I gave them both an uncertain smile in return and headed on back to my office.

So much for eyewitnesses.

It was only about a fifteen-minute wait after that before Vergil finally showed up.

Vergil walked through my front door, gave the belt of his tan uniform a hitch, and took a sad look around. "Well, now," he said, "it doesn't look a whole lot different, now, does it?"

So much for sympathy.

While the guy from the crime lab peppered my office with fingerprint dust, Vergil told me, by way of making conversation, that the coroner had put Phyllis's death at between one and three the previous afternoon, and that she'd been shot with a .38 handgun. Vergil also told me that Orval's story about it being him and Flo on the tape we'd listened to had checked out. "I listened to the whole thing, and Orval called Flo by name quite a few times."

Vergil made it sound as if somebody had held a gun to his head and forced him to listen to that tape. It even looked like he was reddening a little, admitting he'd actually done such a thing. He didn't fool me. I had no doubt that old Vergil here had listened to that tape a lot more than just once. Hell, he could probably recite the thing verbatim. With all the sighs and all the giggles in the appropriate spots.

Vergil told me that Orval mentioned Flo's name mostly toward the end of the tape, when Orval and Flo had themselves a little argument over how much Flo thought Orval owed her for her giggling and assorted other talents. Orval had apparently ended up forking out $150. Giggling, apparently, wasn't cheap.

I couldn't help remembering how sparse poor Phyllis's clothes closets had been.

Vergil went on about Orval and Flo's argument in a real casual tone. Like maybe we could've been talking about the weather. His tone changed some when we moved on to the subject of my office being broken into. "Kinda looks like somebody was looking for something, don't it?" Vergil said. The lines beside his mouth were deepening into caverns.

There was no use to denying it. I shrugged. "It sure looks that way."

Vergil stepped closer to me and lowered his voice, even though the crime lab guy was in the bathroom by then. I assumed the guy was still dusting for prints in there. Either that, or this whole mess had made him even sicker than it had made me. "You know, Haskell," Vergil said, "I'd hate to find out that Will's boy was keeping something from me."

Will's my dad. I believe I've mentioned that my dad's been gone for some nine years now, and that he and Vergil were best friends. Vergil was bringing out the heavy artillery if he was dragging my dad's name into it.

I took a deep breath. "Vergil," I said, "I don't have those tapes. I mean it. I'm not kidding."

Maybe I was a little too emphatic here. Vergil drew a long, exasperated breath that I was afraid might use up all the air in my office. When he was finally finished, he gave me a mournful look and said, "Whatever."

Whatever *that* meant.

No surprise, the crime lab guy finally came up to Vergil and me, and said, "This is just a preliminary finding, of course, but it's my guess that the only fingerprints here are Haskell's. I'll go back and run what I've found through the computer, but I think we're going to find that this place is clean."

Vergil looked over at me, and rolled his eyes. I believe Vergil was making the point here that my office could never be accurately described as *clean,* but since Vergil didn't say it out loud, I ignored it.

I also pretty much ignored what Vergil had to say just before he left. He fixed me with yet another mournful look and intoned, "It surely would be a crying shame if I found out Will's boy was hiding something he shouldn't have picked up in the first place."

I looked him straight in the eye. "Vergil, I don't have the tapes," I said. I almost added, *Read my lips,* but it occurred to me in time that this might not be the most convincing thing in the world to say.

Vergil didn't seem convinced no matter what I said. He sighed, walked out on my landing, sighed yet again, and finally left.

I watched him go. Just about the very second Vergil disappeared from view, another figure appeared, darting out the front door of Elmo's just below me and immediately heading my way. If I didn't know better, I'd say this particular person had to have been standing down there, keeping watch out Elmo's front window, just waiting for Vergil to be on his way.

It was Leesa Jo Lattimore, the waitress at Frank's Bar and Grill. You remember, the woman who preferred dating a *married* guy to going out with me? If I hadn't been made painfully aware of this particular fact, I no doubt would've gotten a lot more enjoyment out of watching Leesa Jo sashay her way up the stairs to my office.

Leesa Jo was wearing the tight black skirt I'd mentioned earlier, a skirt, I might add, which showed off her long bare legs to perfection. She was also wearing a creamy white puff-sleeved blouse with tucks all down her curvy front.

I took a deep breath, watching her climb toward me. Some of the women around these parts, I call a Pigeon Fork 10. These women would probably be a 7 or an 8 anywhere else in the United States, but here in Pigeon Fork, with so many of the women still wearing their hair in beehives and not a few of them looking like maybe they should go out for professional wrestling, these Pigeon Fork 10's are a welcome sight. Leesa Jo, however, was not a Pigeon Fork 10. Leesa Jo would've been a 10 anywhere.

Leesa Jo today looked pretty much the way she always did—blond hair in a thick plait down her back, perky little nose, large blue eyes framed by long eyelashes. Only one thing was different. Leesa Jo's complexion didn't look so creamy today. In fact, it looked downright pink and blotchy.

Leesa Jo had obviously been crying.

Oh God. Have I mentioned how great I am with weeping women? I took a hasty glance around the shambles of my office. Even if there *had* been a Kleenex somewhere in this place, I'd never be able to find it. If Leesa Jo got really damp on me, the best I'd be able to do was a few squares of toilet tissue from the bathroom.

Somehow, that just didn't seem any too cool.

Leesa Jo was already blinking back tears when she got to my landing. I swallowed, watching her. She immediately took one look around my office and decided not to go in. Still standing out on my landing, she said, "Good grief. What happened?"

I started in, telling her, but you could tell she wasn't listening. Right away she interrupted me, waving a small hand distractedly, "Why, that's awful. It really is, Haskell." She was pulling a lace handkerchief out of her purse—a thing I was right glad to see—as she hurried on. "I've had something awful happen to me, too."

That last word sort of had a life of its own. It seemed to go on and on. Too-oo-oo-oo-oo. When that word was finally over, Leesa Jo dabbed at her eyes with her handkerchief and then looked back up at me. Her pretty eyes seemed suddenly hostile for some reason. "Winslow just broke up with me! He said you're looking into Phyllis Carver's murder, and that you suspect him, and that we can't ever see each other again!"

Now, what was I supposed to say to all that? *Good idea?*

Leesa Jo obviously didn't think so. In fact, she was now looking downright angry. Her voice shook as she told me the rest of it. Apparently Winslow had told her about Phyllis's blackmail scheme the same day Phyllis had approached him for the money. "I told him then and there that I didn't care who found out about us!"

I stared at Leesa Jo. How in the hell did Winslow do it? Somehow he'd managed to get himself two, count them, *two* good-looking women who were willing to put up with some major inconveniences in order to keep him in their lives. I

197

hadn't been able to get Claudzilla to put up with *Rip,* for God's sake. In fact, a couple of times during the four years we were married, she'd actually threatened to poison him.

Leesa tearfully hurried on. "But now it looks like Winslow's the one who cares what people think! And all because of *you!*" Oh yeah. Leesa Jo was blaming all this on me, all right. According to Leesa Jo, Winslow had just told her that continuing on with her would make it look as if Winslow had had a terrific motive for murdering Phyllis. Everybody would think he might've killed Phyllis to keep Leesa Jo's reputation clean. Winslow figured that if everybody saw that he could drop Leesa Jo this easily, then no one would think he could possibly kill to protect her.

It made sense to me. What also made sense, I was afraid, was that Leesa Jo really couldn't mean very much to old Winslow. Maybe June Reed knew her husband better than I'd thought when she'd described his "relationships on the side" as "inconsequential."

All this apparently had not yet occurred to Leesa Jo. She now sobbed outright, and then when she finally managed to get herself under control, she glared at me. "But you're wrong, Haskell, to suspect Winslow! He couldn't possibly have killed Phyllis Carver! He was with me at my apartment all that afternoon! We were—we were—"

Leesa Jo's voice trailed off, but I didn't need any help in filling in the blanks. I swallowed, staring at her. *All* that afternoon? Was she talking *hours?* In *bed?* OK. That did it. I was really depressed now.

I hated to ask it, but I actually needed to know. "How many hours was Winslow with you?" My voice was a little weak as I formed the question. On account of my mouth being so dry.

Leesa Jo took her time answering, looking first toward my office door and then over toward the courthouse across the street. When she glanced across the street, I noticed that both Road Map and Overalls jerked to attention. I think I could probably eliminate Leesa Jo as a possible suspect in the trashing of my office. Leesa Jo, I was pretty sure, Road

Map and Overalls would remember. For a second, I thought the two of them might actually wave at her. Instead, they both just continued to sit there on that bench, looking quite a bit more alert—and grinning.

Incidentally, not a pretty sight.

Leesa Jo apparently didn't even see them. She turned back toward me, lifted her chin, and said, "Winslow was with me all that afternoon and then *all night long.*" Obviously Leesa Jo had no idea the exact time of Phyllis's death, so she'd decided to go with what was safe.

I just looked at her. This, after what June had told me about how Winslow always kept up appearances and came home to her every single night?

Of the two women, my guess was that Leesa Jo here was the one doing the lying.

Leesa Jo had evidently said all she came by to say. Other than one final parting shot, as she turned to leave. "So if you think you're going to pin this thing on Winslow, you better think again! He was with *me!*"

She sounded downright proud of it.

After watching Leesa Jo's cute little backside sashay its way down my stairs, I can't say I was all that eager to jump right into cleaning up my office. What I was eager, in fact, to do was jump right off my landing and crash headfirst on the pavement below.

How in the hell did Winslow—not to mention *Orval*—do it?

Thinking of Orval made me remember that I had not yet returned Imogene's phone call. It also made me remember what all June had said. It took me about five minutes to locate my phone, and the whole time I was looking, my stomach was knotting up. I wasn't real sure I wanted to hear what Imogene had to say.

The phone turned out to be lying under a bunch of my books, off in a corner. Its receiver was about a foot away, stretching the cord almost full length. The whole thing looked as if it had just been tossed over there. No wonder Melba had had no phone calls for hours.

Fortunately, I was wearing the same jeans I'd worn last night, so I didn't have to look for Imogene's home number. I just pulled it out of my back pocket, sat myself down on my office floor, and started dialing.

Imogene picked up on the first ring. "Oh, Haskell, thank God you caught me. I was just getting ready to leave for the funeral home. I thought it might be somebody calling up to offer condolences again. This phone's been ringing off the hook. I think everybody in the entire town has called."

I think Imogene said all this without taking a breath. She and Phyllis were definitely sisters, all right.

Imogene wasn't through, either. She hurried right on, "Tell me, did you find out anything from Winslow or Ruta that was interesting?"

I think *incriminating* was the word Imogene meant here, because I went ahead and told her quite a few things I would've described as *interesting,* but you could tell she wasn't real impressed. She was particularly unimpressed with what all June had had to tell me about her and Winslow's "arrangement."

"Oh, Haskell, you don't mean to tell me you believed her! Why, I never heard of such a thing! Do you really think that June Reed doesn't mind if her own husband runs around on her?"

I hated to admit the truth. "I don't know. June sounded pretty convincing to me."

Imogene gave a sigh that sounded a whole lot like Vergil's. "Tell me, Haskell, do you believe everything a pretty woman tells you?"

I guess if I'd wanted Imogene to think I was the cool, suave, debonair type, I should've said something like, "Sure, what did you want to tell me?" But I reckon I've never been that cool. Or suave. Or debonair. Instead of turning what Imogene said into a compliment, I just sort of sat there like a lump, with my stomach hurting. All the time we'd been talking, I'd been looking for a chance to smoothly work the conversation around to asking her about Orval. Now, when the opportunity presented itself, I could hardly get the words out.

"Haskell?" Imogene finally said.

"Well, uh, now that you mentioned it," I said, "June, uh, did happen to tell me one other, uh, little thing." Lord. I sounded like Winslow. I cleared my throat. "What's all this about you and Orval?"

Talk about smooth.

"Orval?" Imogene sounded genuinely confused. "And *me?*" Now she sounded appalled.

I cleared my throat again. My stomach was hurting real bad now. "June told me that you and, uh, Orval were an item."

"What?" Imogene's answer was almost a shout. "Look, I don't know where in the world June got an idea like that. Unless, of course, she was talking about high school. Orval and I went out a couple of times back then. But I found out right away that Orval was *not* for me." There was a long silence, and then I heard her take a deep, ragged breath. "I only wish I'd managed to convince Phyllis he wasn't for *her,* either."

My stomach was still hurting. This phone conversation did not seem to be making either one of us feel any too good.

"Look, Haskell," Imogene went on, "I guess I should've told you in the first place about my going out with Orval, but to tell you the truth, Orval and I dated so long ago, it didn't even occur to me to mention it."

I wanted to believe her, but I wasn't sure I did.

"By the way," Imogene said, "has your office phone been off the hook today? I bet I've called you a dozen times and I kept getting a busy signal."

I wasn't sure if Imogene had intentionally changed the subject, or if she simply considered the Orval topic discussed and done with. Whichever it was, there didn't seem to be any way I could keep on quizzing her about Orval without making it sound like some kind of accusation.

So I dropped it.

No doubt just like Imogene wanted me to.

"Well, yes, I guess you could say my phone's been off the hook," I said, and we moved right on to talking about what had happened to my office. Leaving the Orval topic behind us. When I got finished telling Imogene how the intruder had apparently wiped the place clean of fingerprints, she let out a low whistle. "Good heavens, Haskell, do you think they were looking for Phyllis's tapes?"

"Actually," I said, "I don't just *think* they were looking for them. I know it."

"But, Haskell," Imogene said, "this doesn't make any sense. If Phyllis was killed for the tapes, then why is the killer still looking for them?"

This line of thought had already occurred to me. There was only one answer to Imogene's question. "It could very well be that whoever broke into my office is not the killer."

Even over the phone, I could hear Imogene take a long, disappointed breath. "Then finding out who broke into your office might not help us at all."

I found myself nodding just as if Imogene could see me. "Yes, but it might eliminate somebody from the list."

I did not add, *And considering the list probably includes Winslow, Leesa Jo, June, Ruta, Boyd, Lenard, Orval, and even you, eliminating anybody would be a real help.*

Imogene made me promise to call her the second I found out anything new, and after that, there didn't seem anything else to do but hang up. I would've liked to ask Imogene a few more questions about how she'd managed to forget all about her and Orval dating in high school, but there didn't seem to be any way to do it less subtle than a train wreck.

At that point, I fully intended to spend the rest of the afternoon doing something that I think it should be pretty clear by now is the thing I like least to do. Cleaning my office. But right after I got off the phone with Imogene, it occurred to me that I hadn't eaten since breakfast. And it was now nearly two in the afternoon. Maybe my stomach had not been hurting because I was tense so much as because I was *starving*.

I can't exactly say I hated putting off my cleaning chores for a little while. I headed toward the alley out back where I'd parked my truck.

At this particular point I now fully intended to spend a few quiet minutes at Frank's Bar and Grill, stuffing my face with one of Frank's quarter pounders. Frank's is the closest thing we've got to a McDonald's around these parts. It's not fast food and it's not great food, it's just *food*.

Frank's, as a matter of fact, was a feed store at one time. When the feed store went bankrupt, Frank Puckett bought the place and turned it into a restaurant. The place is still real rustic-looking with its weathered signs on bare wood walls advertising Aubrey's Red Feed and Friskies Dog Food and the like. Frank's also has the distinction of having the only neon sign in Pigeon Fork. It's real little, and red, and it says, "Say bull." The sign hangs in Frank's front window and, in my opinion, doesn't add a whole lot to the decor. Frank, though, seems real proud of it.

Frank's is located about seven miles outside of Pigeon Fork, at the junction where Main Street turns into a state road, so it's a little bit of a drive away. I already had my keys out when I walked around back of Elmo's.

That's when I noticed that The Dalton's red Cadillac was parked in the alley right next to my truck. Evidently Melba's main squeeze had dropped by for a visit. No doubt to see Melba's Madonna outfit for himself. It *was* something you had to see to believe.

I also noticed something else. Dalton's shiny, new, red de Ville made my Ford truck—with its real nice metallic blue paint job, mind you—look like a poor relation.

I guess I stood, keys in hand, and stared at that Cadillac for a good minute or so. Remembering what all Melba had told me earlier.

It didn't take me fifteen minutes to get in my truck, drive over to Toomey's Hardware Store, buy me the kind of voice-activated tape recorder that Phyllis used and some heavy-duty tape, and drive back into the alley.

Sure enough, The Dalton's Caddy was still there. I got out

of my truck and took a good long look around. There was nobody in sight.

I kept right on looking around as I moseyed on over to the Caddy. Then I started really staring at it, leaning this way and that, so that if anybody happened into the alley, they'd just think I was admiring the thing.

The Dalton must be a real trusting soul, or else downright forgetful, because while he'd locked the door on the driver's side, he'd left the front door on the passenger side unlocked. I'd have to remember to mention to him how he ought to be more careful. Anything could happen.

I was in and out of his car in less than a minute.

That heavy-duty tape worked real good, fastening the recorder securely to the underside of the front seat, just like that was what it was made to do.

I reckon I should've been feeling real sneaky a little later at Frank's, while I sat there in one of his booths and ate my lunch. And, in fact, I guess I did feel sneaky. A little. Mostly what I was feeling, though, was determined. I was determined to find out for sure if Dalton was on the level. Hopefully before Melba turned over any money to him.

After I inhaled Frank's Afternoon Special—that's a quarter pounder, a thirty-two-ounce Coke, and a plate full of fries—and I drove on back to my office, I finally got around to doing what I hated. You guessed it. Turning Tornado Alley into just a Bermuda Rectangle again.

While I worked, putting books back into the bookcases, and picking up chair stuffing and whatnot, I more or less kept my mind occupied by trying to decide who, if anybody, would get my vote for Most Likely to Ransack an Office.

If I could assume that whoever did the ransacking had definitely been looking for Phyllis's tapes, then it seemed pretty significant that I'd only told *two* people that I even had the tapes. Ruta. And Boyd. Of these two, Boyd got my vote.

Unless, of course, Boyd should be disqualified on account of his being too lazy to do the job. Which *was* a possibility.

Another person who might've been looking for the tapes could've been—and I hated to say it—Imogene. I wasn't at all sure that she'd totally believed me when I'd insisted I didn't have them. Could she have been looking for the tapes herself in order to keep anyone from ever proving that her sister had been blackmailing folks?

Come to think of it, Orval also might've been looking for the tapes. Maybe he'd been in on the blackmail scam with Phyllis, after all. Maybe it had only been *his* own tape that he hadn't known about.

Was that possible?

It could even be possible that, even though I had not told them directly, Winslow and June could just have assumed I'd taken the tapes. By now, just about everybody in town probably knew I was the first on the scene after Phyllis was killed. Winslow and June no doubt had heard that I was the one who'd discovered Phyllis's body. Maybe that's why June admitted everything about Winslow's affair the way she did. Maybe she thought I had the tapes, and I already knew.

By the time five o'clock finally rolled around, I was pretty much getting around to suspecting everybody. It even crossed my mind that maybe one of the Guntermans had done the dirty deed. Maybe the twins, like Vergil, believed I'd taken the tapes, and they were looking for the next exciting installment.

I decided if I was starting to suspect the twins, I must be really tired. Next, I'd think it was Vergil. Enough was enough. I put my cleaning stuff away, locked up my office as best I could, and headed on home. I wasn't anywhere near done straightening up the place, but at least you could walk into my office without stumbling over something.

On the way home, I tried not to think of a thing. I wanted to simply give it a rest for a while. In fact, I actually tried to just drive along with a totally blank mind.

I did this by pretending I *was* one of the Guntermans.

It was while I was headed up my driveway, however, that something did pop into my head. In fact, it occurred to me, just as I was making the turn in the middle of my driveway, that something was different today. Something I couldn't quite put my finger on. What was it?

I'd already gotten to the top of my hill when it came to me. *Rip wasn't barking.*

I'd driven all the way up my hill, and that crazy dog was not doing his bark-at-the-guy-who-lives-here routine. I swallowed uneasily. I would've liked to think that after all these years of living with me, a small miracle had happened, and my own dog had finally learned to recognize me. Or that maybe old Rip had at last decided that it was probably in bad taste to bark at the guy who feeds you.

I would've liked to think all that, but I knew it wasn't true. If there was ever a dog that was living proof of that old saying about teaching old dogs new tricks, Rip was it. Rip, in fact, hadn't been able to learn new tricks when he was a *young* dog.

I got out of my truck and began hurrying toward the house, my heart now starting to speed up a little. It especially speeded up when I saw that Rip was not at the head of the stairs. This, the dog who'd been sitting there when I got home every single day since the first day we'd moved out here, waiting impatiently for me to carry him down to the yard.

Something was very wrong.

I scanned the deck above. Where the hell was Rip? I went up those steps two at a time.

And then I saw him.

Rip lay motionless on the deck, right next to the corner of the house.

I took one look, and my mind started repeating the same thing over and over. Oh God, oh God, oh God, oh God.

14

Rip lay on his side, his eyes closed. In the middle of his right side, there was a small, dark hole. The blood had caked around the wound, matting the fur. I didn't need to be a private detective to figure out what had happened.

Rip had been shot.

To this day, I don't remember actually running to Rip. It just seemed as if, all of a sudden, I was just there on the deck, by his side, stroking his fur.

Thank God, he still felt warm.

His breathing was so shallow, though. So shallow.

The second I touched him, surprisingly, Rip opened his eyes. He didn't lift his head, though, he just looked at me.

"It's OK, Rip," I said, as I looked him over as fast as I could. "It's OK, boy."

Rip tried to wag his tail, but right away it was clear that the effort was too much for him. He gave one weak thump, gave it up, and closed his eyes again.

My mouth went dry.

The wound in Rip's side looked real raw and ugly, but it wasn't bleeding much anymore. I didn't want to consider whether this was a good sign or a bad one. There was also some dried blood around Rip's mouth, but I couldn't see any cuts or wounds on his head. Or on his front legs, or anywhere else, other than his side. The blood on Rip's mouth was just a small amount, not what he would've gotten if he'd been licking at that side wound. Besides, in the condition he was in, I strongly doubted he could've lifted his head to lick it. The blood on Rip's mouth, in fact, looked to be exactly the amount Rip might've gotten on it if he'd bitten somebody.

I sure hoped whatever part of the anatomy it was that Rip had gotten hold of, it had been something vital.

I knew it was probably dangerous to move Rip, but I also knew there might not be enough time for a vet to get here. Not to mention, to try to find my house. I've had friends wander around in these woods for an hour, going up and down these little country roads trying to find me, and that's *after* I drew them a map.

One thing for sure. I wasn't about to sit around and watch Rip die.

I hated to leave him even for a second, but I needed to run inside to get a blanket to wrap him in. So Rip wouldn't go into shock any worse than he already was. It was then, just as I raced through my front door, that I first realized that my house was now an identical twin to my office earlier.

My blue wraparound sofa lay in pieces all over the room. Books, newspapers, and magazines were thrown all over, my lamps upended, the wooden wire spool I use as a coffee table lying on its side.

At that moment, however, I didn't do much other than just register what had happened. There wasn't time. The house could wait. Rip couldn't.

In fact, the thing about it that bothered me the most right at that moment was that, in all the mess, I couldn't find a blanket anywhere. All the closets where I'd stored my blankets for the summer were now standing empty, their contents littered all over the house.

I ended up grabbing up the bedspread off my bed, racing outside, and wrapping Rip in that.

BED BUGS

The Crayton County Veterinary Clinic is about eight miles on the other side of Pigeon Fork High, so it's usually about a twenty-minute drive from where I live. Of course, I'm not usually driving to the vet particularly fast, being as how I'm always pretty distracted when I go. Rip and I have never gone to this clinic for any reason other than to get his shots updated, so every time I put him in the truck and head that way, Rip knows exactly what's going to happen to him when we get there. Rip always starts howling the second he realizes where we're headed.

I reckon that's why it seemed so strange now, driving to the vet with Rip lying on the seat beside me, not making a sound. I glanced over at him, swallowing hard, and stepped a little harder on the gas. I never thought I'd ever wish that silly old dog would be howling, but the thing was, I'd have given anything for him to be throwing his usual fit.

I made it to the clinic in fourteen minutes tops. By that time, I'm pretty sure my heart was going even faster than my truck.

You could tell the clinic was getting ready to close up. The outside waiting room was empty, and the girl behind the enclosed counter at the far end of the waiting room had already shut the little rippled glass square that she always talks to you through.

"Hey!" I yelled, as soon as I walked through the front door. Rip, when he's feeling fine, is one heavy dog. Now, lying motionless in my arms, he seemed twenty pounds heavier. "Hey, I need some help out here! My dog's been shot!"

Just saying the words made my stomach wrench.

Thank God, I didn't have to waste much time explaining what had happened. Dr. Darlene Carmichael, the fiftyish lady vet, came running out, with one of her assistants right behind her. She took one look at Rip and scooped him right out of my arms.

Doc Darlene, with her curly brown hair streaked with gray and her no-nonsense horn-rimmed glasses, is one of the women around Pigeon Fork who look like maybe they could make a career out of wrestling. She's about six feet tall, at least two hundred pounds, and her upper arms look like hams. Doc Darlene picked up overweight Rip with as much ease as the average woman picks up her purse. Doc and her assistant disappeared with Rip through a white paneled door leading into the back. Doc tried to give me a reassuring look as she went, but there was no way to disguise how worried she looked.

I imagine I looked a lot like her.

After all that hurrying, now there wasn't anything to do but wait.

This part seemed a lot harder to do than the hurrying part. I sat myself down in one of the uncomfortable but no doubt durable metal chairs out in the waiting room, and for a long time didn't do anything but stare at my shoes. After a while, though, just for something to do to keep my mind off what was happening behind that white paneled door, I started looking around at what passes for art in the Crayton County Veterinary Clinic.

In the times I'd been here before, I'd never had to wait for a long time. Being as how Rip is always carrying on so much by the time I drag him through the door, they always take us back pretty much the second we walk in. So I can't say I'd ever particularly noticed this art before.

Now, more's the pity, I seemed to have all the time in the world to fully appreciate it.

I reckon I stared at the artwork on the wall to my left for a good five minutes. It was definitely something you don't see every day. Thank God, I might add. It was a two-foot-high cutaway model of a dog tick. Which showed the tick's insides in what I reckon you would say was better than living color. Being as how I'm pretty sure a tick does not have the colors magenta, turquoise, or purple anywhere inside it.

Of course, I've never actually *looked*.

On the wall next to the big tick, as you went left around the room from where I was sitting, there was an even larger plastic model of a flea. The flea wasn't anywhere near as impressive as the tick, however. The flea's insides were just done in black and white.

The insides of either of these things, I might as well admit, were not something that I've ever had even the slightest curiosity about. In fact, I think I'm safe in saying that I could've lived my whole life, never have seen them, and might actually have been grateful to have skipped it.

I continued to glance around the room. On the wall to my right, directly across from the tick, a large flip chart apparently kept a running count of the number of cases of heartworm in Crayton County this year. It was simple, but dramatic. It said, in bold black marker, "22!!!"

I don't believe Doc Darlene will ever be mistaken for an art connoisseur.

The one thing in her art collection, however, that I found myself actually reading, for want of something, *anything*, to occupy my mind, was the framed poster on the wall directly behind me. It depicted, in full color, the life cycle of a tapeworm.

I believe at this point I don't have to say anything more about how upset I was.

I actually turned myself around in the metal chair I was sitting in so that I could get a better view, and I read that damn poster word for word. In fact, I'd read the entire thing *twice* and had once again gotten to the part where the tapeworm larvae were busily burrowing into the muscles of brightly colored dogs, cats, pigs, cows, *and* fish when Doc Darlene appeared at my side.

"Well, Haskell," she said quietly. "He got through the surgery."

I felt as if every bit of the air in my lungs rushed out at that particular moment.

Doc went right on as if I'd had no reaction at all. I think that she, like me, is real uncomfortable around any emotion, so she just pretends she doesn't see it. "Your dog was shot with a .22. What happened, some moron hunter mistake him for a deer?"

I just looked at her. "It was a moron, all right, but I don't think it was a hunter," I said.

Doc blinked, but she didn't pursue it. Doc Darlene never wants to know any more than you want to tell her. Around these parts that makes her downright odd. "Rip's not out of the woods yet," she went on. "He's lost a lot of blood, and getting that bullet out wasn't easy. Your dog might still die." Doc is also a tad on the blunt side. I think this is because she's accustomed to dealing with creatures that don't require you to carry on extended conversations. If it turns out she has to actually talk things over with a human being, Doc Darlene is real ill at ease. Right now, as she said this last to me, her eyes behind the horn-rims were fixed on the tapeworm poster behind my head.

I nodded my head to show I was listening and all, but to tell you the truth, all that really seemed to get through was that last sentence of hers. *Rip might still die.* I couldn't seem to breathe.

"There's no use in you sitting around here, though. There's not a thing you can do. Just call me tomorrow, and I'll let you know how things are going, OK?" Doc Darlene made it sound as if I were doing nothing more than leaving Rip behind to have his toenails clipped.

I didn't particularly want to go, but Doc Darlene is not the kind of woman you can argue with. She just says what she's got to say, folds her wrestler's arms across her chest, and then stares at you. There's not much else you can do except go along with whatever she just said.

It wasn't until I'd gotten into my truck that I realized I hadn't even called up Vergil yet. To report what had happened.

I kind of hated to tell him. Particularly since it was obvious that somebody had definitely been looking for something. Again.

On the other hand, I knew I wasn't going to be able to sleep, anyway. At least, dealing with Vergil would keep me busy—and keep me from thinking about Rip. And worrying.

About a half hour after I finally located my downstairs phone and gave him a call, Vergil showed up with that same guy from the crime lab that had been at Phyllis's and my office earlier. And sure enough, Vergil did take my mind off Rip. Some.

Vergil also, however, reminded me of Rip. Especially when Vergil's car first came up my driveway. It was getting dark by then, and watching Vergil's headlights bouncing up my hill, I couldn't help being struck by how odd it felt for Rip not to be there, dancing around on the deck the way he always does. Doing his best Cujo impression.

I was swallowing real hard when Vergil headed up my stairs. And maybe blinking a little. I don't think Vergil noticed, though, because he went right by me, took one look at my house, and said, "Lordy, Lordy, Lordy." Then he turned to me. "Sure looks like they were looking for something, don't it?"

I tried to look impressed at his amazing deductive powers.

After that, Vergil and I pretty much went through a rerun of Vergil's visit to my office earlier. Complete with the references to my dad. "Sure is a shame for a thing like this to happen to Will's boy," Vergil said when he'd been there about ten minutes. "Somebody must think you've got something they want."

Vergil gave me a real pointed look when he said that.

I just stared back at him.

"They must be real desperate for it if they'd shoot your dog," Vergil added. "Lordy, Lordy, what a shame." For once, Vergil's mournful tone sounded entirely appropriate to me.

"Vergil," I said, "I don't have those tapes."

"Uh huh," he said, walking off.

I think I could put Vergil down as somebody who didn't believe a word I said.

About the only thing that was different about this visit was Vergil's sneezing. He started in sneezing his head off right after the crime lab guy peppered the place.

"I think I'm getting allergic to fingerprint powder," Vergil told me. His sad eyes were clearly accusing. "You got a Kleenex around here anywhere?"

I don't reckon I have to tell you what my answer was. Vergil ended up going back out to his car, grumbling all the way, and getting one out of his glove compartment. After he got his Kleenex, Vergil wandered around my A-frame, staring mournfully at the mess, and a-chooing to beat the band.

Vergil was maybe on his tenth sneeze when Imogene phoned. It took me a minute or so to answer, being as how I had to step over so much stuff between me and the phone. Maybe it was waiting so long for me to pick up the phone that got her in such an all-fired hurry, but Imogene didn't even give me the chance to say hello before she started talking. "Haskell," she said, "I've got a great idea for flushing out Phyllis's killer!"

Vergil was standing right behind me in the kitchen then, so all I said was, "What?"

"How about if I tell Winslow and Ruta that Phyllis sent *me* a copy of the tapes she made? I could tell them both that the tapes arrived in today's mail. That way the killer would think that there was more than one copy of the tapes in existence, and he'd have to come after *me*!"

I swallowed. Wait a minute. Hold the phone. Imogene wanted to set herself up as a decoy? Was she kidding? Not only would Phyllis's killer come after Imogene, but possibly *everybody* who'd been taped would come after her, too. "Look, this is not a good idea. In fact, it's a real dangerous idea, understand?" I lowered my voice a little since I was sure Vergil was now trying to listen to every word. His sneezing had mysteriously stopped right after my phone rang. What a coincidence.

"Nonsense, Haskell!" Imogene said. "They do this kind of thing on TV all the time!"

I lowered my voice so that now it was barely above a whisper. "Imogene, they shoot people, and rob people, and have car chases all the time on TV, too, but I don't think *we* want to do any of those things." I hurried on, telling Imogene what all had just happened to Rip, not to mention my house. "So don't do it, understand? Don't even *think* about doing it."

There was a long silence, and then Imogene definitely changed the subject. "Haskell, I'm sorry to hear about Rip." Imogene sounded definitely subdued. "I really am."

I would've liked to talk to her a little longer, and maybe hear a few more sympathetic words like the ones she'd just said, except that, out of the corner of my eye, I noticed Vergil was on the move. He was busy wiping his nose, like maybe that was what he was really concentrating on, but he was also taking a few steps around the stuff on the floor and definitely moving closer to me.

"I've got to go; the police are here right now."

Imogene didn't need to be hit over the head. "Oh. Sure," she said. "Call me if there's anything I can do. And I sure hope Rip's OK, you know?"

I knew, all right.

It occurred to me as I hung up that Imogene sure didn't act like a woman with something to hide. Matter of fact, I wasn't sure what to think now. Here I'd been feeling real uneasy about Imogene not mentioning that she'd once dated Orval, and yet, she seemed genuinely adamant about finding her sister's killer. If Imogene had indeed been involved in Phyllis's death, she was either a gifted actress—or totally without conscience.

I also thought of something else. If Imogene had wanted me to be convinced of her innocence, that little phone call was the perfect thing to do.

Vergil looked at me as if he expected me to tell him who that was on the phone, but when I didn't, he didn't press it. He made a couple more references to my dad before he left, but finally he drove off down my hill, with the crime lab guy sitting right next to him.

Like Vergil, the crime lab guy had also been doing his own rerun of the visit to my office earlier. "My guess—and mind you, it's just preliminary——is that the only fingerprints around this place belong to Haskell," he'd said finally, much like he did before, pulling off his rubber gloves and closing his black lab kit with a little snap.

By this time, of course, I'd seen this guy so often in the last day or so, I was feeling like maybe we were family. I stuck out my hand. "Well, thanks, anyway, I sure appreciate it," I said.

The lab guy shook my hand, all right, but his eyes didn't look any too friendly. "Try not to have any more break-ins for the next hour or so, OK?" he said. "I'd like to finish my supper."

I just looked at him. I'd been about to introduce myself and all, maybe find out what his name was, but now I didn't think I'd bother. Nope, I decided right then and there that I'd prefer to just remember this guy as the Asshole from the Crime Lab.

It was after nine when Vergil and Asshole left. I reckon I should've been exhausted by then, what with all that had gone on during the day. The truth was, I was so keyed up, I could hardly stand still. Like Asshole, I had completely missed supper, but I didn't feel like eating. What I felt like doing, of course, was giving Doc Darlene a phone call. I reckon, though, I was real afraid to hear what she might have to tell me.

Come to think of it, even if Rip was OK, what Doc Darlene would have to tell me, if I called her right now, probably wouldn't be any too pleasant. Doc Darlene has a reputation for getting riled when you don't do as she says. I'd heard tell she'd given my neighbors a tongue-lashing for being two days late bringing their cat in for its annual checkup.

I had to face it. Doc Darlene had clearly instructed me to phone *tomorrow*. And it probably wasn't a good idea to piss off the person taking care of Rip.

I took a deep breath, standing in the middle of my living room, staring at the mess around me. If I couldn't find out how Rip was, at least I could try to find out who shot him. To my way of thinking, there were two suspects at the head of the list—Boyd and Ruta. They were the two I'd personally told I had the tapes, so it stood to reason they'd most likely be the ones looking for them. It was a place to start, anyway. I wasn't sure where Boyd lived, but checking out Ruta ought to be real easy.

It turned out to be not only easy, but real quick. I knocked on Ruta's huge oak door about twenty minutes later, and both Ruta *and* Lenard answered it. At almost nine-thirty in the evening, they were both wearing bathing suits, for God's sake, and they stood there in the doorway, with red towels around their necks, dripping a little on the parquet floor in the large foyer.

"What the hell do you want now?" Lenard said, running his huge hand irritatedly over his flattop. "Can't me and my wife even enjoy a little peace and quiet in our hot tub without you bothering us?"

I was doing a fast look-see at the both of them. Lenard was in red-checkered trunks, and Ruta was in a matching spandex swimsuit. Ruta's checkered swimsuit seemed to be having as much trouble containing her massive chest as her pink uniform had earlier. I was pretty sure I was looking at industrial-strength spandex.

Lenard was an equal sight to behold. With his blockhead sitting flat on top of a square-shouldered, squat body, the man looked like he'd been constructed out of Legos. Hairy Legos, at that.

Thank goodness, it didn't take any time at all to see that neither of these folks had anything even faintly resembling a dog bite anywhere on their person.

I gave both Lenard and Ruta a quick smile. "You're right, Lenard," I said, "it was downright rude of me to interrupt your hot-tubbing." And I turned on my heel and left them both staring after me as if I'd just lost my mind.

I stopped at a phone booth just outside of the Crayton County Supermarket down the road, and looked up Boyd

Arndell in the phone book. Surprisingly enough, it gave Boyd's address as Arndell's New and Hardly Used Furniture.

Old Boyd apparently lived above the store. Or maybe he just bedded down for the night in one of the La-Z-Boys.

I drove downtown, and parked in front of Arndell's. It was by now around ten, almost an hour after Arndell's closes, but the furniture and the bicycle and the old humpbacked trunk were still sitting out on the sidewalk. It was pretty easy to figure out why. Boyd himself was slouching in one of the green velvet wing-backed chairs, eyes closed, chin resting on his chest. Zeke must've left Boyd to move everything back inside, and Boyd was obviously throwing himself into his work with his usual gusto.

As I pulled up, the thing that really grabbed my attention more than anything else, though, was Boyd's right hand. Resting on top of the wing-backed chair's arm, Boyd's right hand was swathed in a neat, white bandage.

Boyd didn't even bother trying to hide it. Or maybe he realized it was too late to try. Boyd just raised his head and watched me as I put my truck in park, got out, and walked toward him.

"How'd you hurt your hand, Boyd?" I said, by way of greeting.

Boyd looked down at his hand with the bemused look of somebody who, before that moment, hadn't noticed it was injured. "Why, I—I reckon I got it caught in something."

I stared at him. Something like maybe Rip's *mouth?*

"No kidding," I said. "Like what?"

Boyd gave his hand another bemused look. "You know what, I don't rightly recall."

I took a short, irritated breath. *"You* know what," I said. "My house was broken into today, and Vergil found *your* fingerprints all over it." I hadn't exactly been planning on what I would say. Before I could stop it, my mouth was lying up a storm.

Maybe I should've given it more thought. Boyd stood up, stretched, and then drawled one word. "Bullshit." Boyd's thick lips shaped themselves into something that Boyd probably intended to be an arrogant smirk. It looked more like gas to me. "They couldn't have found no fingerprints of mine," he said slowly, "because I ain't never been in your house, Haskell." His eyes dared me to prove him wrong.

I reckon even lazy Boyd could remember if he'd happened to wear gloves while he was trashing my house, but I wasn't going to let a little thing like being caught in a lie slow me down. I glared right back at him. "Then you wouldn't mind a doctor looking at that hand of yours, would you? Maybe a doctor could help you remember what you caught it in."

Boyd's thick lips sort of twitched at that. He blinked a couple of times, like a weasel suddenly caught out in the sunlight. "All right, dammit, your dog bit me, OK?"

After that, I must've looked exactly like I felt—which was, of course, that I was itching to clobber Boyd right in the mouth—because Boyd immediately started putting some distance between us, his voice turning into a whine. "Fact is, Haskell, I—I ought to sue you! I drove all the way out to your house just to talk to you, and when I went up on your deck, your damn dog jumped me!"

It was all I could do not to jump him myself. "Why would my dog do a thing like that, Boyd? Tell me that." My voice sounded unnaturally calm as I kept moving toward him.

Even Boyd must've realized it was probably the calm before the storm, because a flicker of alarm appeared in his eyes. He moved now so that both wing-backed chairs were between us.

"Because your dog's vicious, that's what! Your damn dog was going for my throat! I had to shoot him in, you know, *self-defense!*"

I found myself gritting my teeth, just listening to him. "Then you admit it? You admit you broke into my house? And shot my dog?" I sidestepped the first wing-back.

"I don't admit nothing," Boyd said. His eyes were darting around now, as if he were looking for a way out. "I—I had to protect myself, that's all. But I never broke into anybody's house. Whoever done that must've broken into your house after I left." While he was denying things, Boyd apparently figured he might as well go whole hog. "And I didn't do nothing to Phyllis Carver, neither!"

I was still moving toward him, clenching my fists. "You shot my dog and just left him there?"

Boyd backed up now until his legs were pressing against the old humpbacked trunk. "Now, Haskell," he said, talking faster, "I would've taken your dog to the vet, I really would've, but—but I was afraid he'd bite me again."

I was pretty sure old Boyd here was making things up as he went along.

"I—I even tried to call you," Boyd added, "to let you know what had happened, but you weren't in your office."

I'll bet.

Up to that moment, I don't think I'd ever fully understood how somebody could ever get to the point where they could actually kill somebody. Now, listening to Boyd, I understood perfectly. There wasn't a doubt in my mind that Boyd had gone to my house with the full intention of hunting for Phyllis's tapes. He'd no doubt been carrying his .22 just in case he ran into any opposition. Like me, for example. Instead, Boyd had run into Rip. Rip had bitten him as he came up my stairs, and Boyd had simply shot him. Just like that.

This slimy little asshole had shot a mentally ill dog so he could ransack my house.

God. It was a good thing I didn't have my own gun, or I might not be able to resist the temptation to show old Boyd here just exactly how Rip must've felt.

There was also now not a doubt in my mind that Boyd had also been the one who'd trashed my office, too.

Proving it, however, was an entirely different story.

Still watching me warily, Boyd was now backing rapidly around the trunk, making his way backwards toward the front door of Arndell's without taking his eyes off me. "I—I just came out to your house, Haskell, because I wanted to beg you not to tell anybody about me and Ruta." Boyd was back to whining again. "I was just trying to protect Ruta's reputation, you know, that's all I wanted to do. You've got to believe me."

The answer to that, of course, was fat chance.

"Sure, Boyd," I lied, "I believe you." I kept right on moving toward him real slow. "I know you were just trying to protect Ruta."

Boyd's fool face actually brightened. Like maybe he actually believed me. "I'm real sorry about what I had to do to your dog, Haskell. You can get another one, you know."

What a comforting thing to say. Apparently Boyd was certain that he'd killed Rip. I swallowed, trying to breathe calmly, and let Boyd keep on talking, even as I moved toward him. "You know, Haskell," Boyd said, his eyes now sly, "I might be *real* generous to somebody who might happen to come across that tape of me and Ruta. Why, I might pay as much as a thousand dollars." Here Boyd actually had the gall to *smile* at me. "To protect Ruta, mind you."

Right. I knew, of course, that Boyd didn't care two cents about protecting Ruta. It was *himself* he was worried about. Because it was a pretty safe bet that if Lenard Lippton ever found out that Boyd was fooling around with his wife, Lenard would cheerfully beat Boyd to a pulp, if he didn't outright kill him.

Right now, making my way toward Boyd around all the stuff in front of Arndell's, I can't say that sounded like a bad idea.

I tried to return Boyd's smile, but it must've come out looking like a sneer or something, because Boyd immediately looked alarmed. He apparently decided that he ought to put a locked door between us right away. He started moving real fast toward Arndell's front door, even as he kept on talking. "I just want you to keep that in mind, Haskell," he said. "A thousand dollars is a lot of money, you know, and all you need to do to collect all that money is get me that tape." That said, Boyd quickly opened the door that was now just behind him, slipped inside, shut it, and clicked the lock.

I was almost within grabbing distance by then, but Boyd had gotten inside before I reached him. Can you believe it? For a lazy guy, Boyd could really move when he wanted to.

Once inside, that slimy little twerp just stood there, watching me through the glass on the other side of the door. Like maybe he was worried I might throw one of the chairs through the glass and come after him.

I'll admit, I was actually tempted. But I got back in my truck, just the same, and I pulled away.

I could always come back here later and have myself another little chat with old Boyd.

In fact, if Rip died, Boyd could count on it.

15

It was close to eleven when I got back to my house. As soon as I opened my front door, I instantly wanted to turn right around and head on back to Arndell's. I took one quick glance around my wrecked living room and concluded that Boyd Arndell needed his face punched in real bad.

I think it pretty much showed the kind of person he was, too, for Boyd to admit that he'd shot Rip, but *not* to admit that he'd ransacked my house. Apparently Boyd considered shooting my dog the lesser offense of the two. Of course, Boyd probably only admitted shooting Rip because he could say that he acted in self-defense. No doubt, if Boyd could've said my *house* had attacked him first, he would've admitted the ransacking, too.

I stood there, just inside my front door, looking around at the mess, and tried not to grit my teeth. Boyd had better be hoping that Rip pulled through, because if Rip didn't, I myself was going to enjoy teaching Boyd the true meaning of the word *attack*.

I reckon I've already made it pretty clear how much I hate cleaning. And yet, at this point, I didn't have much choice. I was pretty sure I wasn't going to be able to get Boyd over here any time soon to clean up the mess he'd made. And I definitely needed to put my bed back together before I got in it.

If I ever did get in it, of course. Even as late as it was, I still didn't feel the least bit sleepy. If anything, I felt almost too wide-awake. Too wide-awake and too worried.

So I took a deep breath, made my way through the debris in my living room, and went on out to my kitchen. There I fixed myself a Coke, took a couple sips, then returned to my living room, and dug in.

I reckon I could've made myself a sandwich, too, while I was out there, but I wasn't any more hungry than I was sleepy. Funny, before now, I probably would've told anybody that spending a night that didn't include having to carry a sixty-pound dog up and down stairs before I went to bed would be a welcome change.

I would've been real wrong.

I spent the next three hours or so putting my house back together. Reconstructing my sofa, righting my upended lamps, putting stuff back in my closets, things like that. After doing pretty much the same thing earlier at my office, this cleaning thing was starting to feel like a habit.

I can't say it was the most fun kind of habit I could've come up with.

Surprisingly enough, almost nothing in my house had been broken. The glass top to my blender turned out to be cracked, and a couple of my books had torn pages. Other than that, everything seemed pretty much OK. Boyd had thoughtfully not bothered to rip open my sofa cushions the way he'd done the chairs in my office. Maybe, as lazy as he was, he'd decided it was too much effort.

As I worked, I tried real hard to think of almost anything other than Rip.

The anything-other-than-Rip that I mainly thought about, of course, was the Phyllis Carver case. As much as I would've loved to pin it on him, it was pretty clear that Boyd must not have shot Phyllis. If he had, why would Boyd still be looking for Phyllis's tapes? Apparently, then, I could assume that old Boyd only shot at *non*humans.

The slimy little jackass.

So who could it have been? Apparently whoever had shot Phyllis had taken *both* missing tapes. Had the killer left behind the one tape of Orval in order to throw suspicion on him? If so, why had the killer taken *both* the other tapes? The answer to that one occurred to me just as I was folding up one of my sheets and putting it away in my hall closet upstairs.

The killer had, no doubt, taken both tapes just in case Phyllis had played these tapes for someone else. That way, he wouldn't implicate himself by just taking the one with his own voice on it.

I picked up another sheet off the floor in my upstairs hall and started folding it. If we eliminated Boyd because he was still looking for his tape, then that only left Winslow and Leesa Jo. And yet, June had told me that she and Winslow had an open marriage—that she knew about Leesa Jo and that she didn't care if Winslow played around on her. So why on earth would Winslow kill for that tape?

It didn't make sense.

There was also another person, of course, that had to be considered. I really didn't want to think it, but she *was* still a suspect. Imogene. June had suggested that Phyllis's seven could be an incomplete *I*. Was that possible? Had Phyllis been trying to tell us that her own sister had killed her? And yet, why would Imogene kill for tapes of Ruta and Winslow? Could Imogene have killed Phyllis to get Orval for herself— and then taken the tapes to throw everybody off? And yet, that didn't explain why she would've left the one tape of Orval behind. Could Imogene have found out about Orval and Flo and decided to pay him back by implicating him in his wife's murder? My God. Could I be that wrong about her?

I had finished my upstairs closet by this time, so I moved

on into my bedroom. Righting the lamps in there, putting stuff back in my nightstand, picking up clothes off the floor. While I was doing that, I remembered something else.

June's reaction when I showed her and Winslow the note Phyllis had left.

I hadn't imagined it. A look of alarm and *recognition* had crossed June's face when she looked at the mark Phyllis had made. I was sure of it. So why would June recognize that mark, and no one else?

I was stuffing books and magazines and old family photographs back into my nightstand when it hit me. June was a church secretary. A secretary, *just like Phyllis.*

Could that be the connection?

If it was, then I did just happen to know of another secretary who might be able to shed a little light on this case.

If, of course, I could get her to stop drawing hearts long enough to look at Phyllis's note.

I closed the drawer to my nightstand, and stood up. Tomorrow, first thing, I was going to show Phyllis's note to Melba. I started putting the sheets back on my bed, and for the first time since I'd found Rip, I actually smiled to myself. Was it possible that Melba, of all people, might actually help me solve a case?

Or had worry over Rip affected my mind?

It was a little after two when I finally fell into bed. My house, of course, was not exactly what you'd call neat by then, but at least if it was ransacked again tomorrow, I'd be able to tell.

The next morning I was surprised when I woke up that I'd actually slept five whole hours. I reached for my phone the second my feet hit the floor.

"Yeah?" The tone of the voice who answered was clearly not cheerful. Maybe I'd interpreted Doc Darlene's instructions to call "in the morning" a little too loosely.

"Doc Darlene?"

"Yeah?" If anything, her tone had taken a nose-dive.

I started talking real fast. "Uh, Doc, this is Haskell Blevins, I'm calling about Rip, my dog? I brought him in last

226

night? He'd been shot, and I was just wondering if maybe you could tell me—"

It seemed suddenly as if I couldn't breathe. I didn't know if I kept blabbering because I was afraid to hear what Doc Darlene might have to say about Rip, or if I was just afraid to stop and give Doc the chance to cuss me out.

Doc interrupted me, anyway. "Hell's bells, Haskell," she said, "do you have any idea what time it is?"

I didn't answer. Besides, I had a feeling she already knew.

"It's seven o'clock in the frigging morning, *that's* what it is. Are you out of your frigging mind? I've been up with your dog all night long, and now that he finally seems to be stabilized, I decided to finally get some frigging sleep. And what happens? *You* call! Well, I never—"

Doc went on and on, using some words that could probably get her phone taken away, but all I heard was that part about Rip being stabilized. I felt like maybe I could take a full breath again.

"Your dog's holding his own, Haskell," Doc finished up by saying, "but he sure doesn't need to be waked up by the phone ringing. No more than I do!" With that, she hung up.

I believe we can safely say that Doc Darlene was not in her best mood.

However, what she'd had to tell me about Rip had put *me* in a much better one.

I showered, got myself dressed, and headed into work with renewed energy. When I got to my office, I didn't go upstairs, though, I just headed straight into Elmo's. Unlike yesterday, I saw Melba right away. Come to think of it, you would've had to *try* to miss her. Sitting at her desk in the back of Elmo's, Melba had managed to outdo yesterday's outfit.

And they said it couldn't be done.

Today Melba had selected a low-cut, tomato red, sequined dress with a metallic gold belt as appropriate attire for office work. Her spiked heels matched her belt, and her lips and nails matched her dress. Also matching her dress were Melba's earrings. These things were, without a doubt, the largest, sparkliest earrings I'd ever seen. With several long strands of sparkling red stones dangling from each lobe, Melba's ears glittered so much, it made you want to squint when you looked at her.

Of course, you might've been wanting to do that, anyway.

Like yesterday, Melba had completed her ensemble by sticking a big bow into the side of her beehive. Today's bow, though, was red satin.

For a moment, I just stood there beside Melba's desk, squinting at her and trying to make up my mind what look she was going for today. Joan Collins? One of the Supremes? Or maybe Liberace?

Melba, of course, had already heard about Rip. Like I said at the beginning, word travels fast in a small town. I imagine Doc Darlene or one of her assistants had mentioned it to somebody or another, and before you knew it, the ever diligent Pigeon Fork grapevine had passed on the news to Melba.

"How's your dog, Haskell, honey?" Melba said the second I walked up. I think I was finally getting used to Melba's tone being so lilting these days. It was the way she kept calling me "honey" that still made me cringe inside.

Before I could answer, Melba started shaking her head, causing her dangling earrings to start up a fearful clatter. Not to mention, causing red lights to ricochet all around the store, like lights off a prism. You might've thought a cop car had pulled up. "You poor, poor, *poor* thing." Melba always pronounces the word *poor* as if it were spelled *pore*. "It's just a crying shame. A *crying* shame."

"Doc Darlene told me Rip was holding his own," I said.

Melba's eyes widened. "You already called Doc Darlene? This morning?" Her voice held awe.

I nodded.

"My goodness," Melba said. She was now giving me the sort of look folks must give Evel Knievel after he's jumped a couple dozen cars. "My, my. You must be real worried to call Doc *this* early." Doc Darlene's reputation as a nonmorning person must've been even more well known around these parts than I'd thought. Melba reached over and patted my arm reassuringly. "I'm sure Rip's going to be just fine, Haskell. Just fine."

Melba was obviously trying real hard to act sympathetic. She was blinking her heavily mascaraed eyelashes, and trying to pout like she was feeling real sad for me, but I could tell there was an undercurrent of excitement behind every word she spoke.

"You just wait," Melba went on. "Rip will be feeling fit as a fiddle by my wedding."

I stared at her—this time without squinting. *"Wedding?"*

Melba outright giggled when I said that. "That's right." She picked up a steno pad off the top of her desk and waved it at me, her red earrings sparkling and clattering away. "Can you believe it? I'm actually planning Dalton's and my *wedding!* We set the date last night."

I swallowed once, and managed to get out, "Why, Melba, I—I'm real happy for you."

Melba's answer was another giggle. "Dalton's not given me a ring yet, of course. He said he was ordering one special-made, but our engagement's official, anyway. We're going to be joined in holy matrimony just three weeks from today!" Here Melba apparently couldn't contain herself any longer. She giggled for a full thirty seconds and finally said, "And, Haskell, I—I'd really like it if you'd give me away."

I think stunned is probably too gentle a word for what I was feeling. I just stared at Melba some more and couldn't say a word for a long, long moment. Of course, what immediately leaped to my mind was the tape recorder I'd put in Dalton's Cadillac. It looked as if I needed to retrieve that thing fast. Maybe it could tell me whether or not I should be happy about Melba's impending nuptials. "Melba," I finally got out, "I'd be honored to give you away." I hoped I sounded sincere. Especially since I wasn't all that sure I was.

I reckon I sounded fine, or else Melba was so deliriously

happy herself, she didn't notice. Melba positively beamed at me.

I couldn't meet her eyes. I was sure if I did, she'd see what I was thinking. Instead, I quickly looked down at the steno pad in Melba's hand. The top page was covered in Melba's familiar handwriting and what looked to be chicken scratches.

A lot of chicken scratches.

"What's this?" I asked.

Melba's eyes followed mine. "I'm making a list of all the things I'll need for the big day! That's why I came in early today. To get started on it!" Melba was so excited, her lilting voice shook a little.

According to Melba, she'd been writing down everything she thought she'd need to get. Things like folding chairs, plastic champagne glasses, paper napkins with her and Dalton's names and the date printed on them. "You'd be surprised, Haskell," Melba said, "how much goes into planning a wedding." She gave another earring-clattering giggle. "There's so *much* to be done!"

"What are all these chicken scratches?" I said.

Melba shrugged her plump shoulders. "Oh, that. Well, whenever I'm in a hurry," she said, "I start writing in both English *and* shorthand. I don't really mean to, it just comes out that way. A lot of secretaries do that. I reckon it's sorta like writing in two languages at the same time."

I was barely listening to her by then. Because I'd just realized that one of the chicken scratches on Melba's steno pad looked exactly like an upside-down seven. This mark was right next to the number 27.

My mouth went dry.

"And this?" I asked again, indicating the mark. "What's this?"

Melba looked positively thrilled that I was showing this much interest in her wedding plans. "That? Why, *that's* our wedding date," Melba said proudly. "Dalton and I will become one on the twenty-seventh!"

I pointed directly at the upside-down seven. *"That's* your date?"

Melba was looking at me a little strangely now, but she went ahead and answered. "That's a short form for the month, Haskell. In shorthand you've got a lot of short forms for words you use real often. Things like days of the week and the months and—"

I didn't hear the rest of what Melba said. I was out the door and hurrying up the stairs to my office before Melba even finished her sentence.

In my office I dialed up Imogene at home. Either Imogene was taking off another day of work, or I'd caught her before she headed into her real estate office.

Unlike Doc Darlene, Imogene sounded downright glad to hear my voice.

"How's Rip, Haskell?" she asked.

I told her what Doc had told me, and then I hurried up some, saying what I had to say before I lost courage. The first part, of course, was the easy part. It was the part where I told Imogene I thought I might have figured out who killed Phyllis, and that I was about to go and check it out.

The other part was a lot tougher. "Imogene, I know I told you that I'd try to keep Phyllis's blackmail scheme a secret, but it looks like it's all going to come out, after all. I'm real sorry, but I wanted you to know before it happens."

There was a long silence. During which I gripped the phone real tight.

Finally Imogene said, "I appreciate your telling me." That was all she said.

I was so relieved she hadn't jumped down my throat that when Imogene asked me right after that to tag along while I went and checked things out, I was saying yes practically before I realized it.

I picked up Imogene at her apartment about ten minutes later. Wearing jeans and a white short-sleeved shirt and Nikes, she may have been dressed real casual, but she looked downright tense. I half expected her to start pumping me on the way, but she didn't say a word. Imogene just sat there beside me, staring at the road ahead, her face real pale.

Then, of course, suddenly we were there. Pulling into Winslow's driveway.

It was after nine by then. June must've still been suffering with that flu bug she and Winslow had earlier, because obviously she'd called in sick again today. She answered the doorbell on the third ring.

Standing there in her foyer, dressed in a blue-flowered housecoat, June didn't look all that happy to see me, oddly enough. "Haskell," she said, "Winslow's not here right now, he's at work, and I don't appreciate a bit your coming by when he's not—" Her voice abruptly cut off when she saw Imogene standing behind me.

"Guess what, June," I said brightly. "We've figured out what that mark on Phyllis's note meant."

That pretty much shut June up. For a second, anyway. Then June swallowed and said, "Why, what do you mean?" June's voice sounded real calm, but something was happening to her mouth. It was doing this kind of shaking thing, as her huge brown eyes traveled from my face to Imogene's and back.

"It's over, June," I said. "I know that mark is shorthand." I went on and explained it to her, just as if I had no idea that she already knew. I'd realized when I was looking at Melba's wedding list that, up to then, I'd been looking at Phyllis's note *upside down*. Phyllis's memo paper had been unruled, so there had been no way to tell which was right side up. When Phyllis had collapsed, knocking pencils and papers off her coffee table to the floor, the note she'd written had apparently landed upside down.

Melba's wedding list had shown me my error.

"But then, you knew that, didn't you?" I said, staring straight at June. "You were standing directly in front of me when I showed the note to Winslow, so you were looking at it upside down yourself. That's how come you saw it right away for what it was. As a secretary yourself, you knew that a mark that looks a whole lot like an upside-down seven is shorthand for the word *June.*"

Behind me I heard an audible gasp. June may have already known all this, but it was news to Imogene.

Imogene moved forward, her face a mask of shock. *"You! You killed Phyllis!"* Even as she said the words, there was disbelief in her voice. As if she couldn't imagine anybody doing such an awful thing.

June didn't even blink. "I don't know what you're talking about." Her lotion voice had been refrigerated once again, as her hand fluttered at the collar of her housecoat. "You're both talking nonsense." She swallowed once more, her mouth doing that funny shaking thing again, and added, "How do you know that Phyllis wasn't in the act of writing an entire name, and she just couldn't finish it?"

Imogene moved so that she was now standing a little ahead of me. "Come off it, June," she said, "we know you did it."

For an answer, June slammed the door in both our faces and turned the lock.

Apparently June agreed with Boyd when it came to putting a locked door between you and folks that were mad at you.

Imogene was all set to pound on June's door and maybe do some hard-core yelling, but I pulled her away. I knew very well, of course, that right now everything we had on June was pretty flimsy. It certainly wasn't enough to get her arrested. "Come on, Imogene," I said. "We don't have enough to take to Vergil now, but I think I know where we might be able to get it."

We headed for Pigeon Fork High, where the secretary with the huge red beehive and the wire rims called Winslow to the office for us. When he saw me and Imogene standing there, waiting for him, Winslow looked for a second like he was going to turn tail and run.

Winslow's eyes, however, flickered to the secretary with the wire rims. The woman was leaning forward at her desk, chin in hand, obviously watching the proceedings with a great deal of interest. That was when Winslow stuck his hand out, gave me a big grin, and said, "Haskell, old buddy, good to see you. What brings you here?"

I didn't shake his hand.

"Well, old buddy," I said. "I just thought I'd drop by and let you know that June's been arrested for killing Phyllis Carver. And she's saying *you* did it."

Here, would you believe, Winslow apparently forgot all about Miss Beehive eavesdropping. "That bitch! *June's* the one that did it! Hell, I didn't know anything about it!"

I just stared at him. "But you sure went along with it after it was done, didn't you, Winslow?"

Winslow stared right back at me for about a half second, and then he did what he'd looked like he was going to do when he first walked up. He took off running. Moving a lot faster than Boyd did last night, Winslow was out of the office and heading down the hall toward the front double doors of Pigeon Fork High before I could finish yelling, "Hey! Winslow! Come right back here!"

Winslow, wouldn't you know it, did *not* come right back.

I sort of thought he might not, so I immediately took off after him, turning to shout back at Imogene as I went, "Call Vergil! Get him out here!"

That was about as many words as I could possibly yell with what breath I had to spare. All the rest of my breath I was using up in great quantities, trying to catch Winslow, who—let's be fair here—had clearly cheated by taking off before I knew we were racing.

Winslow was a pretty good runner, but his legs were shorter than mine. So by the time I'd chased him out the front doors, and into the parking lot, and around the side of the school, and past four school buses, and around back across the blacktopped area where I used to play basketball when I was a kid, I was gaining on him pretty good.

Then Winslow ducked into the alley between the school and the large, dome-topped brick building that houses the gym. This alley eventually opens onto a grassy area that leads to a small subdivision situated in back of the school, so I reckon that's why Winslow turned in there. If he could've gotten through that alley, he no doubt expected to be home free.

He didn't get through the alley, though.

Sitting in a classroom all day long must've not kept Winslow in peak condition, or else maybe I was actually getting some benefit out of climbing steep stairs to my office several times a day. Whatever the reason, I caught Winslow about halfway into the alley, tackled him around the knees, and pulled him to the ground.

If we'd been playing football, I reckon there would've been a flag on the play.

In this case, though, there was no flag. There were, however, a lot of garbage cans, maybe ten or twelve of them, that Winslow and I both fell into.

Let me tell you, I would've preferred the flag.

These ten or twelve garbage cans were all lined up in the alley, and every one of them appeared to be full of what I immediately guessed to be today's school lunch leftovers. And probably yesterday's. And, judging by the smell, maybe the day before that.

By the time Vergil showed up, with the Gunterman twins right in back of him, Winslow and I were wearing most of those leftovers. Having rolled around in them a while, trying to punch each other's brains out.

Vergil, amazingly enough, looked like he was almost *smiling* when he first saw me and Winslow. I'd like to think it was because, by that time, I was sitting on top of Winslow and I'd clearly caught Vergil a criminal, but I'm afraid it might've been because I had browned lettuce and old tomato pieces clinging to my hair, and what looked to be spoiled tapioca running down my shirtfront.

I still say to this day that when Vergil showed up, I was definitely winning, but Winslow probably would argue with that. Being as how I had me a black eye by then and a footprint on the side of my face, where Winslow had been trying to kick his way free of me.

Vergil immediately pulled his gun on Winslow and did his "FREEZE!" yell. In my opinion, he could've yelled a tad quicker and maybe Winslow might not have had the chance to pop me in the eye one more time, but maybe I'm being picky here.

Amazingly enough, Vergil did look downright grateful while one of the Guntermans grabbed Winslow, and the other handcuffed him. "Good job, Haskell," Vergil actually said.

Of course, even at the time I was pretty sure that the reason Vergil was so grateful was that *he* hadn't been the one who had to chase Winslow through the garbage cans. And that, at that moment, *he* was definitely not the one decorated in leftovers.

Imogene came running up right while they were taking Winslow away, and I think she might actually have been intending to give me a hug before she saw my decorations. You could pretty much tell the split second she noticed them, because she stopped as quick as if somebody had just pulled her emergency brake, and just stared at me. Backing away, and screwing up her nose some.

I think Vergil came closer to smiling then than I had ever seen him.

Vergil wouldn't let me sit in any of his police cars, and he didn't want me following him in my truck—particularly "downwind," as he put it—so I wasn't around when he and the Guntermans went to round up June. Vergil told me later what happened, though. June had gotten herself dressed, had packed her suitcases, and was just pulling away in her car when Vergil and the others arrived to arrest her.

No surprise, they found the two incriminating tapes in June's luggage. What was a surprise, however, was what they found when they played the tape of Winslow. It turned out it wasn't a tape of him and Leesa Jo after all. It was Winslow and one of his own students. A sixteen-year-old girl.

No wonder June had killed for that tape. Her entire world was about to crumble. If anyone heard this tape, Winslow not only stood to lose his job, but he'd be prosecuted for statutory rape.

According to Vergil, June told him that she'd kept those tapes to maintain a hold on Winslow. She said she intended to use them to keep him from ever running around on her again.

When I heard this, I couldn't help but whistle. Old June apparently had been shutting down her open marriage.

Vergil also told me that the crime lab found a .38 handgun registered to Winslow buried under the Reeds' house. It checked out to be the murder weapon.

I was right glad when I heard it. Finally that Asshole from the Crime Lab turned out to be good for something.

Of course, the afternoon right after I rolled around in the leftovers, I didn't know any of these things yet. All I knew was that I needed a shower.

With Vergil and the rest on their way to June's house, I headed back to my house to take one. I was about halfway there when a big, red Cadillac pulled up behind me and started honking the horn. Of course, the windows were tinted so heavy I couldn't see real clear who it was, but I had a pretty good idea.

I pulled over.

I'd been expecting to see Dalton get out of the car, but it turned out to be Melba, opening the door on the driver's side. She came stomping up to my truck, her round face every bit as red as her earrings and sequined dress.

I made the mistake of rolling down my window.

"Dalton let me drive his car today, and guess what I found under the seat." Melba said.

I didn't have to guess. I could plainly see that Melba was holding the recorder I'd left in Dalton's car.

"Now, Melba—" I started to say. That, of course, is when I found out that rolling down my window had been a big mistake.

I had no sooner finished saying her name when Melba beaned the recorder right off my forehead. For a split second, little lights actually flickered in front of my eyes. "Who the hell do you think you are?" Melba screamed.

"Your friend," I said.

I don't think Melba heard me. She was stomping back to Dalton's car as fast as her red spiked heels could carry her.

16

I reckon I tried to talk to Melba for a full week after that, but she wouldn't have any of it. She walked right by me as if I weren't even there, all the time I was saying to her back, "Melba? Melba? *MELBA!*" The few times I got her to answer me, what Melba had to say, I definitely did not want to hear.

Melba not only wouldn't answer *me,* she also wouldn't answer my phone. Actually, according to what Imogene eventually told me, Melba *did* answer my phone that week. Technically. Only, just about a half second after she picked up the receiver, Melba hung up on the caller.

Which meant, of course, I didn't talk to Imogene that entire week. Being as how I couldn't get up enough courage on my own to call her, and the few times Imogene later told me that she'd called me, she couldn't get through.

From what she said, Imogene apparently also tried reaching me at home, but I wasn't there much. Most of the time I wasn't in my office, I spent at Doc Darlene's, keeping Rip company. I was there as often as Doc Darlene would let me be.

It took old Rip quite a while to recover. Of course, he's

fine now. Except for one small thing. You know how Rip wouldn't go up and down steps? Now that fool dog won't even go out on the deck. I have to carry him out there, and every time I do, he howls piteously, looking around at the woods, his eyes real nervous. I think Rip has decided that something is laying for him out there.

I can't say I'm surprised.

What did surprise me a little is what Imogene said that following Saturday afternoon, when I finally got up enough gumption to ask her out. It was Melba, of all people, who finally convinced me to call her. Not that Melba was talking to me yet. But it finally occurred to me on that Saturday morning that, for all her shortcomings, at least Melba had had the guts to take a chance. Dalton could very well turn out to be a mistake, but at least Melba wasn't spending all her time at home alone.

Or at the vet's, with a mentally ill dog.

About two minutes after it hit me that *Melba*, without a doubt, had more courage than I did, I was in my truck, driving over to Imogene's apartment. As soon as she opened the door, I blurted out, "What would you say to going out with somebody two years younger?"

Surprisingly enough, Imogene all but beamed at me. "Well, I've always been very immature," she said.

My face actually hurt, I started smiling at her so big.

I also smiled real big when I heard, not three days later, that—in spite of her vehement defense of her true love— Melba had sent Dalton packing. As Melba told me later that same day, "Haskell Blevins, I'm not as stupid as you think I am."

I, of course, was not about to touch that one. I just looked at her, not saying a word.

According to Melba, she'd started calling around, checking out Dalton's shopping center success stories, and found out that he'd made them all up.

Melba also even admitted to me that it was finding my bug in Dalton's car that had started her thinking—after, of course, her mad wore off. When Melba told me this, she gave me a real big hug. "When *friends* start getting suspicious, you can't ignore it," Melba said.

I did notice that she emphasized the word *friends*.

Speaking of which, it's still a mystery to me how my old friend Winslow managed to get two good-looking women to put up with his shenanigans. Imogene, however, has an explanation for it. "Why, Haskell," she told me last night, "Winslow is a *dish*. I mean, Winslow may have looked like a geek back in high school, but that man grew up to be a real hunk. Didn't you notice?"

I can't say that I did.

For a second there, I was actually considering maybe growing my hair long and pulling it back into a ponytail, when Imogene moved closer to me, giving me one of her soft smiles. "There are hunks, Haskell, and there are *hunks*."

I don't know what she meant by that, but the way she said it sounded downright affectionate, so I didn't argue.

We seem to be getting along real fine.

One thing Melba has never told me, but I heard it around town. They say that the morning he left Pigeon Fork, The Dalton was seen with two black eyes—the diameter of which were just about the size of Melba's meaty fists.

I also heard that, coincidentally, Boyd Arndell, the dog-shooter, also left town the same week Dalton cleared out. The way I heard it, somebody called up Lenard and told him all about Boyd and Ruta.

I reckon it's just like I said at the beginning. Word travels fast in a small town.

Especially when you've got a phone.

About the Author

TAYLOR McCAFFERTY is the author of the Haskell Blevins mysteries *Pet Peeves* and *Ruffled Feathers*. She has published short stories in several national magazines and lives in Lebanon Junction, Kentucky, where she is working on a fourth Haskell Blevins mystery, *Thin Skins,* for Pocket Books.

THE HASKELL BLEVINS MYSTERIES

PET PEEVES
BED BUGS
RUFFLED FEATHERS

PRAISE FOR TAYLOR McCAFFERTY'S
<u>PET PEEVES</u>
"OH, JOY, HERE IS A WICKEDLY
DELIGHTFUL FIRST NOVEL from a woman
who should be chained to her word
processor until she promises to give us
many, many more....A new novelist of
this promise is very welcome in a world
that keeps losing its John D. MacDonalds."
—*Washington Times*

Taylor McCafferty

POCKET
B O O K S

AVAILABLE FROM POCKET BOOKS

756